PENGUIN BOOKS

MY FATH[illegible]

'A master prose styl[illegible]

'Up[illegible] clear-eyed honesty' *Daily Mail*

'Offers plen[illegible]st and piquant observations on the vagaries of sex, [illegible]ove and getting old' *Metro*

'Exhilarating . . . brilliance of observation . . . passionate appreciation of life' *Spectator*

'Of living American writers, he was, without question or competition, the most personally adored . . . his aim was to reveal beauty where it was thought least likely to dwell' *New Statesman*

Books by John Updike

POEMS

The Carpentered Hen (1958)
Telephone Poles (1963)
Midpoint (1969)
Tossing and Turning (1977)
Facing Nature (1985)
Collected Poems 1953–1993
Americana (2001)
Endpoint (2009)

NOVELS

The Poorhouse Fair (1959)
Rabbit, Run (1960)
The Centaur (1963)
Of the Farm (1965)
Couples (1968)
Rabbit Redux (1971)
A Month of Sundays (1975)
Marry Me (1976)
The Coup (1978)
Rabbit Is Rich (1981)
The Witches of Eastwick (1984)
Roger's Version (1986)
S. (1988)
Rabbit at Rest (1990)
Memories of the Ford Administration (1992)
Brazil (1994)
In the Beauty of the Lilies (1996)
Toward the End of Time (1997)
Gertrude and Claudius (2000)
Seek My Face (2002)
Villages (2004)
Terrorist (2006)
The Widows of Eastwick (2008)

SHORT STORIES

The Same Door (1959)
Pigeon Feathers (1962)
Olinger Stories (a selection, 1964)
The Music School (1966)
Bech: A Book (1970)
Museums and Women (1972)
Problems and Other Stories (1979)
Too Far to Go (a selection, 1979)
Bech Is Back (1982)
Trust Me (1987)
The Afterlife (1994)
Bech at Bay (1998)
Licks of Love (2000)
The Complete Henry Bech (2001)
The Early Stories: 1953–1975 (2003)

ESSAYS AND CRITICISM

Assorted Prose (1965)
Picked-Up Pieces (1975)
Hugging the Shore (1983)
Just Looking (1989)
Odd Jobs (1991)
Golf Dreams: Writings on Golf (1996)
More Matter (1999)
Still Looking (2005)
Due Considerations (2007)

PLAY

Buchanan Dying (1974)

MEMOIRS

Self-Consciousness (1989)

CHILDREN'S BOOKS

The Magic Flute (1962)
The Ring (1964)
A Child's Calendar (1965)
Bottom's Dream (1969)
A Helpful Alphabet of Friendly Objects (1996)

John Updike

MY FATHER'S TEARS and Other Stories

PENGUIN BOOKS

PENGUIN BOOKS

Published by the Penguin Group
Penguin Books Ltd, 80 Strand, London WC2R 0RL, England
Penguin Group (USA) Inc., 375 Hudson Street, New York, New York 10014, USA
Penguin Group (Canada), 90 Eglinton Avenue East, Suite 700, Toronto, Ontario, Canada M4P 2Y3
(a division of Pearson Penguin Canada Inc.)
Penguin Ireland, 25 St Stephen's Green, Dublin 2, Ireland (a division of Penguin Books Ltd)
Penguin Group (Australia), 250 Camberwell Road, Camberwell, Victoria 3124, Australia
(a division of Pearson Australia Group Pty Ltd)
Penguin Books India Pvt Ltd, 11 Community Centre, Panchsheel Park, New Delhi – 110 017, India
Penguin Group (NZ), 67 Apollo Drive, Rosedale, North Shore 0632, New Zealand
(a division of Pearson New Zealand Ltd)
Penguin Books (South Africa) (Pty) Ltd, 24 Sturdee Avenue, Rosebank, Johannesburg 2196, South Africa

Penguin Books Ltd, Registered Offices: 80 Strand, London WC2R 0RL, England

www.penguin.com

First published in the USA by Alfred A. Knopf, a division of Random House, Inc. 2009
First published in Great Britain by Hamish Hamilton 2009
Published in Penguin Books 2010

1

'Morocco', based on [illegible] November 1979 issue
of the *Atlantic Mon*[illegible] they have here.
'Varieties of Rel[illegible] Prelude to a
Second Marriag[illegible] *Harper's Magazine*;
and 'Germa[illegible] *New Yorker*,
[illegible]

Printed in England by Clays Ltd, St Ives plc

ISBN: 978–0–141–04259–6

www.greenpenguin.co.uk

Penguin Books is committed to a sustainable future
for our business, our readers and our planet.
The book in your hands is made from paper
certified by the Forest Stewardship Council.

To Grandchildren:

Anoff, Kwame, Wesley, Trevor, Sawyer, Kai, and Seneca

and

Adèle, Helen, Alex, Isabel, Lily, Charlotte, and Katharine

Contents

MY FATHER'S TEARS

Morocco

THE SEACOAST ROAD went smoothly up and down, but compared with an American highway it was eerily empty. Other cars appeared menacing on it, approaching like bullets, straddling the center strip. Along the roadside, alone in all that sunswept space, little girls in multicolored Berber costume held out bouquets of flowers—violets? poppies?—which we were afraid to stop and accept. What were we afraid of? A trap. Bandits. Undertipping, or overtipping. Not knowing enough French, or any Arabic or Berber. "Don't stop, Daddy, don't!" was the cry; and it was true, when we did stop at markets, interested persons out of the local landscape would gather about our rented Renault, peering in and offering unintelligible invitations.

We were an American family living in England in 1969 and had come to Morocco naïvely thinking it would be, in April, as absolute an escape to the sun as a trip to the Caribbean from the Eastern United States would be at the same time of year.

But Restinga, where a British travel agency as innocent as we of climatic realities had sent us, was deserted and windy. The hotel, freshly built by decree of the progressive, tourism-minded king, was semicircular in shape. At night, doors in the curving corridors slammed, and a solitary guard in a burnoose kept watch over the vacant rooms and the strange family of pre-season Americans. By day, the waves were too choppy to swim in, and the Mediterranean was not so much wine-dark as oil-black. Walking along the beach, we picked up tar on our feet. When we lay down on the beach, wind blew sand into our ears. Off in the distance, apartment buildings of pink concrete were slowly being assembled, and there were signs that in a month vacationers from somewhere would fill the bleak plazas, the boarded-up arcades. But for now there was only the whipping wind, a useless sun, and—singly, idly, silently in the middle distance—Arabs. Or were they Berbers? Dark men, at any rate, in robes, who frightened our baby, Genevieve. Fantastic as it seems now, when she is so tall and lovely in her spangled disco dress, she was then overweight and eight. Caleb was ten, Mark twelve, and Judith a budding fourteen.

"*Je le regrette beaucoup*," I told the manager of the Restinga hotel, a blue-sweatered young man who wandered about closing doors that had blown open, "*mais il faut que nous partirons. Trop de vent, et pas de bain de la mer.*"

"*Trop de vent*," he agreed, laughing, as if reassured that we were not as crazy as we had seemed.

"*Les enfants sont malheureux, aussi ma femme. Je regrette beaucoup de partir. L'hôtel, c'est beau, en été.*" I should have used the subjunctive or the future tense, and stopped trying to explain.

The manager gave our departure his stoical blessing but

explained, in cascades of financial French, why he could not refund the money we had prepaid in London. So I was left with a little cash, a Hertz credit card, four children, a wife, and plane tickets that bound us to ten more days in Morocco.

We took a bus to Tangier. We stood beside an empty road at noon, six stray Americans, chunky and vulnerable in our woolly English clothes with our suitcases full of continental sun togs bought at Lilywhite's and of Penguins for vacation reading. The sun beat upon us, and the wind. The road dissolved at either end in a pink shimmer. "I can't believe this," my wife said. "I could cry."

"Don't panic the kids," I said. "What else can we do?" I asked. "There are no taxis. We have no money."

"There must be *some*thing," she said. Somehow, my memory of the moment has dressed her in a highly unflattering navy-blue beret.

"I'm scared," Genevieve announced, clutching her knapsack and looking painfully hot and rosy in her heavy gray overcoat.

"Baby," sneered her big sister, who attracted stares from native men everywhere and was feeling a certain power.

"The bus will come," Daddy promised, looking over their heads to the vanishing point where the road merged in the pink confusion of the new buildings the king was very slowly erecting.

A thin dark man in a dirty caftan materialized and spoke to us in a lengthy nasal language. He held out his palms as if to have them read.

"Dad, the man is talking to you," Mark, then prepubescent and now a graduate student in computer science, said, very embarrassed.

"I know he is," I told him, helplessly.

"What's he saying, Dad?" Genevieve asked.

"He's asking if this is the bus stop," I lied.

The man, continuing to speak, came closer, confiding a breath rich in Muslim essences—native spices, tooth decay, pious fasting with its parched membranes. His remarks grew more rapid and urgent, but a light was dying in his bloodshot eyes.

"Tell him to go away." This suggestion came from Caleb, our silent, stoic, sensible child, now a college junior majoring in zoology.

"I think he will," I hazarded, and the man did, shaking his skeletal head at our unresponsive idiocy. Our little family clustered closer in relief. Sand blew into our shoes, and the semicircular halls of the abandoned hotel, our only home in this foreign land, howled at our backs like some deep-voiced, clumsy musical instrument.

The bus! The bus to Tangier! We waved—how we waved!—and with an incredulous toot the bus stopped. It was the green of tired grass, and chickens in slatted coops were tied to the top, along with rolled-up rugs. Inside, there were Moroccans: dusty hunched patient unknown people, wearing knit little things on their heads and knit little things on their feet, their bodies mixed in with their bundles, the women wrapped in black, some with veils, all eyes glittering upward in alarmed amazement at this onrush of large, flushed, childish Americans.

The fare, a few dirhams, was taken noncommittally by a driver, who had a Nasseresque mustache and a jaw to match. There was room at the back of the bus. As we wrestled our ponderous suitcases down the aisle, the bus swayed, and I feared we might crush with our bulky innocence this fragile vehicle and its delicately balanced freight. Deeper into the bus, an indigenous smell, as of burned rope, intensified.

In Tangier, the swaying bus was exchanged for a single overloaded taxi, whose driver in his desire to unload us came into the Hertz office and tried to help the negotiations along. Allah be praised, his help was not needed: the yellow plastic Hertz card that I produced did it all. Had I been able to produce also the pale green of an American Express card, our suspenseful career down the coast, from Tangier to Rabat to Casablanca and then through the narrower streets of El Jadida and Essaouira and Tafraout, would have been greatly eased, for at each hotel it was necessary to beg the clerk to accept a personal check on a London bank, and none but the most expensive hotels would risk it; hence the odd intervals of luxury that punctuated our penurious flight from the Mediterranean winds.

The avenues of Rabat as we drove into the city were festooned in red. Any thought that we were being welcomed with red banners gave way when we saw hammers and sickles and posters of Lenin. A Soviet high-level delegation, which included Kosygin and Podgorny, was being received by the open-minded king, we discovered at the Rabat Hilton. The hotel was booked so solid with Communists that it could not shelter even the most needy children of free enterprise.

But a hotel less in demand by the Soviets took us in, and at dinner, starved, we were sat down in a ring on piled carpets, around what in memory seems an immense brass tray, while a laughing barefoot girl tiptoed at our backs, sprinkling rosewater into our hair. Mark, tickled, made his monkey face.

This sensation of being beautifully served amid undercurrents of amusement recurred in a meadow high above the sea, where, after miles of empty landscape and empty stomachs, a minuscule restaurant, scarcely more than a lean-to, advertised itself with a wooden arrow. We stopped the rented Renault and with trepidation walked across the grass, single-file, feeling again huge, as when we trod deeper into that fragrant bus. We halted when a man emerged from the shack bearing a table, and a boy emerged carrying chairs. With an air of amusement all around, this furniture was set on the grassy earth, in a spot we lightly indicated. From the shed were produced in time wine, rice, kebabs, and Cokes, which we consumed in sight of the Atlantic, of beige cliffs, and of vast pastures grazed by a single donkey. We were the only customers, for all we knew, that this beautiful restaurant by the sea had ever had.

Even on the rough back road to Tafraout, into the stony hills of the Low Atlas, with the gas gauge saying zero and not a house, not a sheep or goat, in sight, a little girl in a dip of the unpaved track held out a handful of flowers. The road here had become one with the rocks of a dry riverbed, so our Renault was moving slowly, so slowly she had time, when she saw we were truly not going to stop, to whip our fenders with the flowers and to throw them at the open car window. One or two fell inside, onto our laps. The rest fell onto the asphalt beside her feet. In the rearview mirror I saw the little girl stamp her foot in rage. Perhaps she cried. She was about the age of Genevieve, who expressed empathy and sadness as the girl diminished behind us and dropped from sight.

In Tafraout, Caleb could not stop staring at a man so badly crippled he seemed a kind of spider, scuttling across the packed earth on his arms, his little body dragged between them. He didn't beg; indeed, he moved about like a local figure of some importance, with urgent business to conduct.

North of Agadir, we were in our motel rooms watching the minutes to dinnertime crawl by, and became aware that the traffic on the road outside had stopped. Policemen had come quickly, and were talking to the driver of a dusty truck, a young man in soft-colored work clothes slumping against his cab with bowed head, nodding, nodding, as the police asked questions. Traffic was held up on both sides of the road. We stayed on our side, mere tourists, but interested. It was difficult to see what had happened. Some kind of bundle was eclipsed by a wheel of the truck. Under cover of the tumult when the police fetched the mother, Mark crossed the road and looked.

He was pale when he returned to our side of the road. He didn't make his comical monkey face. We asked him what there was to see. "You don't want to see it," was his answer.

"It was a little girl," he later told us.

The mother was short and wore black, without a veil; she raced up and down the bare slopes on the other side of the road, splitting the skies with her uncanny keening, her ululating, while men raced after her, trying to pin her down. As they failed to catch her, the excited crowd of them grew, a train of clumsy bodies her grief in its superhuman strength trailed behind her. No American could have made the noise she made; all the breath of her chest was poured upward into the heavens that had so suddenly, powerfully struck her a blow. Ancient modes of lamentation sustained her. Her performance was so naked and pure we turned our heads away. We had not been meant to witness this scene in Morocco. When two men caught her at last and pinned her by the arms, she collapsed in a faint.

We found the climate we had hoped for at Agadir. The beach there was a wide beach but, though the sun and sea were warm enough, almost deserted. We looked for other vacationers to settle near and, seeing none, spread our towels not far from the seawall. Judith wandered a little away from us, gawky and pearly white in her bikini, picking up shells and gazing at the sea, aloof from the company of her parents and her siblings. Genevieve and Caleb began a sand castle. Mark lay back and scowled, concentrating upon his tan.

We only slowly became aware of the Arab in robes lying thirty yards away, his face turned toward us. His face—dark, pentagonal—stayed turned in our direction, staring with some thrust of silent pain, of congested avidity, out of the foreshortened rumple of his robes. Genevieve and Caleb fell silent at their castle. Judith drifted closer to us. None of us ventured to the inviting edge of the sea, across the waste of sand, through the silent shimmer of the Arab's stare. So softly the children couldn't hear, Mommy murmured to me, "Don't look, but that man is masturbating."

He was. Out of his folds. At Judith and us.

I stood, my knees trembling, and organized our rapid retreat from the beach, and that afternoon we located the private pool—admission a mere dirham—where all the Europeans were swimming and tanning safe from the surrounding culture. We went to the pool every day of our five in Agadir. The sun shone and there was little wind. We had found a small hotel run by an old French couple; it was wrapped in bougainvillea, with a parrot in the courtyard and a continental menu.

Not ten years before, on February 29, 1960, an earthquake in Agadir had killed an estimated twelve thousand people and devastated much of the city. We saw no traces of the disaster. In Agadir we rejoined the middle classes. We had money again. I had cabled my London bank, and they had worked out one of their beloved British "arrangements" with a bank in Agadir. The bank building had a prim granite façade, erected since 1960, but inside it had more the flavor of a livestock close. Merchants in shepherds' robes muttered and waited at a long chaotic counter. As each transaction ripened, names were shouted in Arabic. When my own was shouted out, evidently the amount of money cabled from London was called out with it. The muttering ceased. Astonished brown-eyed glances flew along the counter in my direction. I had swelled to immense size—a prodigy, a monster, of money. Blushing, I wanted to explain, as I stuffed the pastel notes into my worn wallet, "I have children to feed."

Genevieve liked to feed the dogs that haunted our hotel. Pets in foreign places are strange: to think, they understand French or Arabic better than you do. And they never look quite like American animals, either: a different tilt to their eyes, a different style of walking. Most of our slides, it turned out, were of these animals, out of focus. The children had got hold of the Nikon.

We escaped from Agadir, from Morocco, narrowly. On a basketball-sized globe of the Earth, you can mark with the breadth of a thumbnail the distance we drove that last day. At the Air Maroc office, they told us there was no space for six persons on any flight from Agadir to Tangier, where we did have rooms at a hotel that night, and airplane reservations to Paris the next morning. There was nothing to do but drive it, the distance it had taken us days to traverse, five hundred miles, eight hundred kilometers, along the northwest shoulder of Africa.

We set out at dawn. We had secured a big bag of oranges and bottles of Perrier water. Daddy drove, hour after hour;

Mommy refused to drive in Morocco, or perhaps the car rental terms excluded her. You children, all four crammed into the back of the little Renault, were quiet, sensing, as children do, real danger, real need.

In some dusty small city, perhaps Safi, I failed to see a red light and drove through it. A whistle shrilled, and in the rearview mirror, as clearly as I had seen the little flower girl stamp her foot, I saw a policeman in a white helmet calmly writing down our license number. His white helmet receded. His gaze followed us. My stomach sank. But the street continued straight, and the pedestrians in their dusty native garb continued indifferently to go about their business. In another day we would be safe in Paris; and the traffic light had been very poorly placed, off to the side and behind some advertising signs. Criminally, I drove on. The boys cheered; the girls weren't so sure.

"Maybe he would just have bawled you out," Genevieve said.

"Fat chance," Mark argued. "He would have put Dad in some awful pokey full of rats and cooties."

"I saw the light," Mommy said mildly, "and assumed you did, too, dear."

"Thanks a bunch," I said, less mildly.

"I didn't see it," said Caleb, our born consoler and compromiser. "Maybe it was yellow, and turned."

"Who saw it and thinks it was yellow?" I asked hopefully.

Silence was the answer.

"Who saw it and what color was it?"

"Red," three voices chorused.

"What do you all want me to do? Turn around and try to explain to the cop? *Je regrette beaucoup, monsieur, mais je n'ai pas vu le, la lumi—*"

"*No!*" another chorus proclaimed, Mommy abstaining.

"You've made your decision," Judith told me, in almost a woman's voice.

"Step on it, Dad," Mark said.

We were already on the outskirts of town, and no police car was giving chase. The empty green pastures, the smooth empty road reclaimed us. Our prolonged struggle down the coast was rerun backwards. Here was the little restaurant in the meadow on the cliff. Here was the place where everybody refused to eat the liver sandwiches that the one-eyed man had cooked for us on a charcoal burner set up beside the road. Here was Casablanca, which didn't look at all like the movie. And here was Rabat. The red banners were down, the Russians had moved on. By now it was late afternoon, and Daddy's neck muscles ached, his eyes felt full of sand, and he had grown certain that his license-plate number was being telegraphed up and down the coast, through the network of secret police that all monarchies maintain. At any moment sirens would wail, and he would be arrested, arrested and thrust deep into the bitter truth of Morocco, which he had tried to ignore, while stealing the sun and the exotica.

Or the police would be waiting for him at the hotel desk in Tangier; already his name would have been traced from Restinga through a trail of one-night stops to the receipt he had signed in the bank in Agadir. Or else there would be a scene at the airport: handcuffs at passport control. Oh, why hadn't I stopped when the whistle blew?

Had my French been less primitive, I might have stopped.

Had we not recently read, in a *Newsweek* at the hotel with the parrot, an article about innocent Americans moldering away in African and Asian prisons, I might have stopped.

Had the United States not been fighting so indefensibly yet inextricably in Vietnam, I might have stopped.

Had it not been for the red flags in Rabat, the masturbating man on the beach, the dead girl by the truck wheel . . . my failure or refusal or cowardice still exists, a stain upon my memories of Morocco.

It was dark when we pulled into Tangier, and the hotel could be reached only through a maze of one-way streets, but the desk clerk had our reservation nicely written down, and no arrest warrant to hand me. The king himself could not have been more tourist-friendly; the gray-haired bellhop (who looked like Omar Sharif) smiled as he accepted my little salad of dirham notes; the waiters in the hotel restaurant bowed as deeply as if we were their only customers. Which, at that hour, we almost were; the trip had taken fifteen hours. We had consumed the full bag of oranges and drunk all the Perrier water. We parted sadly, the next morning, with our loyal Renault, which had never broken down and which we returned covered with dust. The people at Hertz, whose license plate had been so sinned against, scarcely looked up from doing the calculations that, a month later, were to arrive in London out of the ozone of numbers that blankets the globe. We had escaped.

Remember Paris, children? In the raw spring cool of the budding Tuileries, we still clustered close. In the back seat of the Renault, there hadn't been room enough for all four of you to sit back at the same time, so one of you, usually Genevieve, had to sit forward, breathing on my ear. Mommy, strapped in beside me, doled out oranges and water; Caleb and Mark tirelessly debated who was "squishing" whom; Judith, by the window, tried to dream herself away. We had achieved, in Morocco, maximum family compression, and could only henceforth disperse. Growing up, leaving home, watching your parents divorce—all, in the decade since, have happened. But on a radiant high platform of the Eiffel Tower I felt us still molded, it seemed, forever together.

Personal Archaeology

In his increasing isolation—elderly golfing buddies dead or dying, his old business contacts fraying, no office to go to, his wife always off at her bridge or committees, his children as busy and preoccupied as he himself had been in middle age—Craig Martin took an interest in the traces left by prior owners of his land. In the prime of his life, when he worked ten or twelve hours every weekday and socialized all weekend, he had pretty much ignored his land. Years had passed without his setting foot on some corners of it. The ten acres were there to cushion his house from the encroachments of close neighbors, and as an investment against the day when these acres would be sold, most likely to a developer, the profit going to Craig's widow, Grace, who was six years younger than he.

The place, as he understood it, had been a wooded hill at the back of an estate until around 1900. A well-heeled, somewhat elderly man, marrying tardily, built a spacious summer house for his bride and himself on what had been a boulder-framed picnic spot, with enough trees felled to afford a glimpse of the Atlantic, a third of a mile away.

There were old roads on the property, built up on retaining walls of big fieldstones, too steep and with turns too sharp for any combustion-driven car. Horses must have pulled vehicles up these hairpin turns, through these enduring tunnels of green; trees are shy, even after decades, of taking root on soil once packed tight by wheels. Standing on the edge of one of the several granite cliffs he owned, Craig imagined farm wagons or pony carts creaking and rattling toward him, the narrow spoked wheels laboring up swales, now choked with greenbrier, that he imagined to have been roadways, bringing young people in summer muslin and beribboned bonnets and white ducks and straw boaters up, past where he stood, to a picnic high in the woods.

But Massachusetts land was, a century ago, mostly cleared, bare to the wind and sun, cropped by sheep and cows. Perhaps he was imagining it all wrong. The winding roadway ran head-on into a spiky wall of monoliths; how had it climbed the rest of the hill? Near the house, the granite outcroppings bore enigmatic testimony. There were holes drilled here and there, as if to anchor iron gates or heavy awnings. A veranda with a sea view had long ago rotted away, and Craig himself had replaced a dilapidated pillared porch on the front of the house, facing the circular asphalt driveway, once a gravel carriage-turn.

The woods held vine-covered mounds of jagged rock that he took to be left over from the blasting of the house foundations. In the early years of the twentieth century, crews of masons fresh from Italy roamed this neighborhood, building giant walls that were gradually, stone by stone, collapsing. One night a section of retaining wall holding up his wife's most ambitious flower garden collapsed, spilling not just earth and flowers but ashes, of the clinkerish sort produced by a coal furnace, and a litter of old cans and glass jars. The garden's subsoil had been an ash-and-trash dump. When had the garden been created, then? Later than he thought, perhaps—the same era when the concrete wells for the cold frames were poured—sunken beds now roofed by frames of punky wood, crumbled putty, and shattering glass.

In Craig's mind, the property had four eras before his. First, there was the era of creation and perfect maintenance, when the enthusiastic, newly married rich man was still alive, and servants bustled from the stone sinks in the basement out to the bricked drying yard with baskets of steaming laundry, and the oiled cedar gutters poured rainwater down gurgling downspouts into fully functional underground drains. Then this happy man died, and the widow—much younger than he, preferring the society of Boston to her lonely house on the hill—imposed a largely absentee reign, in which one dining-room wall with its hand-printed pictorial French wallpaper was ruined by a winter leak, and the dainty verandas of the summer house, pillared and balustered appendages exposed to the weather, slowly succumbed to blizzards and nor'easters. There came an era when she, too, was dead and the house stood empty. Perhaps most of the neglect and damage should be assigned to this interregnum, which ended just before World War II, when a young and growing family took on the place as a year-round residence. Central heating was installed, and a pine-panelled study was carved from the grandiose front hall, and the brick chimneys were repointed and the leaky roof shingles replaced. Improvements were halted by World War II. The man of the house enlisted to sail the ocean, which was visible from the windows until they were covered with black-out paper.

The hero returned as a rear admiral, and lived in the house until he was eighty and all five of his children had moved on to places and families of their own. From this long and busy era Craig dated most of the oddments he found in the woods—Mason jars, flowerpots, shotgun shells, rubber tires half sunk in the leaf-mold and holding a yellow oblong of scummy water, pieces of buried iron pipe, rusted strands of wire testifying to some bygone fencing project. Tree houses had been built and abandoned amid the rocks and trees. Porcelain insulators and insulated copper strands carried the ghost of electricity; parts of a motorcycle engine, filmed with blackened grease, remembered a time when the steep old roads served a young man's racing game. These acres had absorbed much labor: stacked between pairs of still-living trees, logs cut to fireplace length moldered and grew fungi; Craig's shoes scuffed into view beneath the leaves a sparkling layer of carbon, the charcoal residue of old fires. There were pits that looked dug, and mounds too regular to be natural. Above the railroad tracks, along a path trespassers had worn beside a once-impeccable square-cut wall that now leaned dangerously out over the eroded embankment, he picked up beer cans, plastic six-pack holders, shards of shattered glass, bottles of indestructible plastic. On the lower reaches of the land, where a broad path across pine needles wound downward toward a causeway that would eventually lead trespassers, through several private domains, to a beach, there had been a virtual snowfall of pale plastic litter—styrofoam-cup tops, flexible straws, milk containers. Craig was rewarded, in his occasional harvests with a garbage bag, by finding, hidden in the greenbrier and marsh grass, bottles of a nostalgic thickness, such as he as a child had drunk root beer and sarsaparilla from.

Trespassers and owners and guests had trodden the land,

craggy as it was—trodden and scarred it. In an incident that had been described to him by an ancient friend of the previous owner, an unsteady dinner guest, one icy, boozy night, had climbed into his car and promptly slid into the wall of great stones on a curve of the asphalt driveway. The bumper had knocked out, like a single tooth, a molar-shaped boulder that now sat some dozen yards into the woods—a permanent monument to a moment's mishap, too massive, in this weakling latter age, to be moved back into position. When Craig inquired about bringing the equipment in to move it back, he was told the weight of the backhoe might break down the driveway.

In a seldom-visited declivity beyond this great granite cube, Craig, picking up deadwood, found a charred workglove, stiff as a dead squirrel, with the word SARGE written on the back in the sort of felt-tip marker that didn't come into use until the 1960s. Who had Sarge been? Part of a work crew, Craig speculated, that had carelessly dropped his glove on the edge of a spreading grass fire. Or a woodsman who, while feeding brush into a blaze, had seen his hand flame up and flung the glove from him in pain. Nearer the house, raking up organic oddments in a spring cleaning, Craig spied beneath an overgrown forsythia bush a gleaming curve of white ceramic and, digging with his fingers, found it to be the handle of a teacup. He dug up six or so fragments; the delicate porcelain cup, gilt-rimmed, had been dropped or broken, perhaps by a child who in fright and guilt had buried the evidence in a shrub border. The quality of the cup suggested one of the early eras, perhaps the near-mythical first. Ceramic, unlike metal or wood, is impervious to time and moisture. But the earth, freezing and thawing in its annual cycle, can at last push up to the surface what the culprit thought had been safely buried and forever hidden.

. . .

Craig's dreams, those that disturbed him enough to be remembered when he awoke, tended to return, like a dog to a buried kill, to a rather brief stretch of his life when he was embroiled in a domestic duplicity, an emotional bigamy. There was his first wife, who in these dreams had a certain ceramic smoothness, and his wife-to-be, whose discomfort seemed to occupy several corners of the dream's screen while he scrambled to hold on to every human piece of the puzzle. Curiously, in his dreams he invariably lost the second woman—saw her flee and recede—so that it was with a soft shock that he awakened and realized that Grace, and not his first wife, Gloria, lay beside him in bed, as she had done for twenty years now. His confusion gradually cleared into relief, and he fell back asleep like a living bandage sealing over a wound. His children, now middle-aged, figured in the dream dramas indistinctly, shape-shifting participants in a kind of many-bodied party located halfway up the stairs; the party's main ingredient, however, was not jollity but pain, a pain glutinously mixed of indecision, stretched communications, unexpressed apologies, and scarcely bearable suspense. Craig would wake to find that the party was long over, that he was an old man living out his days harmlessly on ten acres covered by a spotty mulch of previous generations. He rarely got invited anywhere.

The parties had been vehicles for flirtation and exploration, a train of linked weekends carrying them all along in a giddy din; he and his friends were in the prime of their lives and expected that, as amusing and wonderful as things were, things even more wonderful were bound to happen. There were in fact two simultaneous parties, two layers of party—the overt layer, where they discussed, as adults, local politics, national issues (usually involving Richard Nixon), their automobiles and schools for their children, zoning boards and home renovations, and the covert layer, where men and women communicated with eye-glance and whisper, hand-squeeze and excessive hilarity. The second layer sometimes undermined the upper, and with it the seemingly solid structure of the closely intermingled families.

Cocktail parties were lethal melees, wherein lovers with a murmur cancelled assignations or agreed upon abortions. Craig could see in his mind's eye, in an upstairs hall, outside a bathroom, a younger woman, smooth of face and arm, coming at him with her lips shaped to bestow a kiss and saying, softly, "Chicken," when he backed away. But for every moment he consciously remembered from that remote time there were hundreds he had forgotten and that fought back into his awareness in the tangle of these recurrent party dreams. His sensation in these dreams was the same: stage fright, a schoolboy feeling that what he was enacting was too big for him, too eternal in its significance.

He woke with relief, the turmoil slipping from him, his present wife absent from the bed and already padding around downstairs. Sometimes he awoke in a separate bed, because in his old age he helplessly, repulsively snored, and was consigned to the guest room. On his awakening there, his eyes found, on the opposite wall, a painting that had hung in his childhood home—in the several Pennsylvania homes his family had occupied. The painting, a pathetic and precious token of culture which his mother had bought for (if he remembered correctly) thirty-five dollars in a framer's shop, depicted a scene in Massachusetts, some high dunes in Provincetown, with a shallow triangle of water, a glimpse of the sea, framed between the two most distant slopes of sand. Had it been this painting which had led him from that commonwealth to this one, to this hilltop house with its discreet view of the sea a third of a mile away?

Various other remnants of his boyhood world had washed up in the house: his grandfather's Fraktur-inscribed shaving mug; a dented copper ashtray little Craig had often watched his father crush out the stubs of Old Gold cigarettes in; a pair of brass candlesticks, like erect twists of rope, that his mother would place on the dining-room table when she fed in-laws visiting from New Jersey. These objects had been with him in the abyss of lost time, and survived less altered than he. What did they mean? They had to mean something, fraught and weighty as they were with the mystery of his own transient existence.

"I'd give anything not to have married you," Grace sometimes said, when angry or soulful. She carried into daylight, he felt, a grudge against him for snoring, though he was as helpless to control it as he was his dreams. "If only I'd listened to my conscience."

"Conscience?" he said. *Chicken*, he remembered. "I don't know about you, but I'm very happy. You've been a wonderful wife. Wonderful."

"Thank you, dear. But it was just so *wrong*. That time upstairs at the Rosses', the way you loped toward me in the hall, you were scary—like a big wolf out of the shadows. Your teeth gleamed."

"Gleamed?" He couldn't picture it. He had dull, tea-stained teeth; but he recognized that the gleam was something true and precious unearthed from deep within her, giving her past a lodestar, a figment to steer by.

She said, with a blush and downcast eyes, "I shouldn't tell you this, but at times I think I hate you."

I hate you: she did now and then proclaim this, and would

disown the proclamation in the next breath; but Craig saluted the utterance as honest, gouged with effort from the compacted accumulation of daily pretense and accommodation. As well as love one another we hate one another, and even ourselves.

One day after school his younger son had somberly told him that Grace's son, a year behind him at school, had confided that his parents were splitting up. Craig had sickened at the casual revelation, knowing the boy to be imparting news that would soon envelop him; his trusting child was standing on the edge of a widening chasm, a catastrophe his father was in the process of creating.

At the time he kept dreaming of, he had not had stage fright. Strange to recall, he had felt oddly calm, masterful, amid scandal and protest and grief. There had been a psychiatrist encouraging him. His mother, initially indignant, became philosophical, employing postmodern irony and a talk-show tolerance learned through hours of watching television. His children consoled themselves by thinking they would some day grow up and never be so helpless again. In abandoning his family, a man frees up a bracing amount of time. Craig found himself projected into novel situations—dawn risings from a strange bed, visits to lawyers' offices, hotel stays hundreds of miles from home—and reacted like an actor who had rehearsed the lines he spoke, who had zealously prepared for this unsympathetic role, and played it creditably, no matter what the reviewers said. So why the stage fright now, in his sleep? It had been there all along, and was rising up into him, like his death.

Recently he had visited an old friend, a corpulent golfing buddy, in the hospital after a heart attack. Al lay with tubes up his nose and into his mouth, breathing for him. His chest moved up and down with a mechanical regularity recorded by hopping green lines on the monitor on the wall: a TV show, *Al's Last Hours.* It was engrossing, though the plot was thin, those lines hopping on and on in a luminous sherbet green. Al's eyelashes, pale and furry, fluttered when Craig spoke, in too loud a voice, as if calling from the edge of a cliff. "Thanks for all the laughs, Al. You just do what the nurses and doctors tell you, and you'll be fine." Al's hand, as puffy as an inflated rubber glove, wiggled at his side, on the bright white sheet. Craig took it in his, trying not to dislocate the IV tubes shunted into the wrist. The hand was warm, and silky as a woman's, not having swung a golf club for some years, but didn't seem animate, even when it returned the pressure. Our bodies, Craig thought, are a ponderous residue the spirit leaves behind.

One of his childhood homes had been rural, with some acres attached, and while exploring those little woods alone one lonely afternoon he had come upon an old family dump—a mound, nearly grown over, of glass bottles with raised lettering, as self-important and enduring as the lettering on tombstones. Many of the bottles were broken, though the glass by modern standards was amazingly thick, a kind of rock candy, the jagged edge making a third surface, between the inside and outside. Malt-brown, sea-blue, beryl, amber, a foggy white, the broken glass bore the raised names of defunct local bottling works. The liquids the fragments had held were evaporated or had been drunk. For all the good or ill these beverages and medicines did, not so much as a scummy puddle inside an old tire was left. The pile had frightened little Craig, as a pile of bones would have done, with its proof of time's depths, yet in his rural isolation it had provided for him, there in an unfrequented corner of the woods, a kind of glittering, obliviously cheerful company.

On his own acres, wandering, garbage bag in hand, in the lowland beyond the stray rock and the burned glove, he found a number of half-buried golf balls, their lower sides stained by immersion in the acid earth, the cut-proof covers beginning to rot. He remembered how, when first moving to this place, and still hopeful for his game, he would stand on the edge of the lawn and hit a few old balls—never more, thriftily, than three at a time—into the woods down below. They seemed to soar forever before disappearing into the trees. He had never expected to find them. They marked, he supposed, the beginning of *his* era.

Free

"SHE has such lovely eyes." The remark had come from his mother, on one of her visits to the town where Henry and Leila, married to others, lived at the time. She could not have known that her son and Leila were having an affair—one which, like an escaped field fire, kept flaring up each time they thought they had stamped it out. But Leila would have known that this was her lover's mother, and this knowledge would have injected an extra animation, an eye-sparkle, into the conversational courtesies she showed the older woman. Once, Leila's mother had been the visitor to their superheated small town, and Henry had marvelled, looking at the stout, sixty-something woman's profile at the little party her daughter gave for her, that a person so plain and sexless could have produced such a beauty, such a lithe and wanton fomenter of masculine bliss.

His mother's remark had given his illicit passion a ghostly blessing, and the two women did share a love of nature—they knew the names of birds and flowers, and when he and

Leila met it was often in the wild, in a lakeside cottage that a liberated friend, an older woman, lent her, on the woodsy far edge of an adjacent town. The off-season chill, and the musty smells of the canvas and wicker summer furniture and a bare mattress and a disconnected refrigerator, gave way to the aromas of their own naked warmth, as the lake glittered outside the window and squirrels pattered across the roof. Leila under him, he poured his gaze down into her widened eyes, which were indeed lovely—a hazel mixed of green and a reddish brown ringing the black pupils enlarged by the shadow of his head. There was a skylight in the cottage, and he could see its rectangle, raggedly edged with fallen twigs and pine needles, reflected in the wet convexity of her startled, transfixed eyes.

His mother had never warmed to his wife: Irene was too citified, too proper, too stoical. For Henry, she had been a step up, into a family of comfortably well-off lawyers, bankers, and professors, but in the small incessant society of their home her dispensations of intimacy were measured, and became more so rather than less. Henry tried to restrict his appetites to match, and rather enjoyed his own increasing dryness, his ever more effortless impersonation of a well-bred stick. His mother, whose ambitions for him took something florid from her unfulfilled hopes for herself, saw this domestic constriction and resented it; her resentment fortified him when, with Leila more intensely than with several others, he strayed from fidelity and inhaled the wild, damp air of outdoors.

Damp: he never forgot how Leila had abruptly stripped, one sunny but chill October day, and executed a perfect jackknife—her bottom a sudden white heart, split down the middle, in the center of his vision—into the lake, off the not yet disassembled dock and float. She surfaced with her head as small and soaked as an otter's, her eyelids fluttering, and her mouth exclaiming, "*Woooh!*"

"Didn't that kill you?" he asked, standing clothed on the wobbly float, glancing anxiously about for the spying strangers that all these autumnal trees might conceal.

"It's ecstasy!" she told him, grimacing to keep her teeth from chattering. "If you go forward to meet it. Come on. Come in, Henry." Treading water, she spread her arms and butterflied her body up so her gleaming breasts were exposed.

"Oh, no," he said, "please," yet had no choice, as he saw this erotic contest, but to drop his clothes, folding them well back from the splash, and to dare an ungainly, heart-stopping lurch into the black lake water. The pink leaves of swamp maples, withered into shallow boat-shapes, were floating near his eyes when he came up; his submerged body felt swollen and blazing, as if lightning had struck it. Leila was doing an efficient crawl—her tendony feet kicking up white water—away from him, toward the center of the lake. He gasped for breath, doggy-paddling back to the dock, and from this lower perspective saw the trees all around as the sides of a golden well, an encirclement holding him at the center of the circumscribed sky. This was one of those moments, it appeared to him, when a life reaps the fruits that nature has stored up. This was health: that little wet head, those bright otter eyes, that tufted, small-breasted body at his disposal when the electricity ebbed from his veins and their skins were rubbed dry on the towels Leila had foresightedly brought.

But even then the less healthy world intruded. He wondered if Irene would smell the black lake on him, with its muck of dead leaves. She would wonder why his hair was damp. He was not good at adultery, not as good as Leila, because he could not give himself, entirely, to the moment, rushing forward to meet it. His mother's blessing did not save him from gastritis, and an ominous diagnosis from his doctor: "Something's eating at you."

The justice of the phrase startled Henry; his desire for Leila was a kind of beast. It would pounce at unexpected moments, and gnawed at him in the dark. "Work," he lied.

"Can't you ease up?"

"Not yet. I have to get to the next level."

The doctor sighed and said—there was no telling, from his compressed and weary mouth, how much he guessed or knew—"In the meantime, Henry, you have to live on this level. Give up something. You're trying to do too much." This last was said with an emphasis that struck Henry as uncanny, like his mother's blessing out of the blue. The air itself, his illusion sometimes was, hovered solicitously over him, superintending his fate while he plodded on in a fog.

He resigned from his church's fund-raising drive, of which he was co-captain. This, and giving up coffee and cigarettes, made his stomach a little better, but it did not cease to chafe until Leila suddenly, for no reason she ever explained, confessed to Pete, her husband. Within the year, they moved to Florida; within a few more years, the word came back, they were divorced. Her marriage had always been mysterious to him. "He doesn't need me," she had once said, her eyes breaking into rare tears, while she focused somewhere over his shoulder. "He needs my asshole." Henry couldn't quite believe what he heard, and didn't dare ask her to clarify. There were many things, it occurred to him, that he didn't want to know. Though life brought him advancement at work, and vacations in Florida and Maine, and grandchildren, and, with Irene's guidance, an ever more persuasive impersonation of a well-bred stick, there was never another love-beast; such fires burn up the field.

In time Irene died, of cancer in her sixties, and he was free. By way of his friends—those inescapable, knowing friends—he had kept track of Leila, and knew that she was again unmarried, after two post-Pete marriages: the first to an older man who had left her some money, the second to a younger man who had proved, of course, unsuitable. He learned her address, and wrote her a note suggesting he come see her. It had been his and Irene's custom to visit Florida for two weeks in midwinter, staying at a favorite inn on an island off the Gulf Coast—more Irene's favorite than his. The inn smelled of varnished pine and teak, and had stuffed tarpon and swordfish mounted in the long corridors, and photographs of old fishing parties and hurricane damage; on the sunny broad stair landings stood cased collections of shells, the ink on the dried, curling labels quite faded. It smelled of Florida when it was a far place, a rich man's somewhat Spartan paradise, and not yet the great democracy's theme park and retirement home. Yet since Irene's death, after the two years of shared agony, of hospital trekking, of rising and falling hopes, of resolute hopelessness and then these posthumous months of relief and grief and numbingly persistent absence, Henry had grown timid of straying from the paths she had marked out for them to travel.

The inn was on the west coast, below Port Charlotte, and Leila's condo was on the east coast, in Deerfield Beach, above Fort Lauderdale, so it proved an arduous drive, south and then east into the sun, against what felt like a massive grain in the scrubby Everglades landscape. The east-coast congestion—the number of aggressive dark-skinned drivers, the blocks of white-roofed one-story houses laid out for miles on the flat acres of sand—disoriented him. Old age, he was discovering, arrived in increments of uncertainty. Street signs, rearview mirrors, and his own ability to improvise could no longer be trusted. He asked directions three times, steering away from the young people on the bright streets and pulling up alongside skittish and wary seniors, before finding Leila's condo complex; squintingly he doped out the correct entrance and where the parking area for visitors was hidden. He found himself inside a three-story quadrangle, each unit facing inward with a screened sunroom. Piece of scribbled paper in hand, he matched the number there to one on a ground-floor door. When his ring was answered, he had trouble relating the Leila of his memory and imagination to the tiny woman, her nut-colored face crisscrossed by wrinkles, who opened the door to him. Her face had seen a lot of sun in these past thirty years.

"Henry *dear*," she said, in a tone more of certification than of greeting. "You're over an hour late."

"The drive was longer than I thought, and I kept going around and around within a couple blocks of here. I'm so sorry. You always said I was disorganized." From the way she held her face up and motionless he gathered he was supposed to kiss it; he abruptly realized he had brought her no present. It had been the nature of their old relationship for him simply to bring his body, and she hers. Her cheek had a dry pebbled texture beneath his lips, but warm, like a dog's paw pads.

"I can't complain that lunch has gotten cold," Leila said, "since it's cold salad, chicken, in the fridge. I began to think you might not make it at all."

More than once before, he had failed to show up—some sudden obstruction at work or in his duties at home. That her anger never lasted or triggered a permanent rupture had indicated to him that, strangely, he had a hold over her much like hers over him. How much had changed? In her voice he heard hardly a trace of Southern accent, just an erosion of the New England edges. But her manner was edgy enough. Had she become one of those spoiled, much-married women who say whatever rude sharp thing comes to them, take it or leave it, as if sassy were cute? Her clothes—lavender slacks, a peach silk shirt with the two top buttons undone, white platform sandals, magenta toenails—had that Florida swagger, which women anywhere else wouldn't dare at her age.

"Please forgive me," he said, playing his courtly card until the drift of the hand came clearer. His heart had been thumping throughout his long drive, to the point where he imagined an onset of fibrillations, and his panic had grown as he searched the blocks of Deerfield Beach, with their unreal green lawns and ornamental lemon trees. Now that he was here in Leila's presence, a kind of glazed calm, a sweat of suspension, came over him, as it used to when Irene would take a sudden downward turn, or during those endless last nights when there was nothing for him to do but stay awake, hold her hand, and feed her morphine and ice chips. How marvellous he had been, the network of friends confided to him when it was finally over. To himself he had just been correct, obedient to one of the few still-unmodified phrases of the marriage vows, "in sickness and in health."

He became aware, at his back, of splashing sounds. There was a pool in the center of the quadrangle of condos, and Leila's sliding doors were open to admit its sounds, along with those of shuffleboard discs sliding on concrete, cars revving up, palm trees rustling in their antediluvian trance, glasses and ice cubes clinking on a tray somewhere in another screened-in room looking out on the wide shared space. A memory of Leila's little lake, her white body knifing into the cold water, brought him to recognize, as she swayed on her ungainly footgear ahead of him toward her dining area, that she had stayed lithe, though the years had redistributed her weight toward the middle and loosened the flesh of her brown arms. Her salt-and-pepper hair was cut short in this climate and fitted close around her tidy skull, on its supple swimmer's neck. The old beast lived, and sluggishly stirred within him, chafing his stomach; in an abrupt collapse of all the rest of their lives he felt at home with this woman, their two bodies moving phantasmally among the rush-seated chairs, the glass tabletops, the faintly musty furniture of a perpetual summer. "I always did," Leila said. Forgive him. For what? For fucking her? For leaving afterwards, in his own car, spinning dust down the woodsy road in a semi-panic?

Over the chicken salad and white wine, and iced tea and Key-lime pie, they caught up with enough of their decades apart. Her husbands, his spousal tragedy, their scattered children, the expectable aches, the predictable self-denials with which they tried to stay in shape and preserve the sensations of well-being as long as they could. They shared a vanity, it occurred to him, in regard to their physical health.

"Why did you tell Pete, and come south?" he asked at last. "Was it to escape me? Was there no other way?"

It was as if she had forgotten, and had to strain to see such a distant moment. "Oh . . . we'd often talked about Florida, and then the right job for him came up. I had to clean house. You were dirt under the bed. Dear Henry, don't look so sad. It was time." As she turned her head, he remembered her mother's profile; Leila's was now identical.

Leila had, he saw as he watched her talk and gesture, become vulgar, in the way of a woman with not enough to do but think about her body and her means. Yet a vulgar greed for life was part of what he had loved. Her desires had been direct and simple. In two hours they had said enough; they had never been ones for long confidences or complicated confessions. Their situations had been obvious, each to the other, and their time together had been too intense, too rare, too scandalously stolen, for much besides wonderment and possession. Now, as the shadows deepened in her touching condo, with its metal furniture and mall-bought watercolors, and the westering sun reached across the rattan mats toward the room where Leila and her guest sat still at the glass table, having returned to white wine, an invisible uneasiness seized him; he was not used to being alone with her this long, this late into the afternoon. Fuck and run had been his style.

She stood up, firmly on her bare feet. She had eased out of the awkward sandals; the straps had left red welts on her bony blue-veined insteps. They had been blue-veined and tendony thirty years ago. "How about a swim?" she asked.

"So late in the day?"

"It's the best part of the afternoon," Leila said. "The air's still warm, the kids have gone in, hydrotherapy for the cripples is over." She touched her shoulder, as if to begin undressing.

"I don't have a suit."

"You can use one of Jim's. He left three or four." She laughed. "You can let out the waist string. He was just a kid.

He used to strum his knuckles on his abs and expect me to be thrilled."

Henry stood, pleased to be standing, once again, and without hurry, next to Leila—her serious small mouth, its upper lip weathered to a comb of small creases, and her lovely eyes, gleaming like jewels in crumpled paper, bright-hazel remembrances of his mother's desire to have him live, to be a man, on her own behalf. He panicked at the invitation. "I—"

He, too, had been unfaithful, as she had with Jim's abs, with Jim's predecessor's money, with Pete and his uses of her. For two years he had lain beside Irene feeling her disease growing like a child of theirs. He had stayed awake in the shadow of her silence, marvelling at the stark untouchable beauty of her stoicism. In the dark her pain had seemed an incandescence. Toward the end, in the intervals when the haze of painkillers lifted, she spoke to him as she never had, lightly, as to another child whom she did not know well but with whom she had been fated to spend a long afternoon. "I think they might have been just kidding us," she confided one time. "Suppose you don't get to take a trip up to Heaven?" Or again, "I knew I was boring to you, but I didn't know how else to be." In her puzzlement at his tears she would touch his hair, not quite daring to touch his face.

"I'd better get back," he announced.

"Back to what?" Leila asked.

To that inn Irene had loved, with its stuffed fish and nameless saved shells, its bare comforts. To the repose he found in imagining her still with him. Since her death she was wrapped around him like a shroud of gold and silver thread.

"You were always getting back," Leila said. Her tone wasn't rancorous, merely reflective, her tidy head tilted perkily as if to emphasize what she was: a little old lady still game to take her chances, to play her hand. "But you're free now."

Back in her front room, Henry already saw himself out the door, under a circumscribed sky that was rectangular this time. It would be a long drive, against setting sunlight, through the great South Florida swamp. "Well, what is free?" he asked. "I guess it's always been a state of mind. Looking back at us—maybe that was as free as things get."

The Walk with Elizanne

THEIR CLASS had graduated from Olinger High School in 1950, a few years before its name was regionalized out of existence. Though the year 2000 inevitably figured in yearbook predictions and jokes, nobody had really believed that a year so futuristic would ever become the present. They were seventeen and eighteen; their fiftieth class reunion was impossibly remote. Now it was here, here in the function room of Fiorvante's, a restaurant in West Alton, a half-mile from the stately city hospital where many of them had been born and now one of them lay critically ill.

David Kern and his second wife, Andrea, long enough his wife to be no stranger to his high-school reunions, went to visit the sick class member, Mamie Kauffman, in the hospital room where she had lain for six weeks, her bones too riddled with cancer for her to walk. She had been living alone in a house that she and a long-decamped husband had bought forty years ago, and where three children had been raised on a second-grade teacher's salary. Get-well cards and artwork from generations of her pupils filled the room's sills and walls. Mamie was, as she had always been, bubbly and warm, though she could not rise into even a sitting position.

"What an outpouring of love this has brought on," she told the couple. "I was feeling sorry for myself and, I guess you'd have to say, not enough loved, until this happened." She described getting out of bed and feeling her hip snap, feeling herself tossed into a corner like a rag doll, and reaching for the telephone, which luckily was on the floor, with her cane. She had used one for some time for what she had been told was rheumatoid arthritis. At first she meant to call her daughter, Dorothy, two towns away. "I was so mad at myself, I couldn't think of Dot's phone number, though I dial it every other day, and then I told myself, 'Mamie, it's two-thirty in the morning, you don't want Dot's number, what you want is nine-one-one. What you want is an ambulance.' They came in ten minutes and couldn't have been nicer. One of the paramedics, it turned out, had been one of my second-graders twenty years ago."

Andrea smiled and said, "That's lovely." In this overdecorated sickroom Andrea looked young, vigorous, efficient, gracious; David was proud of her. She was a captive from another tribe, from a state other than Pennsylvania.

Mamie tried to tell them about her suffering. "At times I've felt a little impatient with the Lord, but then I'm ashamed of myself. He doesn't give you more than He gives you strength to bear."

In theistic Pennsylvania, David realized, people developed philosophies. Where he lived now, an unresisted atheism left people to suffer with the mute, recessive stoicism of animals. The more intelligent they were, the less they had to say in extremis.

Mamie went on, "I've been rereading Shirley MacLaine, where she says that life is like a book, and your job is to figure out what chapter you're in. If this is my last chapter, I have to read it that way, but, you know, I've had a lot of time to think lying here and—" In her broad, kind face, nearly as pale as her pillow, Mamie's watery blue eyes faltered, becoming quick and dry. "I don't think it is," she finished bravely. Even flat on her back, she was a teacher, knowing more than her audience and out of lifelong habit wanting to impart the lesson. "I'm not afraid of death," she told the visiting couple, smartly dressed in their reunion finery. "It's locked into my heart that—that—"

Yes, what? David thought, anxious to hear, though aware of the time ticking away. He came to this area so rarely now, he sometimes got lost on the new roads, even travelling only a mile. The reunion wouldn't wait.

"That I'll be all right," Mamie concluded. She sensed the anticlimax, the disappointment even, and made an exasperated circular motion of her hand, with its flesh-colored hospital bracelet and IV shunt. "That when it comes, I'll still be there. Here. You know what I'm saying?"

The visiting couple nodded in eager unison.

"It's the getting there," Mamie admitted, "I don't look forward to."

"No," Andrea agreed, smiling her bright healthy smile. She was dressed in a gray wool suit whose broad lapels made her look more buxom than usual.

David searched himself for something to say, but his tongue was numbed by memories of Mamie from kindergarten on: the round-faced little girl being led to the asphalt playground by her round-faced mother, although the other mothers had ceased such escorting; the eager student, knowing all the answers but never pushing them on others or on the teacher, never demanding attention but ready to shine when the spotlight fell on her; the cheerleader and class secretary; the guileless pep girl. Like David, she had been an only child, a fruit of the Depression's scant crop. Like him, she had acquired an only child's self-entertaining skills—drawing, reading, keeping scrapbooks. In their class plays and assembly programs, she always played the part of the impish little sister, while David, for some reason, played that of the father, with talcum powder in his hair. There was no need for talcum powder now; he had turned gray and then white early, like his own mother.

Mamie was saying, "So I say to myself, 'Mamie, you stop complaining. You've had a wonderful life, and three wonderful children, and it isn't over yet.' Dot offered to have me come live with them but I wouldn't do it to her, not in the shape I'm in. Jake offered, too, out there in Arizona. He thinks the dryness would be good for me, but what would I do looking out the window at the desert, unable to open a window because of the air-conditioning? The funny thing is—this will amuse you, David, you were always into irony—the rehab I'll be moving to is the same one with my mother already there. She won't be in my unit, but isn't that ironical? I lived two blocks from her most of my life, and now I'll be on the floor just under her."

The yearbook had not predicted that any of their parents would be alive in 2000. "My goodness—your mother must be ninety," David said.

"And then some. Who would have thought it, the way she smoked? And she wasn't averse to a drink now and then either."

"She was always very nice to me," he recalled. "Even without you being there, I could hang out in your house, waiting for my father to get done at school with his extracurricular stuff. Your mother and I'd play gin rummy."

"She always said, 'David will go places.' "

In memory he saw her mother at the kitchen table like a tenement solitary glimpsed from a passing train—smoke unfurling from a Chesterfield in a glass ashtray, a fanned set of cards in her hand, a glass of some tinted liquid beside her other elbow. She had pasty, deeply dimpled elbows, and she and her daughter shared curly brown hair, and full, talkative lips, curved up at the corners. For all the bubbly welcome with which the two females of the house had received David's visits, there had been a melancholy nap to the furniture, a curtained gloom. It was a semi-detached house with no windows on one side and those on the other staring at a neighbor's windows not six feet away. The man of the house, a small, almost rudely untalkative lathe operator, was slow, in the evenings, to come home from work. Mamie's sunny manner, her busy happiness in high school—the long shiny halls, the organized activities, the tides of young life regulated by bells—partook of the relief of escape. Like David's father, who taught there, Mamie had made a home of the broad, chaste communal setting. David's fondness for her had never crossed the border into the mildest sexual exchange.

"Speaking of going places," David said.

"Yes," Mamie said quickly, recovering her briskness, "you must be off. It kills me not to be there; I swore I'd show up even if it had to be in a wheelchair. But my doctors said it wasn't to be. You two have a wonderful time. David, be sure to say something nice to Sarah Beth about the decorations and favors. She *slaved* to find all those things in the class colors."

. . .

Sarah Beth, a shy, skinny girl who had become a stringy, aggressive old woman, had indeed slaved. The effect was dazzling—swags of maroon and canary yellow, floral centerpieces to match at every table, the walls thronged with enlarged photographs taken more than fifty years ago of schoolchildren in pigtails and knickers, and then of teenagers in saddle shoes and pleated skirts, corduroy shirts and leather jackets. The boys looked mildly menacing, with their greased pompadours and ducktails and flagrantly displayed cigarettes, a pack squaring their shirt pockets and an unfiltered singleton tucked behind one ear. The girls, too, with their thickly laid-on lipstick and induced blond streaks, had a touch of killer—of determination to get their share of the life to come.

Now, although that life was mostly over, the function room was full of human noise, gleeful greetings and old-fashioned kidding: "God, ugly as ever! Who's your friend, or is that a stomach?" Sarah Beth, who without Mamie here was thrown into the chief managerial role, came and seized David above the elbow and turned him away from studying the photographs on the wall to face a smartly dressed woman with button-black eyes and hair to match, cut short and tastefully frosted.

"Do you know who this is?" Sarah Beth asked. Her tone was so aggressive his mind seized up. The mystery woman's features, in her smooth plump face, had an owlish sharpness, and her jet-black, decisively shaped eyebrows gave her a frowning look, though she was smiling hopefully, trying silently to sing her identity to David across the decades. He was reminded of walking to elementary school, when Barbara Moyer and Linda Rickenbacker would steal his cap and his rubber-lined book satchel and nimbly keep these possessions out of his reach until tears stung his eyes and he ran the other way in a tantrum; then the girls would chase him, to give him back what they had grabbed.

Now, again, he was being ganged up on by girls. The seconds stretched. Plump women of sixty-seven or -eight have a family resemblance. He stammered—an old problem, long outgrown—when he began to mouth the name of a girl, Loretta Haldeman, who, he realized in mid-stammer, this could not be, for Loretta had attended a reunion five years ago wearing steel-rimmed spectacles with one opaque lens; an eye had given out. This woman with her bright stern stare was being presented as a treat, a delicacy, a rarity. Sarah Beth offered a hint: "This is the first reunion she's come to." He tried to remember who, among the popular girls, always annoyed the class organizers by never coming, by not coming for fifty years, and thus through the powers of deduction rather than of recognition he named her: "Elizanne!" It was a name like none other, pronounced, they learned as children, to begin with an "ay" sound, like the mysterious "et" in "Chevrolet." It bespoke an ambitious, willful mother, to brand a daughter with such a name, in so conservative a county.

Elizanne stepped forward to be kissed; David aimed at her cheek, though from the way she puckered she would have taken him on her mouth. "How lovely to have you here," he said, a bit blankly. She had not been one of the showier girls in the class, though she had aged better than most. Her dress was teal silk and understated, expensive and suburban; her husband, that ultimate accessory, was tall and genial, with a trace of Southern accent—a man of business, retired or all but. The two of them were together embarked, David imagined, upon a well-earned sunset career of determined foreign travel, of grandchild-sitting and health-club attendance, of hard-working American leisure modelled on the handsome aging couples in commercials for Viagra and iron supplements. Elizanne had, he sensed, gone places. Her face displayed, along with that demure quick smile he could now remember—a smile that darted in and out—a good sense of herself, an established social identity momentarily set aside, for this occasion, like a man's jacket folded into an airplane's overhead bin. Though he was happy enough to see her, he had little to say to her, and less than that to the tan and drawling husband, to whom they must all seem, David imagined, Pennsylvania Dutch hicks. This man's indulgent witness was inhibiting, and David, anxious to join in his class's old-fashioned fun, soon drifted away.

Only toward the end of the evening, with their spouses lost in the crowd, did Elizanne come up to him. There had been the bumbling monologue by the unofficial class clown, the e-mailed greeting from the unable-to-attend class president in Florida, and the touching message from Mamie that Sarah Beth read aloud. The microphone amplified the catch in her throat. "We had the best of it," Mamie had written. "No drugs, no gangs, no school shootings, respect for our teachers, and faith in America." Then the Frankhauser twins, now stooped and heavy of step, performed a soft-shoe routine last presented in senior assembly. Sarah Beth methodically thanked all the committee members and warned that a hat would be passed for the outstanding Fiorvante's wait-staff. Butch Fogel announced how to find tomorrow's picnic, at Shumacher's Grove, though the TV weathermen were predicting rain. The hired entertainment, a female keyboard player with a bassist, sang old songs freighted with nostalgic content for somebody, no doubt, but not quite for them.

Their songs had been overlookable oddities tucked into the late Forties and early Fifties, just before Presley and doo-wop and rock rendered obsolete everything before them—the swing bands, the crooners, the iron-coiffed female vocalists, the novelty numbers and moony heart-wringers, to which one did a sluggish box step, as if sleepwalking. There was a little dance floor at Fiorvante's, and five years ago, one couple dared venture onto it with their version of the jitterbug, and others followed. Now—nobody. The Olinger High School Class of 1950 had given up on dancing.

As the classmates began to shuffle, in a kind of panicked unison, toward the door and whatever fate the next five years would bring, Elizanne came up to David, resting a hand on his forearm and speaking with a firm, lilting urgency, as if she were speaking to herself. "David," she said, in this running murmur, "there's something I've been wanting for years to say to you. You were very important to me. You were the first boy who ever walked me home and—and kissed me."

In this dimmed function room, her eyes, their stern glare softened and widened by the act of confession, sought his, causing her lids with their starry wealth of black lashes to lift. Her eyebrows were released from their frown. Her face, so close and foreshortened, seemed arrived from a great distance. She might have had a drink or two—Fiorvante's had its bar just outside the function room—but she was sober enough, and now so was he, to be shocked, amid the reunion's loud adult courtesies, by this remembrance of their young selves, their true, fumbling, vanished selves.

"I remember that walk," he said. But did he?

Elizanne laughed, a bit coarsely—a modern suburban woman's knowing laugh. "It got me started, I must tell you, on a lot of—whatever. Kissing, let's say." This innocent generation had aged into the sexual revolution, and had hurried to catch up.

David tried to ignore the experienced, sardonic woman she had become. The forgotten walk was coming back to him. The shy, leisurely passage, in dying light, through Olinger, and the standing close, still talking, at the door of her parents' house, and then his lunge into the kiss, and her equally clumsy yet fervid acceptance of the kiss. He had loved her, for a season. When? Why had the season been so short? Had they kicked fallen leaves as they walked through town, along the Alton Pike with its gleaming trolley tracks, into the rectilinear streets of brick row houses, and then on to Elmdale, the section where the streets curved, and the houses stood alone on their lawns, the lawns weedless and the houses half-timbered and slate-roofed and expensive, to the house where Elizanne lived? Had it been spring, shot through with sudden green and yellow, or summer, when bugs swarmed and girls wore shorts, or winter, when your cheeks stung? He was stricken to have her imply, with a knowledgeable laugh, that she had gone on to kiss others. She had added something he didn't quite catch, in the noise of reunion farewells or in his growing deafness, about "what you all wanted"—a sadly cheap and standard sneer, he felt, about male sexuality, which in that place and era had been a massive, underpublicized impetus that most boys dealt with alone. But the sneer itself dated her, and took them back.

"You were so," he breathed, groping for the word, "dewy." This he did remember, amid so much he had forgotten—her dewiness, a quiet, fuzzy moisture about her skin, her near presence. "I'm glad," he added, going into dry adult mode, "it was a successful initiation."

Darkly her eyes held his for a second, then flicked away,

searching for her husband in the dispersing crowd. She realized that David couldn't express what was there to express, and gave his forearm a squeeze through his coat sleeve and removed her hand. *Good-bye, for fifty more years.* "I just wanted you to know," she said.

Wait, he thought, but instead said, quite inanely, "Thank you, Elizanne. What a sweet thing to remember. Hey, you look great. Unlike a lot of us."

That night, twisting with the reunion's excitement next to Andrea in their bed at the Alton Marriott, and for days following, he tried to recapture that walk which had ended in a kiss. Elizanne's house and neighborhood had been more expensive than his, and that had intimidated him. She was not for him. Before too long he got his first real girlfriend, from the class below theirs, who let him hold her breasts, and partially undress her, slick as a fish in the parked car. How old would they have been, he and Elizanne? Sixteen, perhaps fifteen. Had it been after a football game, or a school dance? He had not really been very sociable, nor, after they moved to the country when he was fourteen, was he free to drift around Olinger as he pleased, though he continued at Olinger High, riding back and forth with his father.

She was in the marching band, he remembered. He could see her in her uniform, her hair bundled up under her cap and her female body encased, somehow excitingly, in the gold-striped maroon pants and jacket. The baton twirlers in their high white boots and short flippy skirts were followed by a maroon unisex mass, and Elizanne was in that phalanx. What did she play? He thought clarinet, but this might have been an echo of her coloring; unlike the other class brunettes, with their highlighted waves of brown, she had truly black hair, with lashes and eyebrows to match. The skin of her face had been luminously white in contrast. A fuzz on her upper lip made two little smudges.

Remembering the dark fuzz, most noticeable in the downward view, brought him another piece of memory: dancing with her, holding her close as they shuffled, her corsage and strapless taffeta bodice and the taffeta small of her back with its little ridges and his feet and armpits and shoulder blades in the rented summer tux all melting into one continuum of sweat while the streamers overhead drooped and the mirror ball flung its reflections frictionlessly across the floor and the band, its muted trombones sobbing, finished its rendition of "Stardust" or "Goodnight Irene." His and Elizanne's cheeks felt pasted together, and yet when the music stopped he didn't want to let go; he continued, pantingly, to drink her in, her foreshortened demure face with its smudged upper lip and dewy expanse of décolletage, the white edges of her strapless bra outlining her gentle bosom.

How often had they danced like that? Why hadn't more come of it? As long as he could remember, the other sex had been sending out formidable scouts in his direction—mothers and grandmothers and teachers, and Barbara and Linda stealing his cap on the way to school, and fellow classroom goody-goodies like Mamie and Sarah Beth wanting to compare their homework with his. Then the surface of femininity, that towering mystery in whose presence his life must be lived, had yielded to a slight pressure. Without a word, a word that he could remember, Elizanne had submitted to his inept attentions, and indicated a demure curiosity in what he might do for her.

The walk: for days after the reunion his mind could not let go of the walk that she reminded him they had taken. In the distorting lens of old age it loomed as one of the most momentous acts of his life. The geography of Olinger had been woven into him, into the muscles that pushed his bicycle and pulled his sled. His parents took walks on Sunday afternoons, and he had tagged behind them until his legs balked. One way turned left, down the alley by their hedge and into the new streets, in regular blocks, across the main thoroughfare, the Alton Pike, with its gleaming trolley tracks. The town was older south of the Pike, where David's house sat in a ragged neighborhood of mixed architecture and vacant lots, some of them planted in corn. He preferred the tightly built blocks north of the Pike; identical brick semi-detached houses, with square-pillared porches and terraced front lawns, had been put up, street after street, during the Twenties. Friends like Mamie lived in these cozy neat blocks, where grocery stores or hobby shops or an ice-cream parlor or a barber shop were tucked into the front rooms of homes. He loved the houses' tightness, their uniformity, which seemed a pledge of order and shared intention missing from his own patchy neighborhood.

Beyond this section, where a harness-racing track had once tied up sixty acres, contractors in the years before the war had positioned handsome limestone and clinker-brick single houses on streets curving up the side of Shale Hill. David's walk with Elizanne must have taken him from the high school or its grounds along the Pike through the blocks of semi-detached houses, which above their porches held picture windows where seasonal decorations—orange-paper pumpkins and black-paper bats for Halloween, Christmas tinsel, Easter baskets—announced the residents' fealty to the Christian calendar. The trees along the streets changed from horse chestnuts in the old section where he lived to dense lines of Norway maples on the solidly built-up rectilinear streets to drooping, feathery elms and blotchy-barked sycamores, locally called buttonwoods, on the streets that curved. These trees were higher, airier; there was more space and light in the section where Elizanne lived, as if you were ascending a hill, as indeed you were, but a gently sloping hill of money, of airy privilege. And yet she had let him kiss her, there by her thick-panelled front door, with its two-tone chime doorbell, and had remembered that kiss for more than fifty years, and spoke of it as her admission ticket to the wonderland of sex.

If Mamie was right and we live forever, David thought, he could imagine no better way to spend eternity than taking that walk with Elizanne over and over, until what they said, how they touched, whether or not he dared hold her hand in his, and each hair of the fine black down on her forearms all came as clear as letters deep-cut in marble. There would be time to ask her all the questions he had been too slow-witted to ask at their fiftieth. Was this her first husband, or the last of a series? Had she had affairs, in that suburb of her choosing? Had there been a lot of necking, as he had heard there was, on the band bus back from the football games? Was it in the bus where she went on with her kissing, the groping that comes with kissing, the flush and hard breathing that come with groping? Whose girlfriend had she been in her junior and senior years? He dimly remembered her being linked with Lennie Lesher, the track star, the five-minute miler with his sunken acne-scarred cheeks and tight ridges of hair soaked in Vitalis. How could she have betrayed him, David, that way? Or was it with those faceless members of the band? Why had they, David and she, drifted apart after walking through Olinger into the region of more light? Or had it been night, after a dance or a basketball game, her white face with its strong eyebrows and quick smile a nocturnal blur?

Elizanne, he wanted to ask her, *what does it mean, this enormity of our having been children and now being old, living next door to death?* He had been the age then that his grandsons were now. As he had lived, he had come to see that for a man there is no antidote to death but a woman; yet from where, he wanted now to ask Elizanne, does a woman draw this antidote, her cosmic balm? And does it work for her as well?

For days he could not let her afterimage go, but in time he would, he knew. He could not write or call her, even if Mamie or Sarah Beth provided him with her address and number, for there were spouses, accumulated realities, limits. At the time, obviously, there had been limits in their situation. He had had little to offer her but his future of going places, and that was vague and distant. The questions he was burning to ask would receive banal answers. It was an adolescent flirtation that had come, like most, to nothing.

"Well, here we are," she announced. The streetlights had just come on.

"So soon!" he exclaimed. "You have a n-n-nifty-looking house."

"Mother's never liked the kitchen. She says it's gloomy, all those dark-stained cabinets. She wants us to move to West Alton."

"Oh, no! Don't move, Elizanne."

"I don't want to, Heaven knows. She thinks they have better schools in West Alton. A better class of student."

"*My* m-mother made us move to the country and I hate it."

"You can't stay in Olinger forever, David."

"Why not? Some do."

"That won't be you."

Her gaze clung to his in her seriousness. Her eyebrows frowned, slightly. He expected her to turn away and go through the heavy door into her house, but she didn't. He explained, "I ought to get back to the school, my p-poor father's p-p-probably looking for me. It must be past five." The light died earlier each day. It was October; the sycamore leaves were turning, slowly, brown creeping into their edges.

"Tell me honestly," she said, as if to herself, rapidly. "Did I talk too much? Just now, walking."

"No, you didn't. You didn't at all."

"That's what I do when I let myself relax with someone. I chatter. I go on too much."

"You didn't. It was like you were singing to me."

Her face had not exactly come closer to his, but its not turning and moving away made it feel closer. Cautiously he bent his face into hers, a little sideways, and kissed her. Elizanne's lips took the fit snugly, warmly; she pressed slightly into the kiss, from underneath, looking for something in it. David felt caught up in a stream flowing counter to the current of everyday events, and began to run out of breath. He broke the contact and backed off. They stared at one another, her black eyes button-bright in the sodium streetlight, amid the restless faint shadows of the half-brown big sycamore leaves. Then he kissed her again, entering that warm still point around which the universe wheeled, its load of stars not yet visible, the sky still blue above the streetlights. This time it was she who backed off. A car went by, with a staring face in the passenger window, maybe someone they knew—a spy, a gossip. "And there was even more," she said, giggling to show that she was poking fun at herself now, "that I wanted to say."

"You will," he promised, breathlessly. His cheeks were hot, as if after gym class. He was worried about his father waiting for him; his stomach anxiously stirred. David felt as he had when, his one weekend at the Jersey Shore the past summer, a wave carrying his surfing body broke too early and was about to throw him forward, down into the hard sand. "I want to hear it all," he told Elizanne. "We have t-tons of time."

The Guardians

Little Lee's soft brain swam into self-consciousness in a household of four adults, with carpets that smelled of shoe soles, and a coal furnace that chuffed in the cellar, and dusty front windows that gave onto the back side of a privet hedge and a street where horse-drawn wagons sometimes clip-clopped along among the swishing automobiles. Lee heard them early in the morning: farmers going to market. On the opposite side of the street, asphalt-shingled row houses stood above concrete retaining walls, looking down at Lee's house like the choirs of angels in the songs at Christmas. Christmas was a time when an expectant cold light invaded the house and made the people within it very clear: Grampop, Granny, Daddy, and Lee's mother, who was, as it were, too important to have a name.

Grampop was amazingly old, even when Lee was a baby. He would sit on the cane-backed sofa and hold stately discourse there with a visitor equally old, crossing and recrossing his legs, exposing a length of hairless white shin and the high black top of a buttoned shoe. Sometimes above the shoe Lee saw not white skin but the white of long cotton underwear, which only very old-fashioned country people wore. Unlike Daddy, Grampop wore a hat—gray, with a sweat-darkened band inside and two big dimples on the crown where he pinched it. When he entered the house, he would take the hat off and hold it pinched delicately between his thumb and forefinger; he would softly gesture with the hat in his hand as if it were a precious extension of himself, like his voice or his money. Once, Lee learned early, Grampop had had a great deal more money than he did now. These were hard times, depressed times, though the house was big and long, in its long hedged lawn: flowering shrubs in front and on the sides, and a grass terrace behind, a lawn broken by cherry trees and an English-walnut tree, and then a vegetable garden, a pear tree, a burning barrel, and a chicken house. Grampop had the chicken house built when he moved here. He smoked cigars, but his daughter, Lee's mother, couldn't stand the smell in the house, so he smoked outdoors, sitting in a lawn chair, or standing under a tree in a sweater, one elbow cupped in the hand of the other arm, surveying the world around him, a world on which his grip had faltered.

Granny, too, had lost her grip; her hands were bent as if holding something invisible, and waggled, with a disease that she had. Yet still she kept busy, cooking the meals and weeding and hoeing in the garden and watching out for Lee's welfare. When he, growing inch by inch, finally managed to climb up onto the lowest branch of the walnut tree, she stood directly below him and told him to get down. She wore glasses that sat cockeyed on her little hook nose, and these glinted in the afternoon light, tilted up toward Lee while he wondered if he should tell her that, though he had discovered he could get up, he hadn't yet learned how to get down. She looked very far beneath him. Her white hair flew out from her sharp small face like an exploding milkweed.

It was she who beheaded the chickens, on a log that stood upright in the chicken yard. When Lee once, on a sudden unstoppable bidding from within, while he hurried up the alley behind his backyard, went to the bathroom in his shorts, it was she who cleaned the yellow mess off his legs and told him it wasn't worth crying so hard about. It was she who pointed out that certain of the neighborhood children—the Halloran brother and sister, especially—were not suitable playmates. Granny, Lee's mother let him know, hadn't always been enfeebled: she had run Grampop's tobacco farm for him in their country days and had been one of the first women in the county to get a driver's license.

The family had owned a car when Lee was born, a green Model A Ford, but before he was old enough to go to kindergarten the car had disappeared, and was not replaced with another. That was how poor they had become. They were so poor that Grampop went to work for the borough highway crew and Granny cleaned the houses of her relatives—she had many; she had been the baby of twelve children—to bring in a few extra dollars.

Daddy worked, too, of course. He put on one of his suits almost every weekday and went off into the world beyond the front hedge. But the work he did there—adding up figures for other men, bookkeeping for a fine-gauge silk-stocking factory—didn't bring very much money home. The men who worked on the factory floor, as machinists and full-fashioned knitters, earned more, Lee became aware when he began to attend school with their children. These fathers were robust, cheerfully rude men with a pleased look about their eyes and a teasing crease about their mouths that Daddy didn't have.

Also, he didn't have a belly, the way workers and farmers did. Even Grampop had a belly, on which he would rest the wrist of the hand holding his cigar while he stood in the yard smoking. Often Lee and his grandfather were the only family members out there as the warm spring night crept in. There was a dewy weight to the air that pressed a wave of sweetness from the darkened bed of lilies-of-the-valley, and caused a scattering of cherry blossoms to fall. The old man would lift his head, listening to the birds' last chirpings. His glowing cigar end would somersault as he tossed it into the peonies. It did not occur to Lee that he, Lee, was the reason his grandfather stood there—"to keep an eye on the youngster."

It did occur to Lee, though not in words he could say, that he was a bright spot in a demoralized household. In the houses across the street—the narrow row houses lined up like gaunt, asphalt-shingled angels—the children outnumbered the parents, and the sounds of screeching and weeping that escaped the walls showed that a constant battle was being waged on near-equal terms. In Lee's house, the only sounds of battle arose between his parents. Some complaint, or set of complaints, lay between them. Otherwise, he felt the four adults as sides of a perfect square, with a diagonal from each corner to a central point. He was that point, protected on all sides, loved from every direction.

Yet there were scrapes, scoldings, childish tantrums, vows to kill himself to make everyone else sorry, various ways in which he let his guardians down. Once, irritated at how his hair kept falling over his eyes as he tried to copy a comic strip while lying on the floor, he had taken his toy tin scissors and cut some off; his mother acted as if he had cut off a finger or his nose. Haircuts, in general, were dangerous. For one thing, the chief barber at the shop they went to was a rabid Roosevelt-hater, and gusts of shrill debate swirled around Lee's hot ears as he huddled embarrassed on the chair, on a board laid across the broad porcelain arms. For another thing, his mother was usually dissatisfied with the haircut when he came home. Of the three barbers in the shop only Jake, the Roosevelt-hater, could cut Lee's hair to her satisfaction. When he pointed out to her that Jake's political opinions were the opposite of theirs, she said yes, but he was an artist.

His mother had this idea of art, of artistry, on her mind. She would sit crayoning with Lee on the floor, her weight gracefully propped on her arm, her legs folded within her nubbly wool skirt, but for the knees, white and round, that peeped from underneath. She praised Lee's little drawings beyond, he felt, their worth—or, rather, she penetrated into that secret place within him where they were valued very highly.

There was something disproportionate, something hotter than comfortable, about his mother. She had copper-colored hair and freckles and a temper. Sometimes after a fight that had rattled through the house all one Sunday afternoon, his father would say to Lee, with a certain sheepish pride, "Your mother. She's a real redhead." When Lee was even a little late coming home for supper from playing in the neighborhood, anger would show in a red V between her eyebrows. The sides of her neck would blush. More than once she whipped him, with a switch cut from the base of the pear tree, on the backs of his legs. It not only hurt but felt like a forced, unnatural exercise; it made him want to keep his distance. He liked his mother best when she sat alone at the dining-room table playing solitaire under the stained-glass chandelier, focusing on the turn of the cards, talking to herself, or when she pushed the lawnmower around the yard like a man. Their yard seemed huge, with its shaggy, fragrant bushes (hydrangeas, bridal wreath, viburnum) encroaching greedily upon each other and upon the lawn, forming secret shady spaces, dirt-floored caves where not even a weed could grow. He liked hiding in these caves, getting his shorts dirty.

At about the age of six, when first grade was teaching him how to read, he created a masterpiece of comic art—a drawing of their side hedge where the brick walk made a gap, one leafy edge slit so that a face on a long neck could be poked through, back and forth, imitating Betty Jean Halloran peeking to see if he was at home, available to play. She was tall for her age, and shy. Perhaps she sensed his grandmother's disapproval of her family, which lived down the street in a house without plumbing, just a pump on the back porch. Lee expected this paper trick to please both his female guardians, but his mother, studying the drawing and making the head poke out once or twice, conveyed without saying so that he had been cruel, because Betty Jean after all was a faithful friend, one of the few friends he had.

His being an only child was part of the soreness, the murmuring quarrel, between Daddy and his mother. Perhaps she would have been better off marrying one of the big-bellied full-fashioned knitters; at least there would have been less worry about money. But no, there was something sensitive and wary in her nature that shunned the world around her. Daddy did not shun it—on days when he didn't do accounting, he went off to teach Sunday school or watch a Saturday softball game on the school grounds—but he always returned, and he indulged his wife and son in their conspiracy about art, a way to push back at the world without touching it. When he heard them talking about art, he would say, "It's miles over my head," obviously not believing it, believing instead that it was beneath him, who dwelt high and clear among numbers.

What he did not know but Lee did and his mother sensed was that crayoning was Lee's way of getting away from her, from all his guardians, into a realm quite his own, where love did not fall upon him but descended from him, onto the little creatures, the humanoid animals, the comically unchanging comic-strip characters that he copied, his nose a few inches from the carpet that smelled of shoe leather.

When Grampop entertained his old-man guests on the cane-backed sofa, they sometimes, in their mutual pleasure at the conversation, kicked up little balls of fluff from the same faded carpet. Lee's mother complained about this, her face getting not quite as red as it did over the smell of cigars. Lee felt her heat, the afterglow of her unpredictable passions, most intensely in the piano room, which blended into the living room through an archway with side pillars and a band of ornate stick-and-beadwork overhead. This passage of carpentry was the grandest thing about the house, and his failure to succeed at piano lessons, though he took them for years, was the most distinct disappointment he made his mother suffer. The piano area, with its sheet music and brass candlesticks on top of the upright, belonged to his mother; the kitchen, with its warping linoleum and black stone sink, to Granny; the front room, with its sagging sofa and dusty view of the neighbors, to Grampop; and the front vestibule and door to Daddy, who was always going out or coming in.

As Lee lay on the carpet, his guardians in their attitudes

of suspended discomfort felt like the four corners of the ceiling far above him. The shelter they formed held through Depression and world war, and even his adolescence and his constantly outgrowing his clothes did not disturb the configuration, though Grampop underwent a cataract operation that made him hold his head very still while Lee read the newspaper headlines to him, and Granny stooped and her hands shook more and more and Parkinson's disease slowly stopped up her speech, and his father turned gray and had to find another accounting job when the hosiery mills went south after the war, and his mother put on weight, and the bushes in the yard grew taller and wilder, and Betty Jean Halloran became a beauty with a racy reputation and had long since stopped peeking around the hedge.

He had always dreaded one of his guardians' dying, disappearing into an unbelievable nothingness, ripping away a corner of his childhood shelter. As if knowing this, they contrived to stay alive until he was safely away at college and beyond, protecting him to the last from anything too ugly or frightening. They died, at tactfully spaced-out intervals, in the order of their births. Grampop was over ninety, and healthy and walking within two days of his death; he felt queasy and went to bed on the first day, and on the second day believed the bed was on fire and, in escaping it, fell dead to the floor. Lee was at college when he heard about this. Granny lingered in bed another year, unable to talk or sit up on her own finally, and was found one morning by her daughter, asleep for good, her sharp nose and deep sockets smoothed into a youthful beauty of the bone. Lee by now was pursuing an M.F.A. degree in Iowa City. For some years Daddy shuttled in and out of hospitals with angina, and nonfatal heart attacks; his young doctor confided to the widow that he "gave them all a rough hour" at the end. Lee was living in San Francisco at the time, pursuing art and his identity as an artist, and was relieved that he could not get to the bedside in time to see his father struggling for life, for air. His mother, like her father, dropped to the floor one day—the kitchen floor, the dishes just done and set in the strainer. She had moved from the long old house to a newer, smaller one, all on one level; her red hair went pure white, and she became mild and whimsical and good-tempered in her solitude, and never rebuked Lee with the rarity of his visits. Her once-a-week cleaning lady saw the body on the floor through the back-door window, and the police and undertakers and clergy did the rest, while Lee flew in from Taos, where he had moved when San Francisco didn't work out.

Now all were gone. Of that early-twentieth-century household, only Lee was left. The coal bin in the cellar, the shelves of homemade preserves, the walnut icebox, the black stone sink, the warping kitchen linoleum in the pattern of little interlocking bricks, the stained-glass dining-room chandelier shade, the front-hall newel post with ribs around it like the rings of Saturn or Plastic Man's telltale stripes, the narrow back stairs that nobody used and that became a storage space choked with cardboard boxes and appliances to be repaired some day, the windowless stair landing where they had huddled in the pitch dark during mock air raids, the long side porch where hoboes had knocked for handouts, the pansy-faced calico cat that came to the porch to be fed but was too wild to come into the house, the tawny wicker lawn chair where Grampop would sit in the twilight with his cigar, watching the fireflies gather—only Lee was left to remember any of this.

As part of his self-consciousness, while old age overtook his once-infantile brain, he made occasional efforts to envision his situation as science proved it to be. He would look at the half-moon and try to see it not as the goddess Diana or as a comic-book decal but as a sphere hung in empty space, its illumined side an infallible indication of where the sun was shining on the other side of the earth's huge round mass. He tried to imagine the surface under his feet as curved, and hurtling backwards toward sunrise. With a greater effort, he tried to imagine empty space in something like its actual vastness, each star light-years from the next, and the near-absolute vacuum of interstellar space containing virtual particles that somehow generated an energy the reverse of gravity, pushing the stars and the galaxies faster and faster apart, until the universe would become invisible to itself, cold and dark forever and ever, amen. He tried to picture organic life as Darwin and his followers described it, as not a ladder of being, climbing toward ever more complex and spiritual forms, but as a flat swamp, a diffuse soup of insensible genes whose simple existence, within however ignoble and grotesque and murderous and parasitic a creature, tended to perpetuation of those creatures, without the least taint of purpose or aspiration. It was all in the numbers, as Daddy had said. What was was, and tended to be the same, generation after generation.

There was comfort in this, Lee thought. His guardians were still with him. They were within him, extending their protection and care. From Grampop—who had had a quaint, tentative gesture of lifting his thin-skinned hand as if to bestow a blessing or to ask for a moment's halt from the powers that be—he had inherited longevity, and from Granny a country toughness, a wiry fiber that had only slowly bent beneath age and disease. His father's receding realism was his, and his mother's intent, dissatisfied heat. His guardians were within him, propelling him like a tiny human crew within a tall, walking armature of DNA. They would not steer him wrong; his death would come tactfully, and was nowhere near close.

The Laughter of the Gods

Benjamin Foster—an ungainly name, carrying in the bearer's own ears a certain formal, distant resonance, as if he were a foster child—took an interest, once his father was dead, in how his parents had met, courted, and, deepest in the darkness, conceived him. His mother told him, "We met in the registration line the very first day of college, and the second we clapped eyes on each other we started laughing. And we didn't stop laughing for the whole four years."

"Didn't you date other people, ever?"

" 'Dating' seems to mean more now than it did in the Twenties, but no, not really. Nobody else would have anything to do with us. That was our feeling. That was our fear. We were held together by fear, your father and I, a fear that nobody else would have us. We were freaks, Benjy."

She looked up, unsmiling but mischievous. Old age had made her tongue more reckless than ever, as if she were testing the echo off the walls of the house, where she lived with a deaf and lame old collie.

In the past their child, their only child, had tried to reassure himself that his parents had not been freaks in college by looking into their yearbook, called *The Amethyst*, bound in padded purple—the year 1925, the college a small Lutheran one on the Pennsylvania bank of the Delaware. The college was named Agricola, after Johann Agricola, an early associate of Luther's and, in regard to the burning issue of antinomianism, Luther's adversary for a time.

The senior photos and write-ups were arranged not in alphabetical order but as if at a dance, boy paired with girl on facing pages. His parents were thus paired, as were their faithful friends the Mentzers, when Mrs. Mentzer was still a Spangler. Benjamin's mother, under her maiden name of Verna Rahn, was shown with glossy thick bangs. Elsewhere in the yearbook she appeared in a riding outfit with boots and jodhpurs, in a tubelike party dress and a glittering headband, and in a middy blouse with dark neckerchief—the uniform of the hockey team, for which she was listed as co-captain and "right inside." She had been class secretary, her young son learned, and president of the hiking club, "a certain blue-eyed damsel from Firetown, Pa.," one with "a true innate love of nature" who could "ride a horse at break-neck speed." The motto the yearbook editors assigned her was "Fair as a star, when only one is shining in the sky."

His father's motto was "The cause of wit in others," his nickname was "Foss," and his write-up was rather joshing, calling him a "ray of sunshine" and asserting that "No fewer than a baker's dozen of the fair sex have fallen victims to his winning and jovial disposition." The yearbook even more far-fetchedly claimed that his native town in New Jersey had "become famous on account of his brilliance." Yet the photocopied college records that at some point had been tucked into the yearbook showed him getting mostly C's and even D's, whereas Verna Rahn pulled in A's and B's; she was especially adept in Latin, though Benjamin had never heard her utter a single phrase of it. The college's purpose had been, it seemed, to produce ministers and marriages; pages at the end were devoted to a diary recording the year's flirtations and pairings. The lead item on a page titled "Jokes" was:

> Frosh (after attending one of Dr. Rutter's hygiene lectures)—"Some terrible things can be caught from kissing."
> Second Frosh—"Right! you ought to see the poor fish my sister caught."

"And yet," Benjamin pointed out to his mother when she was in her seventies, "you and Daddy didn't marry right after college. You didn't marry for how many years after graduation?"

"Three. We were giving each other time to get away, but nothing better occurred to us. We had no imagination, Benjy. We were cowards."

In trying to imagine their attraction, their need to pair off, Benjamin would begin with the fact that they were both tall, his father two inches over six feet and his mother no less than five nine, awkwardly large for a woman of her generation. She put on weight over the years, but in the yearbook she was slender; young, she looked like him, Benjamin thought, and as he grew old he looked more and more like her—faintly shapeless in the face, with a sly, flirtatious expression to the mouth, as if he were prepared to take back whatever he had just said. From his mother he had learned the social arts of teasing and side-stepping.

. . .

His parents loomed large in his first memories of them—giants in their underwear, shambling with their white flanks and patches of hair to the bathroom and back. His little room was tucked behind theirs, at the back of the house, but he was often in their bed, it seemed, sick or frightened of the dark. It was a maple four-poster painted blue-gray and stencilled with a silver crescent moon and several clumsy stars. Benjamin and his mother had done it together; she had made the stencils and he held them while she applied paint. The bed was too high for Benjy to climb into by himself at first; once he could hoist himself up he was often there, as at an observation post, while his mother and father moved about him in semi-nudity, with a docile mute air they lacked when fully dressed.

Until he was old enough to make the tub feel crowded, he took baths with his mother, to save hot water. More than sixty years later, he could still recall the sight of his legs receding in the narrow watery space beside her, his feet squeezed between one of her hips and the porcelain side of the tub. To rinse his shampooed hair she would hold his head under the faucet until he thought he must drown. His parents, he realized when he was old enough to grasp some social history, were cultural products of the progressive Twenties, conditioned to expect a socialist revolution and to be unashamed of their bodies. What was natural, his mother believed, was healthy and good, even though germs and parasites could be argued to come from Nature as surely as, say, spoonfuls of cod-liver oil. The horrible lasting aftertaste as the thick transparent liquid oozed down his esophagus: that was Nature to little Benjamin—that and hay fever and the cat catching robins at the birdbath. He would find their feathers splayed in the grass. He was drawn entirely to the unnatural: to the radio, the movies, the newspapers, the blimp or skywriting airplane that once in a while appeared in the skies over their small town.

When he was thirteen they moved to a farmhouse eleven miles away; in these smaller quarters their bodies were placed in closer proximity. His grandparents occupied one room upstairs, and Benjamin's parents the other, leaving him a bed in a space next to the stairs; his grandfather would tug his toe in the morning on the way downstairs, if it stuck out from the blankets. The walls were thin, and he could hear his parents murmur, sigh, and turn over on their creaking bedsprings. There would be a patting noise and his father's voice making a noise, "*Ooo-ooh*," in appreciation, Benjamin gathered in the dark, of his mother's bulk. "Your mother should have gone onto the burleycue stage," he would tell his son, as they drove into town together, "instead of marrying me. She had the figure for it, but not the temperament. A better man than I would have talked her into it."

It was under the permissive blanket, somehow, of their country intimacy that Benjamin began to masturbate. It happened one night that, because of the primitive laundry facilities in the basement, he had no clean pajamas, and had to go to bed in his underwear. The unaccustomed sensation of his skin on the sheets stirred him into discovery. A quite magical realm, tight and fresh, opened up; at the climax he would feel as if he were somersaulting, the witness inside his head turned upside down. The sensation, if it had been a sound, was shrill, piercing through this world into another: not a dirty world but clean, the saying went, as a whistle. He was too innocent to think about the stains he left on his sheets, and once his mother did mention them in a fit of temper, but the gap between his mother and those upside-down sensations was so vast that his mind couldn't bridge it and went blank, so he made her no answer. He was never able, in later life, alone or within the body of a woman, to recover quite that initial, upending intensity—that experience of a sweetening, narrowing tightness yielding, as it were, a glimpse of icy, annihilating light beneath his feet.

Benjamin never doubted that his mother loved him better than she loved her husband. This knowledge gave him with his father the tolerant good humor with which one treats a defeated rival. When his father was dead, and Benjamin middle-aged, he tended to cut short, or turn his back on, his mother's offered outpourings of marital resentment. Even the wealth of sympathy cards—Earl Foster had been a courthouse bureaucrat, a Sunday-school teacher, a man of good will and good works—had inflamed her sense of grievance, in the way that becoming at last rich aggravates the injustice of having been short-changed all the years before. She let the tinted envelopes pile up, many unopened, on an old brass tray on a side table, and in the days after the funeral made no move to answer them: "What can I say except agree he was a saint? If he was such a saint what does that make me?"

"A fellow saint?" Benjamin suggested, wary of what he had long ago learned to recognize as his mother in a dangerous mood.

"Not by a far cry. Have you ever heard the expression 'Street angel, house devil'? That was your daddy."

"What did he do devilish?"

"You don't want to hear it. Or do you? Maybe you should."

"No, you're right, Mother, I don't."

Sitting stubbornly at the kitchen table in her black widow's dress with its green jade brooch, she went on, "When we first met, at college, my dad still had his money, and dressed me in what was considered high style, in what to your father's eyes looked like too broad a check, with too bright a bow at the neck. He was from New Jersey, and his people were terribly conservative, as you know—Presbyterians, down to the bone."

"I know." Though in fact his father all the while he knew him had been a Lutheran deacon; he had done his best to blend into his wife's locale.

"That was why he laughed at me; he said I looked like a Ziegfeld girl at a barn dance. And then," she went on, "the weekend we got married, the last day of August and terribly hot, Dad had come down a peg or two in the world, and for some reason the best thing I could find to put on was this wool suit that turned out to be *suf*focating—I nearly fainted on the train, and sweated big spots into it. My mother-in-law was reported to have said she thought only colored people got married in August. She was sick with diabetes already, the whole ceremony had been rushed together so she wouldn't hear of it ahead of time, and when she did she fainted dead away. At least the other Fosters said she did. Your daddy was meant to be the one who didn't get married and would support their mother in her decline. I realized when the others told me—it must have been my sister-in-law, she was always free with her news—I realized there were two kinds of women, the kind who really did faint and those who just nearly did, like me. When we got into our tiny stateroom in the Pullman, your father said I smelled like a pig."

"Oh, no!" Benjamin felt obliged to protest, at the risk of tipping her into an even more menacing, unpredictable temper.

"He was right," she said, "I was drenched, and ruined the dress. 'Pig' wasn't the worst word he ever used. Our so-called honeymoon, that whole first year when I was following him around with the surveying crew, all through the coal regions, we kept staying in these cheap boarding-houses that were really cathouses. You'd meet the girls on the stairs dragging up customers almost too drunk to walk. In the daytime everybody except me was sleeping. I got a world of reading done—all the Russians, Balzac, Flaubert. I never could take to Dickens—too jokey. One of the madams told me that what you look for in a girl is a high arch to the foot. That tells you all you need to know. I had flat feet, though she was too polite to point it out. I couldn't compete with your father's ideas of those girls on the stairs—thank Heaven I got pregnant with you and could come home to my father's house. I wish all these people scribbling how your father was such a saint could have heard his language when it was just the two of us stuck together, like dogs in rut."

She gestured with disgust at the stack of sympathy notes in the brass tray, and when Benjamin left the next day they had vanished, unanswered.

He had hungered, through his childhood, for the signs of happy union that he saw in the parents of his friends, a secret physical prosperity that oozed into society as respectability's hard-earned good cheer. His parents almost never went out to parties, and when they did his father was usually sick from the rich food and unaccustomed liquor. He had a Presbyterian stomach. But their old college friends the Mentzers held an annual New Year's party, which included other couples mated at Agricola, and off his parents would go into the dark with what Benjamin imagined as their old collegiate gaiety. At other reunion occasions he had heard Mrs. Mentzer, the once-beautiful Ethel Spangler, call his father "Fossie" with a fond purr that almost materialized the unimaginable conqueror of "no fewer than a baker's dozen of the fair sex."

It was with a daughter of this crowd, not the Mentzers' but the Reifsneiders', that Benjamin had his first real date—his first parentally approved appointment with the fair sex. He was old enough to drive, by a few months, and went off in a sports jacket, necktie, and clean shirt carefully harmonized by his clothes-conscious mother. He and Ada Reifsneider went to the movies and afterwards to the West Alton all-night diner for hamburgers and ice-cream sodas. They attended different high schools and didn't have much to talk about except their parents and the movie they had just seen, yet they managed well enough so that, parked in front of her dark house, he felt entitled to kiss her, which she seemed to expect. Her sallow face had regular features, but her lips were hard and cool, with a chill of prepared willingness he did not feel he had earned. He had felt clumsy, overdressed, and not quite right, and assumed that her sense of him agreed with his. He never called her again, though she was pretty enough. Whatever it was that must be discovered, the path was not through his parents' college days.

His mother in all the years he knew her had never had a haircut or gone to a hairdresser. Her hair had been going gray as long as he could remember; she bundled it behind in a bun held with hairpins that he frequently found on the floor, when he lived boyishly close to the carpet. When she was a girl, she more than once told him (she told him everything more than once), her own mother would do up her hair in braids wound so tight on the top of her head that she wanted to scream. It frightened Benjamin, at night, to see her take out her pins and let her hair down and walk around the upstairs in her slip, looking like a graying witch, just her nose and her eyes peeping out through the curtain of her hair. Years later, in the late Sixties, he picked up a plump young hooker in the bar of a Chicago hotel. When they were done, she put her silvery minidress back on and walked around his room combing out her hair, long and uncontained in the Sixties style, and it came to him that this was how a woman was supposed to look, like Eve or Mary Magdalene in an admonitory old woodcut.

There was a hint of admonition, too, in the underwear drawer of his mother's bureau, its tumble of flesh-colored straps and intricate metal fastenings like a web of apparatus in a torture chamber. Her girdle and its stocking fasteners—flesh-colored buttons, and wire loops shaped like snowmen—left cruel dents in her flesh, and on one of her feet the little toe was quite bent over the others by years of tight, pointy shoes.

At night, upstairs in the country house, his father, describing the adventures of his day in the city world, would mumble, and she would begin to laugh, and he would mumble again, and her laughter would be goaded to a half-suppressed shriek, an escape like that of steam, ending in a whimper begging for mercy, and he would mumble once more, and then in the contagion of her renewed glee he, too, would laugh, a few reluctant chuckles that ended the story. In the morning, when Benjamin asked her what had been so funny, she would say, "It's too hard to explain. It's not so much what your daddy says as how he says it that sets me off sometimes. I don't believe he even means to be funny at first; his life has been really a sad one."

Yet his parents didn't radiate sadness, though their misery and helplessness—their state of being *trapped*—was a frequent theme of their conversation. After Benjamin's grandparents were both dead, a new bed was installed in the vacated room, but as far as Ben knew his parents rarely used it, staying in the too-high, noisy-springed one with the moon and stars stencilled onto the blue-gray headboard. When, summers, he visited with his growing family, there were too many bodies for the beds, and his parents would sleep on a flat farm wagon in the barn. They made so comical a sight there, uplifted on huge spoked wheels, surrounded by mounds of baled hay and rusted equipment, under motley layers of spare blankets and quilts, that his children would run out first thing in the morning, through the dew of the lawn, to catch their grandparents still thus abed, and cheer themselves with the hilarious, comforting sight. The old couple would sit up in greeting, both wearing black wool watch-caps, donned for warmth and to keep dust and dove droppings out of their hair. Pigeons cooed and thrashed in the upper reaches of the barn like left-over bits from their dreams.

As his mother's widowhood stretched past a decade and into its fifteenth year, it was as if her son, who tried to visit her for a few days every month, had always been the only man in her life. When she spoke of her husband, it was in the tone of startled reminiscence with which she might suddenly recall the dark-eyed little Schlouck boy with whom she had walked to the one-room school down the sandy dirt road that passed along the edge of her parents' farm and over the rise to the main road. "My mother thought his people were too dark," she would say. Or, of her husband: "He was so hipped, after his heart began to act up, on paying in his extra thousand to the county retirement fund. He said he could see daylight for the first time in his life."

"Daylight?"

"I don't know how much daylight he thought he had left for himself. But he wanted to leave me *set.* Just like the driving. I hadn't driven since my father sold their Biddle and moved into town. But he forced me to drive, he even had me take a course from a high-school instructor, and get my license. He knew that without it I couldn't hang on out here."

"So he *was* a saint," said Benjamin, ironically.

She missed the irony. She said solemnly, "He wanted to be. His mother had been terribly religious, so full of good works she would forget to feed her own family. But he had these doubts. We all had, back then. We read Mencken, Shaw, H. G. Wells, Sinclair Lewis. Nothing was sacred. We laughed at everything, even at school, where half the professors were ordained, and half the boys were aimed that way. Of course, we were young—we could afford to laugh. Your father was such a kidder, so good-humored around people who didn't know him, it shocked me at first when he'd get these terrible bouts of depression. 'The blues,' he called them. He'd sit in a chair and not move. Everything disappointed him, especially me."

"Oh, no, I don't think so!" The protest was courteous; Benjamin had grown up with the impression that his parents' marriage had been a mistake, partially redeemed by his birth.

"Except my mother," his mother went on, looking past him from within the tattered wing chair where she now spent most of her days, rousing herself only to feed the pets and change television channels. "He *admired* her. She had a quickness I didn't; she could make money. It had been her management of the farm that had made my father rich, for a while, until he lost it on his friends' stock tips. That was our tragedy, if your father and I had one: we didn't know how to make money. And he was the only one of my suitors she ever approved of. The funny thing was, like Sammy Schlouck, he was dark. He could take a tan, your father, unlike you and me. We have the type of skin that can only burn."

"Maybe that's what the attraction was. Opposite skin types."

She ignored the idea. "*Was* there an attraction? Or were we just looking for people who would maintain the suffering that we figured we deserved? We both felt embarrassed at having been born. My parents had wanted a boy, and Daddy was the youngest of four, he always felt he was 'one more mouth to feed.' We hadn't had happy childhoods, either of us. Now you, you did. We were both amazed to see it. We didn't understand how you did it."

"I had loving parents," Benjamin gallantly suggested. Parents, he didn't say, who had no one else to love.

"No," she argued, perversely, "it was something in you, you produced it out of yourself, in this miserable household. Ethel Spangler, after she married Howard Mentzer but before they had a child of their own, came to the house for an afternoon and when she left said to me, 'I hope this child gets some love in his life some day.' "

Benjamin laughed, incredulous and gratified. "What a thing to say! And yet you and Daddy kept on with her all those years."

"People used to hang on to each other," said his mother, "for fear that was all there was. Now, they let go and latch on to somebody else just like the first."

This was a dig—Benjamin had divorced and remarried twice—but he let it glide by. He saw his mother as the dispenser of more truth than he could bear. When he was seven or eight, and graduated from the shared bathtub, he asked her, having been invited to satisfy his curiosity about the facts of life, if in a woman wee-wee came out of the same place as babies did. Gently, frankly, like the progressive spirit she was, she answered him, but his embarrassment was so intense it quite blotted out her answer, leaving his question to hang in his memory as a perpetual humiliation.

When she died, a long lifetime welled up through its leavings. In a small cedar chest opened by a key in her desk drawer, he found, wrapped in a ribbon faded from red to pink, a bundle of letters his father had written to her in the three years between college graduation and their marriage. They were ardent, stiff, earnest. Phrases swam up from the thin creased paper, scented not only with cedar but with, Benjamin imagined, the salt air of Florida, where his father had spent eighteen months: *want to do right by everybody concerned . . . certain you are the mate the good Lord meant me to have . . . Ma has her ups and downs and is brave as Hell . . . Ed says the business climate here is bound to turn around, people always pull in their horns after a hurricane . . . miss you every day and especially after work . . . if, God forbid, she takes a turn for the worse . . . be with you on the old cane-back sofa in Olinger and kick back my heels and share a good laugh . . . almost chuck it all up and head north on the next freight train but . . . the docs say she has the determination of a saint or a mule . . . can hear your voice as sure as shooting . . . the sunsets come on so quick because of the latitude . . . I'm still your Sheik and you my Agnes Ayres . . . ninety-eight in the shade over by Arcadia . . . or die trying . . .* Benjamin could not bear to read continuously, it was like his mother's too-detailed answer to that childish question of his; his mind shied away. His father's handwriting even then, before he got his master's degree and a teaching job, had a schoolteacher's patient legibility; he formed each letter carefully, lifing his pen in the middle of a word. When his mother had at last died, he had already come back up north. The salmon upstream: *or die trying*.

An embossed chocolate box shaped like a heart held proof that his mother had at least once cut her hair. *Verna Rahn's Haircut*, she had written in her little backslanted hand, *June 18, 1926. (Moths ate some of it!)* So this was its second packaging; bound with black thread, it was so long Benjamin didn't dare pull it from the box, which still smelled, very faintly, of chocolate. He let the hair stay in its thick coil, nested in tissue paper. Its color was an innocent pale shade of brown with no gray in it—light brown, like that of Jeannie in the song. A *country* shade, he felt. Experimentally he touched it, and moved his hand quickly away, as if he had presumed to stroke something alive.

And he found, folded at the bottom, under crocheted blankets and lace tablecloths and an Agricola pennant of purple-and-gold felt, something that he could never have given his mother but that his father had: a varsity football sweater, heavy-knit of yellowed white, the chest stiffened by its broad letter, the sleeves pinned up with oversized safety pins that were still there, their rust stains spread into the thick yarn. Another pin, in the back, took a tuck. This sweater, and the pins that had adjusted its fit on her slender body, gave off heat and implied the chill of vanished winters—mild moist Pennsylvania winters, young couples strolling the campus with open coats and unbuckled galoshes, their laughter making small white clouds.

His father had come to college on a football scholarship, though he always maintained he was too tall and skinny for the game. He had kept playing through a series of broken noses that became a feature of his mashed and melancholy face. Photographs survived, of him crouching purposefully in the unpadded leather helmet of the time. Under the folded sweater there was a game program that included Agricola's schedule; the team had played, amazingly, Cornell and Columbia and Rutgers. The little college had been overmatched—cannon fodder. His father had given his mother his all. He had clothed her in his pain, and their son had tagged on behind, uncertain what was so funny, but happy to be jealous.

Varieties of Religious Experience

There is no God: the revelation came to Dan Kellogg in the instant that he saw the World Trade Center South Tower fall. He lived in Cincinnati but happened to be in New York, visiting his daughter in Brooklyn Heights; her apartment had a penthouse view of lower Manhattan, less than a mile away. Standing on her terrace, he was still puzzling over the vast quantities of persistent oily smoke pouring from the Twin Towers, and the nature of the myriad pieces of what seemed white cardboard fluttering within the smoke's dark column, and who and what the perpetrators and purpose of this event might have been, when, as abruptly as a girl letting fall her silken gown, the entire skyscraper dropped its sheath and vanished, with a silvery rippling noise. The earth below, which Dan could not see, groaned and spewed up a cloud of ash and pulverized matter that slowly, from his distant perspective, mushroomed upward. The sirens filling the air across the East River continued to wail, with no change of pitch; the cluster of surrounding skyscrapers, stone and glass, held its pose of blank mute witness. Had Dan imagined hearing a choral shout, a cry of protest breaking against the silence of the sky—an operatic human noise at the base of a phenomenon so inhumanly pitiless? Or had he merely humanized the groan of concussion? He was aware of looking at a, for him, new scale of things—that of Blitzkrieg, of erupting volcanoes. The collapse had a sharp aftermath of silence; at least, he heard nothing more for some seconds.

Ten stories below his feet, too low to see what he saw, two black parking-garage attendants loitered outside the mouth of the garage, one standing and one seated on an aluminum chair, carrying on a joshing conversation that, for all the sound that rose to Dan, might have been under a roof of plate glass or in a silent movie. The attendants wore short-sleeved shirts, but summer's haze, this September morning, had been baked from the sky, to make way for the next season. The only cloud was manmade—the foul-colored, yellow-edged smoke drifting toward the east in a solid, continuously replenished mass. Dan could not quite believe the tower had vanished. How could something so vast and intricate, an elaborately engineered upright hive teeming with people, mostly young, be dissolved by its own weight so quickly, so casually? The laws of matter had functioned, was the answer. The event was small beneath the calm dome of sky. No hand of God had intervened because there was none. God had no hands, no eyes, no heart, no anything.

Thus was Dan, a sixty-four-year-old Episcopalian and probate lawyer, brought late to the realization that comes to children with the death of a pet, to women with the loss of a child, to millions caught in the implacable course of war and plague. His revelation of cosmic indifference thrilled him, though his own extinction was held within this new truth like one of the white rectangles weightlessly rising and spinning within the boiling column of smoke. He joined at last the run of mankind in its stoic atheism. He had fought this wisdom all his life, with prayer and evasion, with recourse to the piety of his Ohio ancestors and to ingenious and jaunty old books—Kierkegaard, Chesterton—read for comfort in adolescence and early manhood. But had he been one of the hundreds in that building—its smoothly telescoping collapse in itself a sight of some beauty, like the color-enhanced stellar blooms of photographed supernovae, only unfolding not in aeons but in seconds—would all that metal and concrete have weighed an ounce less or hesitated a microsecond in its crushing, mincing, vaporizing descent?

No. The great *No* came upon him not in darkness, as religious fable would have it, but on a day of maximum visibility; "brutally clear" was how airplane pilots, interviewed after the event, described conditions. Only when Dan's revelation had shuddered through him did he reflect, with a hot spurt of panic, that his daughter, Emily, worked in finance—in midtown, it was true, but business now and then took her to the World Trade Center, to breakfast meetings at the very top, the top from which there could not have been, today, any escape.

Stunned, emptied, he returned from his point of vantage on the penthouse terrace to the interior of Emily's apartment. The stolid Anguillan nanny, Lucille, and Dan's younger granddaughter, Victoria, who was five and sick with a cold and hence not at school, sat in the study. The small room, papered red, was lined with walnut shelves. The books went back to Emily's college and business-school days and included a number—Cold War thrillers, outdated medical texts—that had once belonged to her husband, from whom she was divorced, just as Dan Kellogg was divorced from her mother. Had Emily inherited the tendency to singleness, as she had inherited her father's lean build and clipped, half-smiling manner? Lucille had drawn the shade of the study window looking toward Manhattan. She reported to Dan, "I tell her to not look out the window but then the television only show the disaster, every channel we switch on."

"Bad men," little Victoria told him eagerly, her tongue stumbling—her cold made her enunciation even harder to understand than usual—"bad men going to knock down *all* the buildings!"

"That's an awful lot of buildings, Vicky," he said. When he talked to children, something severe and legalistic within him resisted imprecision.

"Why does God let bad men do things?" Victoria asked. The child's face looked feverish, not from her cold but from what she had seen through the window before the shade was drawn. Dan gave the answer he had learned when still a believer: "Because He wants to give men the choice to be good or bad."

Her face, so fine in detail and texture—brutally fine—considered this theology for a second. Then she burst forth, flinging her arms wide: "Bad men can do anything they want, anything at all!"

"Not always," Dan corrected. "Sometimes good men stop them. Most of the time, in fact."

In the shadowy room, they seemed three conspirators. Lucille was softly rocking herself on the sofa, and made a cooing noise now and then. "Think of all them still in there, all the people," she crooned, as if to herself. "I was telling

Vicky how on Anguilla when I was a girl there was no electricity, and telephones only for the police, who rode bicycles wherever they went on the island. The only crime was workers coming back from three months away being vengeful with their wives for some mischief. The tallest building two stories high, and when there was no moon people stay safe in their cabins." Then, in a less dreamy voice, one meant to broadcast reassurance to the listening child, she told Dan, "Her momma, she called five minutes ago and work is over for today, she coming home but don't know how, the trains being all shut down. She might have to be walking all that way from Rockefeller Center!"

Dan himself, before returning to Cincinnati today, had been planning to take the subway up to the Whitney Museum and see the Wayne Thiebaud show, which was in its last days. Dan relished the Disney touch in the artist's candy colors and his bouncy, plump draughtsmanship. Abruptly, viewing this show was impossible—part of an idyllic, less barricaded past.

"So we'll all just wait for Mommy," he announced, trying to be, until Emily arrived, the leader of this defenseless, isolated trio. "I know!" he exclaimed. "Let's make Doughboy cookies for Mommy when she comes home! She'll be hungry!" And he leaned over and poked Vicky in the tummy, as if she were the Doughboy in the television commercials.

But she didn't laugh or even smile. Her eyes beneath her bangs and serious straight brows were feverishly bright. She was burning to know what new and forbidden thing was happening on the other side of the window shade. And so was Lucille, but she denied herself turning on television, and Dan denied himself another visit to the terrace, to verify his desolating cosmic intuition.

. . .

Emily was home in an hour, safe and aghast and sweating with the unaccustomed exercise of marching down the East Side and across the Manhattan Bridge in a mob of others fleeing the island. Dan's daughter at thirty-seven was slim and hard and professional, a trim soldier-woman a far cry from her indolent, fleshy mother. She turned on the little kitchen TV right away and was not pleased by the smell of fresh-baked cookies. "We're trying to train Victoria away from sweets," she told her father, and when he explained how he and Lucille had sought to distract the child, commanded, "Let her watch a little. This is history. This is huge. There's no hiding it." In the Heights, she told them, auto traffic had ceased, and men with briefcases, their dark suits dusted with ash, were stalking up the middle of Henry Street. She hid the warm cookies on an out-of-reach shelf; she sent Lucille off to pick up Victoria's older sister, Hilary, at her day school; she gave a supermarket shopping list to her father while she went to the bank to withdraw plenty of cash, just in case society broke down totally. Vicky went with her.

Dan found early lunch hour in progress on Montague Street. Voices twanged over the outdoor tables much as usual, though self-consciously, somehow, as if unseen television cameras were grinding away. The street scene seemed enacted; even the boys loafing outside of the supermarket appeared to be conscious of a new weight of attention bearing upon them—the importance, in the thickened air, of survivors. The air smelled caustic and snowed flurrying motes of ash. Sensory impressions hit Dan harder than usual, because God had been wiped from his brain. In his previous life, commonsense atheism had not been ingenious enough for him, nor had it seemed sufficiently gracious toward the universe. Now he had been shown how little the universe cared for his good will.

He entered the supermarket and pushed his cart along. The place was not crowded with panic shoppers, but rather empty instead, and darker than usual, sickly and crepuscular, like one of those pre-Christian afterlives, Hades or Sheol. A few people moved through the aisles, past the bins of bagels and shelves of high-priced gourmet snacks, as if for the first time, haltingly; they scanned one another's faces for a recognition that was almost there, a greeting on the tips of their tongues. Incredulity edged toward acceptance. They were coping, they were not panicking, they were demonstrating calm to the enemy.

Dan returned to the apartment laden with plastic bags, two on each hand; the handles, stretched thin by the weight of oranges and milk and cranberry juice, had dug into his palms. Emily had come back with plenty of cash and several plans. Already, signs advertising communal events were going up on lampposts: there were blood donations up at the Marriott, near Borough Hall, and a special service at Grace Church at six. In the subdued camaraderie of the crowd at the Marriott, the father and daughter filled out laborious forms side by side and were told, by bullhorn, to go home, the blood bank was overflowing: "There is no more need for the present, but if any develops we have your names." The fact had dawned that there were almost no mere injuries; the bodies were all minced in the two vast buildings' wreckage.

At the church, where he and the four females he escorted found room in a back pew, Dan marvelled at the human animal: like dogs, we creep back to lick the hand of a God Who, if He exists, has just given us a vicious kick. The harder He kicks, the more fervently we cringe and creep forward to lick His hand. The great old church, a relic of post–Civil War ecclesiastical prosperity, was for this special occasion full, and the minister, a stocky young woman wearing a bell of glossy, short-cut hair, announced in a clarion voice that at the moment several members of this congregation were still among the missing. She read their names. "Let us pray for their safety, and for the souls of all who perished today, and for the fate of this great nation." With a rustle that rose into the murk of the stony vaults above them, all bowed their heads.

Dan felt detached, like a visiting Martian. His sense of alienation persisted in the weeks that followed, as flags sprang from every Ohio porch bracket and *God Bless America* was written in shaving cream on every shop window. Back in Cincinnati, having returned, two days later than planned, by bus, he looked across a river not to smoking towers but to Kentucky, where each pickup truck sprouted a soon-tattered banner of national pride and defiance. Heartland religiosity, though its fundamentalism and bombastic puritanism had often made him wince, was something Dan had been comfortable with; now it seemed barbaric. On television, the President clumsily grasped the rhetoric of war, then got used to it, then got good at it. The nightly news showed how, in New York City, impromptu shrines had sprung up on sidewalks and outside of fire stations across the city. Candles guttered under color Xeroxes of the forever missing, memorial flowers wilted in their paper cones and plastic sheaths. Dan found himself aggrieved by the grotesque and pitiable sight of a great modern nation attempting to heal itself through this tired old magic of flags and candles—the human spirit stubbornly spilling its colorful vain gestures into the void.

Some days before Dan's revelation, a stocky thirty-three-year-old Muslim called, like millions of his co-religionists around the world, Mohamed, briefly hesitated before ordering a fourth Scotch-on-the-rocks in a dark unholy place, a one-story roadside strip joint on an unfashionable stretch of Florida's east coast. His companion, a younger, thinner man named Zaeed, lifted his slender hand from the table as if to protest, then let it weightlessly fall back. Their training regimen had inculcated the importance of blending in, and getting drunk was a sure method of merging with America, this unclean society disfigured by an appalling laxity of laws and an electronic delirium of supposed opportunities and pleasures. The very air, icily air-conditioned, tasted of falsity. The whiskey burned in Mohamed's throat like a fire against which he must repeatedly test his courage, his resolve. *It is God's kindled fire, which shall mount above the hearts of the damned.*

On the shallow stage, ignored by most of the customers scattered at small tables and only now and then brushed by his own glance, a young woman, naked save for strategic patches of tinsel and a dusting of artificial glitter on her face, writhed around a brass pole to an irritating mutter of tuneless music. She was as lean as a starveling boy but for the protuberances of fat that distinguish women; these, Mohamed knew, had been swollen by injection to seem tautly round and perfectly doll-like. The whore was entwining herself upside down around her pole, and scissoring open her legs so that a tinsel thong battered back at the light. Her long hair hung in a heavy platinum sheet to the stage floor, which was imbued with filth by her sisters' feet. There were three dancers: a Negress who performed barefoot, flashing soles and palms the color of silver polish; a henna-haired slut who wore glass high heels and kept fluttering her tongue between her lips and even mimed licking the brass pole; and this blonde, who danced least persuasively, with motions mechanically repeated while her eyes, their doll-like blue outlined in thick black as in an Egyptian wall-painting, stared into the darkness without making eye contact.

She did not see him, nor did Mohamed in his soul see her. Zaeed—with whom Mohamed was rehearsing once again the details of their enterprise, its many finely interlocked and synchronized parts, down to the last-minute cell-phone calls that would give the final go-ahead—had been drinking sweet drinks called Daiquiris. Suddenly he excused himself and hurried to the bathroom. Zaeed was young and resident in this land of infidels less than two months; its liquor was still poison to him, and its licentious women were fascinating. He had not grown Mohamed's impervious shell, and his English was exceedingly poor. The whore's globular breasts hung down parallel to her lowered sheet of hair while her shaved or plucked crotch twinkled and flashed.

Through half-shut eyes and the shifting transparencies of whiskey, Mohamed could see a semblance to the ignorant fellahin's conception of Paradise, where sloe-eyed virgins wait, on silken couches, among flowing rivers, to serve the martyrs delicious fruit. But they are manifestations, these houris, of the highest level of purity, white in their flesh and gracious in their submission. They are radiant negatives of these underfed sluts who for paltry dollars mechanically writhed on this filthy stage.

Another slut, the middle-aged waitress, wrinkled and thickened—a pot of curdled lewdness, of soured American opportunities—was waving a slip of paper at him. "Going off-duty . . . finish up my tables . . . forty-eight dollars." Her twanging "cracker" accent was difficult to penetrate, and from her agitation he gathered that this was not the first time this evening that he had offended her.

He did not see why he should hurry to pay. Zaeed was still

in the bathroom, and the sandwiches they had ordered were still on the table, uneaten. That was it: she had offered some time ago—an hour? ten minutes?—to clear the table and he told her he was not done, though in truth the food disgusted him. It was, like everything in this devilish country, excessive and wasteful—an open hot roast-beef sandwich, not rare but gray, now cold and limp on its bread, dead meat scattered beneath his hands, as far beneath them as if under the wings of an airplane. The disgusting sandwich had been served with French fries and coleslaw, garbage not fit for a street dog. Yet he kept thinking he would turn to it, to muffle the burning of the whiskey while he spoke to Zaeed, hardening the younger man's shell for the great deed that had been laid out like a precision drawing in a German engineering class. Mohamed had studied engineering among the unbelievers, absorbing the mathematics they had stolen centuries ago from the Arabs.

He must eat. The day, the fateful morning, of culmination was approaching, and he must be strong, his hands and nerves steady, his will relentless, his body vital and pure, shaven of its hair. The greatness of the deed that was held within him pressed upward like a species of nausea, straining his throat with a desire to cry out—to proclaim, as had done his prophetic namesake the Messenger, the magnificence, beyond all virtues and qualities imaginable on earth, of God and His fiery justice. *For the unbelievers We have prepared fetters and chains, and a blazing Fire. Flames of fire shall be lashed at you, and melted brass.*

The blonde whore flicked away the sparkling thong and with spread legs waddled about the pole showing her shaved slit, an awkward, ugly maneuver that won scattered cheers from the jaded tables in the darkness. Zaeed returned, looking paler. He had been sick, he confessed. Mohamed abruptly felt a great love for his brother in conspiracy, the younger brother he had never had. Mohamed had been raised in a flowery Cairo suburb with a pair of sisters; it was to keep them from ending as sluts that he had dedicated himself to the holy jihad. They were too light-headed to know that the temptations twittering at them from television and radio were from Satan, designed to lure them into eternal flame. Their parents, in their European clothes, their third-rate prosperity measured out in imitation-Western goods, were blind to the evil they wrought upon their children. Hoarding their comforts in their heavily curtained, servant-run house in Giza, they were like eyeless cave creatures, blind to the grandeur of the One Who will wrathfully reduce this flimsy world and its distractions to a desert. Mohamed carried that sublime desert, its night sky clamorous with stars, within him. *When the sky is rent asunder; when the stars are scattered and the oceans roll together; when the graves tumble in ruin; each soul shall know what it has done and what it has failed to do.*

The waitress had returned accompanied by a man, a hireling, the bald bartender in a yellow T-shirt advertising something in three-dimensional speeding letters, a beer or perhaps a sports team, Mohamed could not quite bring it into focus. Zaeed looked worried; he exuded the sickly sweat of fear, and his movements betrayed a desire to leave this unholy place. Mohamed quenched the boy's alarm with a touch on his forearm and stood to confront the hireling in the speeding T-shirt. Standing so quickly dizzied him but did not weaken his wits or dull his awareness of the movements around him. A fresh female on the stage, the *abdah* with bare feet again, dressed in filmy scarves that would soon come off, altered the light of the place, diluting its darkness as the spotlight played upon her. Pale faces, natives of this forsaken coast, turned to witness Mohamed's quarrel with the hirelings. Within him his great secret felt an eggshell's thickness from bursting forth. More than once, small mishaps and moments of friction—a traffic ticket, an INS summons, a hasty slip of the tongue with an inquisitive neighbor seeking, in that doglike American way, to be friendly—had threatened to expose the whole elaborate, thoroughly meditated structure; but the All-Merciful had extended His protecting hand. The Great Satan had been rendered stupid and sluggish; its sugary diet of freedom had softened its mechanically straightened teeth.

Mohamed felt himself mighty in his power to restrain his tongue, that muscle which summons armies and moves mountains. He produced his wallet and opened it to display the thickness of twenties and fifties and even hundreds, depicting in dry green engraving the dead heroes of this Jew-dominated government. "Plenty to pay your fucking bill," he told the threatening man in the yellow T-shirt. "And look, my good man, look here—" Not content with the cash as a demonstration of his potency, Mohamed showed, too swiftly for a close examination, the card registering him in flying school and another, forged in Germany, stating him to be a licensed pilot. "I am a pilot."

Impressed and mollified, his antagonist asked, in the languid accents of a tongue long steeped in drugs, "Hey, cool. What airline?"

Mohamed said, "American." It was an inspired utterance that, in the utterance, became blazingly true, as the suras of his namesake, the Prophet, became true when they blazed from the Messenger's mouth, promising salvation for believers and for the others the luminous boiling Fire. He had been not some ridiculous crucified God but the perfect person, *insan-i-kamil*. Mohamed's assertion sounded so just, so prophetic, he repeated it, challenging his bald, drugged enemy to contradict him: "American Airlines."

From where Jim Finch sat in his cubicle, about a third of the way into the vast floor—a full acre—populated by bond traders and their computer monitors, the building's windows held a view of mostly sky, cloudless today. If he stood up, he could see New Jersey's low shore beyond the Statue of Liberty. From this height, even the Statue, which was facing the other way, looked small, like the souvenir statuettes for sale in every Wall Street tourist trap. Jim lived in Jersey—three children and four bedrooms on an eighth of an acre in Irvington—and from where he lived he could see, picking his spots between the asphalt rooftops and leafy trees, where he worked. To impress the kids he tried to locate his exact floor, counting down from the top, though in truth it was hard from that distance to be certain; the skyscraper was built of vertical ribs that ran individual floors and windows together. Steel tubes, like a row of drinking straws, held it up, and that made the windows narrower than you felt they should be, so the view from his cubicle was more up and down than sideways. Today the windows were a row of smooth blue panels, except that curling gusts of smoke and flickering pieces of paper strangely invaded the blue from below. Some minutes ago, deep underneath him, while he had been talking to a client on the phone, there had been a thump, distant like a truck hatch being slammed down on West Street, and yet communicating a shudder to his desk.

His cell phone rang. Jim's motion of snatching it off his

belt was habitual and instant, like a snake's strike. But instead of business it was Marcy, back in New Jersey. "Jim, honey," she said, "don't hate me, I forgot to say, you went out the door so fast, when you pick up the cleaning on the way home could you swing by the Pathmark and pick up a half-gallon of whole milk and maybe check out their cantaloupes."

"O.K., sure."

"The ones last week went straight from green to punky, but they said there'd be better ones in on Monday. There should be a little give to the skins but your thumb shouldn't leave a dent." He watched a piece of charred insulation foam rise into view and then float away. "For the milk there's plenty of skimmed for ourselves but Frankie and Kristen, the way they're growing, they just wolf the whole kind down; she's as bad as he is. Honest, I meant to pick some up but the cart was already so full. *Sor*ry, hon."

"Hey, Marcy—"

"Any dessert you'd like for yourself, buy it. And maybe—be sure to check the sell-by date—a half-dozen eggs, the *large* size, not the *extra*-large. But don't forget Annie has that event at the church hall tonight, six-thirty, the beginning of indoor soccer, she's *very* nervous and wants us both there."

"Honey—"

"The new young assistant minister scares her. She says he's uptight—he wants too much to win."

"Hey, Marcy, could you please for Chrissake shut up?"

There was a hurt silence, then her voice tiptoed back. "What is it, Jim? You sound strange."

"Something strange happened a couple minutes ago, I don't know what. There was this thump underneath us; I thought it was on the street. But everything shook, and now there's smoke you can see out the windows. Hold on." Cy

Walsh, the man in the cubicle across from his, was signalling for his attention, and tersely told him some things that Jim relayed to Marcy. "The interior phone lines seem to be all out. People have come back saying the elevators aren't working and the stairs are full of smoke."

"Oh my God, Jim."

"Nobody's panicking, I mean almost nobody. I'm sure it'll work out. I mean, how bad can it be?"

"Oh my God."

"Honey, stop saying that. It doesn't help. They'll figure it out. I can't keep talking, they got to start moving us somewhere. Hey. Marcy. You won't believe this, but the floor's warm. Actually fucking *warm.*"

"Oh, Jimmy, *do* something! Hang up whenever you have to. I've always hated those flimsy-looking buildings, and you being up so high."

"Listen, Marcy. What phone are you on? The upstairs portable?"

"Yes." Her voice trembled, putting extra syllables into the word, *ye-ess*, like a child scared she has done wrong and will be punished. Across the miles between them they shared the sensation of being scolded children—a rubbed, watery feeling in their abdomens.

He asked her, "Go into Annie's room and look out the window. Tell me what you see."

While he waited, there was human movement among the desks, herd movement with bumps and shouts, but he didn't feel it had a direction he should join. A rising smell, a tarry industrial smell, oily and sickening-sweet, reminded him of airport runways and the vibrations you see around the engines while waiting to take off.

"Jim?"

"Still here. What can you see from Annie's window?"

"Oh God, I can see *smoke*! From sort of near the top; it's the tower on the left, the one you work in. Jim, I'm scared. There's a kind of black ink running down between the grooves. What can it be? Remember that missile that maybe brought down that plane off Long Island?"

"Honey, don't be dumb. Some kind of malfunction, it must be, within the building. There's enough wiring in the walls to fry China if there's a short. Don't worry, they'll figure it out. They have guys paid a fortune to sit around and plan how to handle contingencies. Still, I must say—"

"What, Jimmy? What must you say?"

"I was starting to say it's getting hard to breathe in here. Somebody just smashed a window. Jesus. They're chucking chairs right through the windows. Hey, Marcy?"

"Yes? *Yes?*"

"I don't know, but maybe this isn't so good."

"The smoke is coming from a floor somewhere under yours," she offered hopefully, shakily. "I can't count how many."

"Don't try." Her voice was a connection to the world but it was entangling him, holding him back. "Listen. In case I don't make it. I love you."

"Oh my God! Don't say it! Just be normal!"

"I can't be normal. This isn't normal."

"Can't you get up to a higher floor and wait on the roof?"

"I think people are trying it. Can you tell the kids how much I love them?"

"Ye-ess." Breathlessly. She wasn't arguing, it wasn't like her; her giving up like this frightened him. It made him realize how serious this was, how unthinkably serious.

He tried to think practically. "All the stuff you need should be in the filing cabinet beside my desk, the middle drawer. Lenny Palotta can help you, he has the mutual-fund data, and the insurance policies."

"God, *don't*, darling. Don't think that way. Just get out, can't you?"

"Sure, probably." People were moving toward the windows, it was the coolest place, the place to breathe, at the height of an airplane tucking its wheels back with that little concussion and snap that worries inexperienced passengers. "But, just in case, you do whatever you want."

"What do you mean, Jim, do whatever I want? You're not making sense."

"Shit, Marcy. I mean, you know, live your life. Do what looks best for yourself and the kids. Don't let anything cramp your style. Tell Annie in case I miss it that I wanted to be there tonight." Of all things, this made him want to cry, the image of his plump little solemn daughter in soccer shorts, scared and pink in the face. The smoke was blinding him, assaulting his eyes.

"Cramp my style?"

"My blessing, for Chrissake, Marcy. I'm giving a blessing on anything you decide to do. It's all right. Feel free."

"Oh, Jim, no. *No*. How can this be *hap*pening?"

He couldn't talk more; the smoke, the heat, the jet-fuel stink were chasing him to the windows, where silhouettes were climbing up into the blue panels, to get some air. Cy Walsh was already there, in the crowd. Jim Finch replaced the phone on his belt deftly; he instinctively grabbed his suit coat and sprinted, crouching, across the hot floor to his co-workers clustered at the windows. They were family, they had been his nine-to-five family for years. They were problem-solvers and would show him what to do. Like an airplane seizing altitude in its wings, he left gravity behind. Connections were breaking, obligations falling away. He felt for these seconds as light as a newborn.

The nice young man beside her told her he was in sales management, on his way to a telecom convention in San Francisco, but he played rugby on weekends in Van Cortlandt Park, in the Bronx. It surprised Carolyn that there were any rugby games in the United States. Ages ago in her long life, after the war, she had spent a year in England and been taken to a rugby game, in Cambridge, and remembered heavy-thighed men in shorts and striped shirts struggling in the mud, under the low, damp, chilly clouds, pushing at each other—there was a word they had used she couldn't remember—and for spurts carrying the slippery oval ball in a two-handed, sashaying way that looked comically girlish to a woman accustomed to the military precision and frontal collisions of American football. To those same eyes it seemed curious that they played nearly naked, in short shorts, and yet no one, at least that day, got hurt.

The introductory courtesies came early in the flight, out of Newark. The plane had sat stalled on the runway for half an hour but then had pushed into the air and climbed and banked so that the huge wing with its skinny little aerial on the tip threatened, it seemed to her elderly sense of balance, to spill them back onto the sun-streaked flat Earth of streets and housetops and highways below. It was a remarkably clear day. Carolyn had flown a great deal in her life, more than she had ever expected to as a child, when flying was something heroes did, test pilots and Lindbergh, and the whole family would rush out into the yard to see a blimp float overhead. Her first flights had been to college, in Ohio, into the old Cleveland-Hopkins Airport, in bumpy two-engine prop planes, early Douglas all-metals. Daddy, a great man for progress, flew the family for a week's spring vacation to Bermuda from New York on a British Air four-engine flying boat, and then put her on a Pan Am Boeing Clipper to London for her post-graduate year abroad: there had been a fuelling stop in Greenland, and actual beds where you could stretch out, and meals, with real silver, that people were too nauseated and anxious to eat. After marriage to Robert, she flew to the Caribbean and Arizona and Paris on vacations, and on some of his lecture trips as he became distinguished, and on three-day visits to her children when they married and scattered to places like Minneapolis and Dallas, and on matriarchal viewings of new grandchildren—to all the ceremonies that her descendants generated as they grew and aged. After Robert died, she had given herself an around-the-world tour, a widow's self-indulgence in her grief that no one could begrudge her, though her children, with their inheritance in mind, did raise their eyebrows. They couldn't understand the need, after sharing a life with a person for all these years, to get away from everything familiar.

All in all she couldn't begin to count how many hundreds of thousands of miles she had flown, but she had never really liked it—the plane's panicky run into lift-off, like some cartoon animal churning its legs and gritting its teeth, and the abrupt sudden banking, tilting and leaning on invisible air, and the changes in the sound of the engines nobody in the cockpit explained, and the sudden mysterious sharp jiggling over the ocean, your coffee swinging wildly in your cup, your heart in your throat. The planes had gotten bigger and smoother, to be sure. Some of those early flights, looking back, were little better than the rides in amusement parks designed to be terrifying—those little silver turboprops that bounced over the Appalachians with the tiny rivers below catching the sun, the stubby island-hoppers out of San Juan where you walked up the steep aisle and the lovely black stewardesses gave you candy to suck for pressure in your ears. People used to dress up as if for a formal tea, even—could it be?—with hats and white gloves. Now these big broad jets were like buses, people wore any old disgusting thing and never looked up from their laptops and acted personally injured if they didn't land on time to the minute, as if they were riding solid iron railroad tracks in the sky.

The nice young man, once the pilot's drawl had given permission to move about and use electrical devices, had asked her if she would mind, since there were so many empty seats, if he moved to another and gave them both more room. She thought his asking was dear, it showed a good old-fashioned upbringing. She watched him set up a little office for himself in two seats across the aisle, and then she studied the terrain five miles below, familiar to her from those first nervous, bouncy flights of hers, to Ohio so many years and miles ago. She recognized the Delaware, and then the Susquehanna, and while waiting for the stewardess with her rattling breakfast cart to reach the mid-section of the plane Carolyn must have dozed, because she awoke as if rudely shaken; the airplane was jiggling and bucking. She looked at her watch: 9:28. Hours to go.

She seemed to hear, far in the front, some shouting over the roar of the engines, and the plane dropped so that her stomach lurched. Yet the faces around her showed no alarm, and the heads she could see above the seatbacks were still. The plane stopped falling, and a voice came on the sound system that said, as best as she could understand, to remain seated. The pilot's voice sounded changed—tense and foreign. Where did the drawl go? He said, as best as Carolyn could hear, "Ladies and gentlemen: Here the captain. Please sit down, keep remaining sitting. We have bomb on board. So—sit."

Then a young man was standing in front of the first-class curtain. He was slender, and touchingly graceful and hesitant in the way he used his hands; he appeared to have no weapon, yet had gained everyone's attention, and the clumsy change in the way the plane was being handled connected somehow to him. He had an aura of nervous excitement; his eyes showed too much white. His eyes were all that showed; a large red bandana—a thick checked cloth, almost a scarf—concealed the lower half of his face and muffled his voice. Then another young man, plumper, came out from behind the curtains wearing another bandana and a comic apparatus around his chest; he held high one hand with a wire leading to it. He shook this hand and cried the word "Bomb! Bomb!" and then some other words in his own musical language, not trusting any other. People screamed. "Back! Back!" the thinner boy shouted, gesturing for everybody to move to the back of the plane.

Carolyn realized that these boys knew hardly any English, so the men in front trying to argue and question them were wasting their breath. Some of the men were standing; they had been made to leave first class. Then all of them began obediently to move back down the aisle, hunched over, Carolyn thought, like animals being whipped. The strawberry blonde seated two rows in front of her—the top of her head like spun sugar, tipped toward that of the boy next to her, her husband possibly, though couples weren't necessarily married now, her own grandchildren demonstrated that—

reached out in passing and touched Carolyn on the shoulder. "You don't have to move," she said softly. She was already far enough back, she meant.

"Thank you, my dear," Carolyn responded, sounding old and foolish in her own ears.

They—the passengers, with three female flight attendants, though there had been four—settled around her, in stricken, fearful silence at first. But when the boy with the bomb and the boy without one didn't move back with them, staying instead in front of the first-class curtain, as if themselves paralyzed by fright, the noise of conversation among the passengers rose, like that at a cocktail party as the alcohol took hold, or in a rainy-day classroom when discipline washes away. Here and there people were talking into their cell phones, including the rugby player across the aisle, who had disbanded his little office on the lunch trays. His hand as it held the little gadget to his ear looked massive, with its red knuckles and broad wedding ring. His shirt had French cuffs with square gold links; French cuffs meant something, her son-in-law had tried to explain to her, in terms of corporate hierarchy. You could only wear them after a certain position in the firm had been attained.

The engines spasmodically wheezed, and a sudden tilt brought Carolyn's heart up into her throat; the plane was turning. The great wing next to her window leaned far over above the gray-green earth. The land below looked like Ohio now, flatter than the Alleghenies, and there was a smoky city that could be Akron or Youngstown. A wide piece of water, Lake Erie it must be, shone in the distance, betraying Earth's curvature. The sun had shifted to her side of the plane, coming in at an angle that bothered her eyes. A cataract operation two years ago had restored childhood's bright colors and sharp edges but left Carolyn's corneas sensitive to sunlight.

The plane must be heading southeast, back to Pennsylvania. She tried to think it through, to picture the plane's exact direction, yet was unable to think. Her own fatigue dawned on her. The flight had been scheduled to leave at eight, and that had meant setting the alarm in Princeton at five. The older she became the earlier she awoke but still it was strange to go out into the dark and start the car.

Her skin had broken out into sweat. Her body was terrified before her mind had caught up. What was foremost in her mind was the simple wish, fervent enough to be a prayer, that the plane be taken, like an easily damaged toy, out of those invisible hands that were giving it such a jerky, panicky, incompetent ride.

Carolyn wondered why the boys up front, hijackers evidently, were letting so many passengers talk on their telephones; perhaps they thought it was a way to keep them calm. The one without the bomb came down the aisle a little way, then retreated; in warning he held up something metallic, a small knife of some sort, the kind with a cruel curved point that slides open to cut boxes, but what showed of his face, the eyes, seemed either frightened or furious, pools of ardent dark gelatin hard to decipher without the rest of the face. His mind seemed elsewhere, somewhere beyond, all that eye-white showing. He wore black jeans and a long-sleeved red-checked shirt that could have been that of a young computer whiz on his way to Silicon Valley. She had two grandsons in dot-coms; they dressed like farmhands, like hippies decades ago, when young people decided that they loved the earth when what they loved most was annoying their parents. But this boy had no pencils or pens in his shirt pocket, the way her grandsons did. He had that baby knife and eyebrows that nearly met in the middle, above his distracted, glittering gaze. Why wouldn't he look anybody in the face? He was *shy*. He must be a very nice boy, at home, among people he could speak to intelligibly, in his own language, without cloth across his mouth.

How humiliating, this sweating she was doing into her underwear. She would smell when she got off the plane, under the wool dress she had put on thinking it was always cool in Tiburon, where her daughter lived, however hot it was in Princeton. The redwoods, the Bay breezes: she realized she might not reach them today. They would land at some obscure airport and a long standoff of negotiations would begin. When they began to release hostages, however, an old lady would be among the first.

The captain came on the loudspeaker again: "There is bomb on board and we go back to the airport, and to have our demands—" She lost the next words in his guttural accent. "Remain quiet, please," the pilot concluded. Her watch said 9:40. Despite the captain's request, eddies of communication moved through the crowded back of the plane: hand signals, eye motions, conversations increasingly blatant and emphatic as the nervous young hijacker's obliviousness dawned on everyone. The stewardesses began to talk as if still in charge. People in first class had glimpsed something in the cabin; word of whatever it was spread back, skipping around Carolyn inaudibly yet chilling her damp skin. Others were learning things through their cell phones that they urgently had to share. The young businessmen in their white shirts held conferences, talking to each other across the heads and laps of women and the elderly. Growing impatient, some of them stood, making a huddle, right near her, around the seat of that nice rugby player. Not a huddle, a *scrum*—that was the word they had used in England.

She tried to eavesdrop, and heard nothing but passionate muttering, rising to the near-shout of men energized by a decision. The distinct word "Yes" was repeated in several men's voices. They had voted. The plumper of the two hijackers, having lowered his bandana to his throat so a pathetic small mustache showed, moved down the aisle, gesturing for people to be silent and sit down, while the apparatus he had strapped himself into looked more and more absurd and rickety. The plane was still rocking in those unseen hands, jerking and tilting, but the rugby player stood up with the others—he was taller than she had realized, in scale with that huge wrist jutting from his French cuff—and they faced forward. She accidentally caught his eye; he smiled and gave her a thumbs-up. She heard a voice, another young man's, say, "You guys ready? Let's *do* it."

Some seats behind her, a woman began to sob. Carolyn guessed it was the young woman who had touched her arm some minutes ago, but her instinct was to tell her to shut up, the plane was bouncing so, she just wanted to adhere to her seat and close her eyes and beg for the motion, the demented speed, to stop. The roaring engines made the hubbub within the plane hard to sort out. The plump young man with the bomb disappeared behind the broad shoulders and white shirts of the stampeding American men. The other one, with his little hooked knife, also sank under the scrum, his silly towel of a veil torn away to reveal a red-lipped mouth open in protest. First fists and then feet in shoes silenced his ugly yells. *Crush him*, Carolyn thought. *Kill him*.

The white shirts pushed through the blue first-class curtain. The engines did not drown out the thumping, crashing sounds from behind the curtain, the unexpected clatter of the serving cart, and a male voice shouting "Roll it!" while a fearful gabble from the passengers still in their seats arose around her.

The airplane lurched more violently than ever before,

rocking and dipping as if to shake something loose, and Carolyn felt, as sharply as if the wires and levers controlling the great mechanism were her own sinews and bones, that control had been lost, something crucial had been severed. From the wing came a high grinding noise; through her porthole she saw the flaps strain erect, exposing their valves. The vast tapering wing, with its stencilled aluminum segments and its little aerial at the very tip, seemed to stand on end; the entire stiff intricate entity bearing her and all these others was heeling beyond any angle of possible recovery. The terrible largeness of everything, the plane and the planet and the transparent miles between them, amazed her much as the shocking unclouded colors of the world had amazed her after her cataract operation. Her body was hanging sideways in the seat belt, so heavily her ribs ached. Through the scratched plastic window the earth in its rural detail—a few houses and outbuildings, a green blob of woods, a fenced field, a lonely road—swung across her vision while her ears popped, and she realized that, nightmarish though it was, this was real, the reality beneath everything, this surge into the maw of gravity. Her brain was flung into wordlessness; she was upside down, and the tortured engine near her ears was making everything shake. She was meeting the truth that her parents and husband and all the protectors of her long protected life had implied: the path of safety is narrow, it is possible to fall from it. *Mercy,* Carolyn managed to cry distinctly inside her pounding head. *Dear, Lord, have mercy.*

Dan stood outside his daughter's apartment, on the sooty tiled terrace from which he had seen the first tower collapse. In the six months since then, news events had tended to corroborate his revelation. A demented woman in Texas was being tried for systematically drowning her five children. Catholic priests were revealed to have molested their immature charges in numbers larger than ever imagined or confessed. Almost every week, somewhere in the United States, angry or despairing or berserk fathers murdered their wives or ex-wives and their children and then, in inadequate atonement, killed themselves. Meanwhile, in Afghanistan, war had been proclaimed and pursued, with its usual toll of inane deaths—colliding helicopters, stray bombs, false intelligence, fatal muddle unmitigated by any Biblical dignity of vengeance or self-sacrifice. The masterminds of evil remained at large; the surrendered enemies appeared exhausted and confused—pathetic small fry. They complained about the climate of Cuba and their captors' failure to provide them with sympathetic mullahs. They claimed, and others stridently claimed for them, their international legal rights. Religious slaughters occurred in India and Israel, fires and floods and plagues elsewhere. The world tumbled on, spewing out death and sparks of pain like an engine off the tracks.

His younger granddaughter, his fellow witness to the most publicized of recent disasters, solemnly informed Dan that all the dogs of New York City had bleeding paws, from looking through wreckage for dead people.

Emily, the tough-minded survivor of divorce, had not prevented the child from gathering what she could from the newspapers and television: "It's turned her into a real news hawk," she dryly explained. "Hilary, on the other hand," she went on, "has refused from Day One to have anything to do with it. It wasn't ladylike, she decided, and disdained it all. She says such things aren't appropriate for children. She can actually pronounce 'appropriate.' But for Vicky, it would have been unhealthy, really, Daddy, to try to shelter her from what everybody knew, what all her schoolmates would be talking about. After all, compared to children in Bosnia and Afghanistan she's still pretty well off."

"Not *all* the dogs, Victoria," Dan reassured his granddaughter, "just a few trained for a certain special job, and wearing little leather booties that nice people made for them. Most people are very nice," he promised her.

The child stared up at him pugnaciously, a bit doubtful but wanting to agree. In six months, she had grown; her eyes, a translucent pale blue beneath level bangs, entertained more subtle expressions. At moments, especially when she was thinking to herself, he could see, in the childishly fine perfection of her face, the seeds of feminine mystery and of her mature beauty.

Lucille, within earshot, said, so the child would overhear, "Vicky, she so interested in *all* the developments. She know how that terrible mess almost cleaned up now, and the two blue floodlights there as a monument, we see them every night."

Victoria explained to her grandfather, "They mean all the people in there have gone up to Heaven."

By daylight, from the terrace, the Twin Towers of the World Trade Center were simply not there. Their stark form, like that of two cubes projected skyward by some computer command, had registered but delicately above the old-fashioned brick thicket of lower Manhattan. Rectangular clouds of glass and aluminum, they had been wiped from the city's silhouette. They were not there, but Dan was here, and God with him; his conversion to atheism had not lasted. His church pledge needed to be delivered in its weekly envelopes; a minor committee (Property Maintenance and

Improvement) of which he was a member continued to meet. The Episcopal church, high in Cincinnati but not evangelical, presented a stream of Cranmer's words in which the mind could lose itself. Dan would have missed the mild-mannered fellowship—the handshakes under the vaulted ceiling, the awkward passing of the peace. Why punish with his non-attendance, in protest of something God and not they had done, a flock of potential probate clients for whom periodically chorusing the Nicene Creed was part, and not the very least part, of getting along, of doing their best, of being decent citizens? He would miss the Sunday-morning congregation, the smell of waxed pews and musty kneeling cushions, the radiators that knocked on winter Sunday mornings after a week of cool disuse, the taste of the tasteless wafer in his mouth.

While he stood there ten stories above the Brooklyn alley (where the two attendants, in the mild March air, again sat joshing at the entrance to their parking garage), the towers' distant absence seemed a light throwing a shadow behind him, a weak shadow, but inextricable from his presence—the price, it could be said, of his being alive. He was alive, and a shadowy God with him, behind him. Human consciousness had curious properties. However big things were, it could encompass them, as if it were even bigger. And it kept insisting on making a narrative of Dan's life, however nonsensically truncated the lives of others—crushed in an instant, or snapped off on the birthing-bed—had been.

Emily and Victoria, his progeny, his tickets to genetic perpetuation, ventured out gingerly onto the terrace, to be with him in the open air. "Amazing," his daughter said, seeking to read his thoughts, "how the not-thereness remains so haunting. Sometimes you still see the towers in old ads, where the admen haven't noticed or taken the trouble to airbrush them out of the background. It feels illicit. A lot of these yuppie movies and TV serials have a shot of them, from SoHo or the Staten Island Ferry or wherever, and I hear they've been collected on tape, like the kisses in *Cinema Paradiso*. They've become a kind of cult."

Victoria eagerly volunteered, "Some day, when all the bad men are killed, they'll put them *back*, just ex*act*ly the way they were." She gestured appropriately wide and high, standing on tiptoe.

Dan tended to discourage other people's illusions, though he was cherishing of his own. "I don't think that would be very sensible," he stated to the child. "Or very American."

"Why not American?" Emily asked, with an oppositional, possibly aggrieved edge. If her parents hadn't divorced, her marriage might have held together; a bad precedent had been set.

"We move on, don't we?" Dan tactfully answered. "As a nation. We try to learn from our mistakes. Those towers were taller than they needed to be. The Arabs weren't wrong to feel them as a boast."

Hilary, barefoot, peeked out from one of the penthouse doors, but did not venture out onto the sooty tiles. She admonished them, "Children shouldn't see what you're all looking at. It's scary."

"Don't be scared," her younger sister told her, and then half to Dan: "My teacher at school says the lights are like the rainbow. They mean it won't happen again."

Spanish Prelude to a Second Marriage

"You'll get lost," she told him. "The same way you do in Brookline or the South End. It's your style, you think it's cute. But look outside! It's pouring cats and dogs."

He ignored the cliché. She thought in clichés, but that wasn't the worst of sins. "How can I get lost?" he replied. "I can see the cathedral from here." They were staying in the Hotel Alhambra Palace, overlooking Granada, Brad Quigley and his longtime companion, Leonora Katz, experimenting to see if a vacation together might nudge their long relationship into marriage or a break-up. She was in her fifties; he was sixty; they worked in different firms within the limpid backwater of Boston finance and had known each other, at first merely collegially, for fifteen years. Her position and income were equal to his; her professional accomplishment shielded them both, to an extent, from the overhanging question of any legalized connection. There was almost no reason why they couldn't go on as they were, with separate apartments, incomes, and friends. And yet . . . a small, brisk brunette, she was growing, he could see, brittle, her gestures jerkier, her temper quicker to flare, her judgments snappier and yet prone to sudden reversals and self-doubts. Since exercise classes and conditioning gyms had become the fashion, Leonora looked too thin—deprived. Her fine-boned beauty conformed to the low-maintenance style of Cambridge and Beacon Hill. She did not deign to dye the gray from her hair, which was left long and pulled into a tight roll at the back, and the squint lines in her face were deepening, exaggerating an increasingly frequent expression, that of a slightly deaf person who blames you for not speaking louder.

"My mother would want me to go," he said. "*Mi madre.* She would want me to see the tombs of Ferdinand and Isabella. She loved them so."

"Don't I know it," Leonora said, though the two women had never met. The only other time Brad had been to Spain, twenty years ago, had been with his mother, an unpublished writer who was doing research for a romantic novel concerning the two legendary monarchs and their only surviving child, the love-crossed Joanna the Mad.

It had been a strange trip, beginning with a humiliating, to Brad, embarrassment when the busy clerk at the Madrid hotel, slipping in English, had called his mother "your wife." The clerk had quickly, sizing them up, corrected it with a self-critical chuckle to "your mother," but for Brad a confusion between his mother and his wife held an abysmal plausibility. Not that his mother looked the part, she was gray-haired and stout; but he was forty, and freshly divorced, and what wife, really, would he ever know as well as he knew her? Even as a fetus he had been attuned to her moods and inner workings; she loomed to him less as another person than as an overarching weather. To dilute their relationship he had proposed that they invite along his fifteen-year-old daughter, Belinda, who had taken the divorce the hardest.

Something fraught and sad about the whole expedition had kept him awake in his hotel room every night, he remembered. His task had been to drive his companions each day out from Madrid to one of the towns—Segovia, Avila, Valladolid, Toledo—where his mother had found a clue, a hint of treasure, in the writings of Prescott and Washington Irving and John Foster Kirk, whose histories had enchanted her in college. Though she could read some Spanish, she was shy of speaking it, and it fell to Brad to negotiate their tourism: "*¿Por favor, señor, dónde está el convento?*" His mother would gaze at some tombs within the convent, and take a few notes. Once, she reached out and touched the marble foot, worn glossy by other touches, on a funerary sculpture of a long-deceased noblewoman. "What a dear little pointed shoe," she said.

Yet he could not believe she was finding what she wanted, the key to crack open that opaque, late-medieval world and get it to spill its colorful mysteries into reach of her pen. The cities surrounding the traces of history were noisy with traffic and ringed with the stark sheds of burgeoning industrial development; post-Franco Spain was hastening to cast off its romantic isolation and the picturesque backwardness that had attracted centuries of infatuated travellers. Belinda, helplessly adolescent, still bearing some baby fat, endured hours in the back of the little rented Fiat and politely tried to interest herself in the stultifying relics, from the Escorial to the castle and aqueduct in Segovia, that her grandmother had come so arduously far to see. All the girl asked, as reward for her patience during this week's ordeal, was to visit the disco of the Madrid hotel, and this her guardians granted on the last night. While her insomniac father at last slept soundly in his room, she returned around midnight, rosy and giddy and full of strange tales, for her grandmother's ears, of Spanish boys—how they danced, how they somehow communicated with her, how happy they seemed to see her.

Separating from Leonora made Brad nervous; they had been constantly together for six days. He had been struck these days by a feminine querulousness that their peaceful intermittent evenings together in Boston did not reveal. So long the manager of her own life and of other people's millions, she distrusted his management of their trip. In Seville, he kept leading her, she felt, astray—his map-reading took them up narrow medieval streets abuzz with motor scooters and speeding taxis. She was afraid of falling into the traffic, or having her bag snatched by a passing pair of Gypsies on a Vespa. She forbade Brad to give money to beggars, lest he attract a band of feather-fingered pickpockets. She was convinced that all taxi drivers were cheating them, even if their meters were turned on and audibly ticking. Her demands taxed his poor Spanish beyond its means: "Ask him what those extra charges are for. Tell him he's going the long way around." She found scarcely endurable the cacophony of competing tour guides in the Alhambra, and in Córdoba complained, five centuries late, that the Spanish had crassly built a cathedral in the middle of the marvellous mosque, with its serene forest of marble pillars. She had acquired the notion that one should not drink the faucet water in this country; *sin hielo* had become one of his phrases, not always comprehended, and for her sake he was always sidling into dark, private-seeming bars and buying a plastic bottle of *agua minerale*.

So it was with a relieved sense of private adventure that he set out, beneath his umbrella, on the puddled little lane that led to the town from the hotel. It twisted down through hair-pin turns; the cathedral quickly sank from sight behind tall shuttered housefronts and, as she had predicted, he became lost. The tiny lettering on his map required fishing his reading glasses from the pocket of his reversible parka; the map became wet and he kept drifting downward, hoping for a clarifying park or monument. At last he emerged into a broad boulevard roaring with commuter traffic. Only a few pedestrians hurried past, under umbrellas. Even when inspected through reading glasses, the map offered no clue to where he was on it. Granada was more of a metropolis than the song suggested. A swarthy beggar, perhaps a Gypsy pick-pocket sitting out thin rainy-day pickings, jeered at him from the doorway of a closed bank. Brad was too proud, and too mournfully pleased with his drenched and solitary condition on this errand of obscure filial piety, to ask for guidance. His instinct was to walk uphill, back toward the hotel, itself lost from sight, where Leonora forlornly waited. For her sake he at last went to a news kiosk and asked the woman in charge, "*¿Por favor, señora, dónde está la catedral?*" She gestured brusquely and gave the impatient answer, "*Derecho,*" which meant either to the right or straight ahead. He damply plodded on, missing the loving goad of his mistress's tongue.

The cathedral, its blank side blending into secular façades, almost slipped by him. He entered by a small door that opened near the altar. There were many more visitors inside than he had expected on this foul day, including several busloads of Japanese in transparent plastic raincoats. The recumbent effigies of the Catholic Sovereigns were easy to find, though hard to examine, lying high above the floor of the nave on pompous marble sarcophagi. Brad joined a line of Japanese who seemed to know the ropes and found himself stepping down into a crypt beneath the sarcophagi. There, in a small vaulted space, behind bars, an arm's length away, five plain, black, toylike lead coffins held the remains of King Ferdinand; Queen Isabella; their unbalanced daughter, Joanna; Joanna's unfaithful husband, Philip the Handsome of Burgundy—he died at twenty-eight, and his widow kept the embalmed body in her bedroom for years—and, in the smallest hexagonal lead box of all, the dust of a child, a child left out of guidebook history, which did record that Joanna's madness had not impaired her fertility: two emperors and four queens could claim her as mother, and her insanity flickered down through generations of Hapsburgs.

Whatever, Brad wondered, had made his own mother think that she could encompass in a work of her imagination these pious, benighted, casually cruel monarchs? She would speak of Juana la Loca as of a lovable eccentric cousin, and of Ferdinand as of the masterful husband she herself had never had. Now she herself was in a box, cherrywood underground instead of lead in a low-ceilinged crypt, but her body reverting to its skeleton all the same. Her body in Spain had been overweight, and dressed in wintry American clothes, so that as Brad remembered her she sweated, pink-faced at the long lunches with him and Belinda on the hot sidewalks by the provincial plazas while they waited for the convents and churches to reopen, her bifocals misting as she consulted her guidebooks and notebooks. Yet, brave soul, she never complained of discomfort, or that she had come all this expensive way and was not finding what she wanted. Now her spirit, not as mad as Cousin Juana's but certainly fanciful, had brought him again to Spain, dragging with him poor nervous, brittle Leonora, who didn't trust even the faucet water. He must be nicer to Leonora, he resolved, emerging into the rain and climbing back to the hotel, and then never repeat this misadventure. He would break off the relationship as soon as they were back in Boston. The clouds overhead were breaking up, exposing exclamatory fragments of blue: an El Greco sky.

In Madrid, which they had saved for the second week, she seemed to relax; it looked to her like a grander Boston, with a bigger Public Garden and more centrally located art museums. Her taut dark looks and severe hairdo led several pedestrians to address her in Spanish, mistaking her for a native; she liked this, blushing as she protested, "*No, no, gracias—soy americana.*" More quickly than he, she learned her way around. In the Prado she found for him a little Goya, an odd painting of a dog, which he had remembered from his previous trip, on view in a kind of basement. It was not to be found among the Goya portraits of the royal court on the first floor. Girlishly proud of her Spanish managerial skills, Leonora led him up, through the tourist throngs, to the third floor, where the savage paintings of Goya's depressive last phase had been sequestered, like a mad person in the attic. He had remembered a complete dog, perhaps thinking of one by Francis Bacon. In reality the painting was titled *Perro semihundido—Half-Sunken Dog*—and showed only a Thurberesque dog profile and a lot of yellow blank space. Brad wondered why he had treasured this memory for two decades. "I couldn't let you not find your little dog," Leonora said, he thought a bit possessively. "You've always talked about it."

"I have?" He felt as if he had never been in Madrid before. He could not spot the hotel where he and his mother and daughter had stayed, on a wide straight street where he had been politely, wordlessly given a ticket for making a U-turn. Only the grounds of the imperial palace—cropped cypresses seen from a balustrade—rang a faint bell; the mismatched trio twenty years ago had walked there the first groggy afternoon. Resting his arms on the balustrade, he had distinctly told himself, *I'm in Spain.* An exotic formality and gloom had seemed to arise from the gardens, with their boxy patterns of privet and truncated inky-green cypresses. Entry was forbidden, as Brad remembered it. The King was still youthful and revered, and Spain was clinging to his image as a safeguard against a return of civil chaos. Now the King was a beefy, good-natured sexagenarian, the Prime Minister was a Socialist, euros had replaced pesetas as the coin of the realm, and the palace gardens were open to the public. Brad descended with Leonora into the once-forbidden grounds; they seemed innocuous, chilly, and empty, just another piece of tourist Europe, as impersonally accepting of them as the hotel clerks who took their unmated passports and handed them back without a flicker of Counter-Reformation puritanism. Spain had rejoined the pagan, Mediterranean world.

Leonora had become more kittenish than she was in Boston. "Wasn't that clever of me," she insisted as they left the Prado, "to find your little dog for you?"

"*Perro,*" said Brad, relishing the trilled double "r." "Yes, it was very clever, dear."

From Madrid he and Leonora took a day trip to Toledo, by train. Their mood, near their vacation's end, had turned light-hearted. She did not furiously object when, in the station, he gave a few coins to a Gypsy with a dirty-faced infant sleeping in her arms. He had been to Toledo once before, but by car, with his—not wife—*madre* and his *hija*. They had had a flat tire on the way, and his doping out enough instructions to replace it with the spare had been one of his few Spanish triumphs. The flat tire was all he remembered of that excursion except for an old ochre bridge, with studded wooden doors, that they had walked across in sunshine, with Toledo massed behind them on a steep, congested hill.

Today, too, was sunny. The train climbed through vineyards and freshly green fields for an hour and then stopped outside the city, on the other side of the river. He and Leonora followed a set of twittery English women, who seemed to know the ropes, to a red bus that quickly filled; a large group of others from the train crossed the street and trooped away on a diagonal road. Watching them disappear, Brad envied them their secret—a sort of short cut, with no bus fare. The bus, stymied by some torn-up streets, dropped them off at a spot Brad could not locate on the map; he became as lost as in Granada in the rain, while Leonora lost patience at his side. She needed a bottle of water, and was fearful of being robbed in the narrow, twisting streets. "Amazing," he admitted, "how these Spaniards hide their cathedrals."

"But this is the biggest Gothic cathedral in Spain!" She was almost wailing. "You're the only man in the world who could totally not find it!"

When they did come upon it, and prowled amid its five huge aisles, he could not find in himself any memory of having been here before. Surely he and his mother, now as dead as Queen Isabella, and his younger daughter, now married and the mother of three, had marvelled together at the exquisite choir stalls, the towering altarpiece, the elaborately robed carved Madonna dating from the old Visigothic church, and, most memorable of all, the Baroque hole, a piece of sky lined with Heavenly figures, incongruously broken into the Gothic vaulting behind the altar in the eighteenth century. It was as if they had been blind. They would have been weary after their escapade with the tire, and his mother would have had her checklist of sights to feed her fiction. Where had they parked? It was hard to imagine his overweight, overheated mother laboring up and down the streets and stairs that he and Leonora dutifully traversed, from the old Jewish Quarter in the west of the city to the Museo de Santa Cruz in the east. As they wearily leaned on a balustrade, he saw his bridge, glowing golden in the late-afternoon light.

The train back to Madrid left in an hour, at six. "I bet," Brad told Leonora, "if we crossed that bridge, and walked to the left, we'd come to the railroad station."

"What makes you think that?"

"I think this map shows it."

"You think. Why are there no people on the bridge? It goes nowhere."

"They wouldn't let a bridge stand that went nowhere. Remember all those people who didn't get on the bus but crossed the street and walked away diagonally? They must have been walking to this bridge. Here it is, on the map. It's called the Puente de Alcántara."

"How do we get down to it?"

It was a reasonable question, so Brad thought she was going to be reasonable. They were standing at a considerable height above the river; several busy thoroughfares intervened. "I don't know," he confessed. "Maybe into that parking lot. I think I see some steps down."

Leonora wanted to please him, but her long years of being single had hardened a habit of self-preservation. "You *think*," she said. "You don't *know*."

"I know that bridge. We were all on it together."

"That was ages ago; you're not even sure of that, I can tell from your voice. Look across the river: there's no road on that side. Brad, I have news for you. I'm taking the bus. I know where it leaves from. If you want to try your precious bridge, I'll meet you at the station. Give me my return ticket."

"Oh, shit, never mind," he told her. "We'll go back and take the stuffy, expensive bus together. But it could have been a lyrical experience." At heart he was relieved that he didn't have to plod down in search of the entry to the bridge, and that by defying him she had put some space between them; they were in danger of becoming inseparable.

Back at the bus stop—a triangular square bustling with young Europeans stripped to their shorts and backpacks—Brad widened the distance by regressively yielding to his desire to buy, at one of the portable stands surprisingly prevalent in the somber old city, the Spanish equivalent of a Good Humor bar—chocolate-covered ice cream on a stick. "Don't," Leonora begged. "The bus will come."

"No, it won't," he said. There was a type—vanilla inside a frosty brown skin bumpy with small bits of nuts—that he especially craved. He rarely saw them for sale in downtown Boston, where men in business suits don't generally patronize Good Humor wagons. "Want a bite?" he offered, poking the treat at his companion, with her gray-streaked hair and censorious frown.

"I certainly do not. Eat it fast—you're not allowed to eat on buses. What a baby!" And Leonora softly shrieked, with a panic deserving a graver emergency, when the bus pulled up in the next minute. In the squeeze at the door, he held the half-finished popsicle behind his back, so the driver wouldn't see. Leonora was horrified, as they took seats in the rear, that he was still gnawing at the stick, with its fast-melting burden. She elaborated: "You're a disgusting, selfish baby."

He waited to reply until he could say, "There. All gone. Nothing spilled. You may apologize whenever you want." To be more annoying still, he asked her, "What do I do with the stick? Could you put it in your purse? *Please?* Pretty please?"

The bus, avoiding the torn-up streets on its way out, crossed the river on a smooth highway bridge and pulled up across from the station within ten minutes. Enjoying his new, bumptious role of hostile bad boy, Brad said to Leonora, "O.K., smartie. We're here forty minutes early; I hope you're happy."

"I'm not *un*happy," she said. Her anxious fury had abruptly given way to a softer, more experimental mood. Rather than cross the street to the station, she pointed at a vending machine on their side, a few steps away. "Maybe you can get me a bottle of water." The insertion of the euro and the responsive thump of the cold bottle was a transaction satisfying to them both; after two weeks in this country, they were learning the ropes. "Let's walk down a little," Leonora said, "to where you think you saw those people going to this bridge you say was so great."

"I didn't say it was great, it was just something I remembered. One of the terrifyingly few things."

The street turned an oblique corner and became, on the side nearer the river, bucolic and scarcely trafficked. Beyond a low stone wall the riverbank held tall grass dotted with poppies and white, daisylike flowers of a medieval simplicity.

The walk was short, scarcely a city block long, to the end of the old bridge, with its fortified gates, its ochre arches. The road they had just travelled had been invisible, slightly sunken, *semihundido*, from the other side. "So—I was right," he said. But, looking across the river, Brad saw that Leonora had been right about access from the parking lot; he couldn't see any stairs. The approach would have been long and diagonal, on weary feet. "O.K., thanks," he said. "Let's go catch the train."

"No, I want you to walk on the bridge. There's time. How silly I was, Brad, not to trust you—it was so *close*. I'm embarrassed to have been so stubborn. So un-simpatico." The bridge had been unpopulated when they had viewed it before, but now whole families, from small children to patriarchal, black-clad men with canes, were strolling and dawdling between its waist-high walls. Leonora insisted on pulling her little camera from her purse and photographing Brad posed at the far end, with its elaborate tower and gate. The ancient tall wooden doors, cracked and darkened, still bore the studs, heraldic metal florets in rigorous rows, that had been nailed into his memory. Here they had once stood, in the same warm dust, his mother and daughter and he, his perspiring mother saying something to make the moment amusing, or writing something in her notebook, but exactly what was long lost, and her novel had never been published.

Leonora put her camera away and stood closer to Brad, in the heat the old stones radiated, than necessary—a European, rather than an American, conversational distance. "Now, wasn't I nice," she flirted, "to find you your dear mother's bridge, after you were so mean?"

She had given him a bridge. "Oh yes, very," he said. "You were very nice. I won't be mean ever again." Her pale pointed face in its hopeful uncertainty, its shy determination to be winning, had shed years; it had drawn so close he smelled the shrimp paella they had shared for lunch, and the liquid dark of her Spanish eyes swallowed him with its plea.

Delicate Wives

VERONICA HORST was stung by a bee, and it should have produced no more than a minute of annoyance and pain, but she, in the apparent bloom of health at the age of twenty-nine, turned out to be susceptible to anaphylactic shock, and nearly died. Fortunately, her husband, Gregor, was with her, and threw her fainting body, with its dropping blood pressure, into their car and sped careening through the heart of town to the hospital, where she was saved. When Les Merrill heard about the event, from his wife, Lisa, who was breathlessly fresh from a session of gossip and women's tennis, he was stung by jealousy: he and Veronica had had an affair the previous summer, and by the rights of love he should have been the one to be with her and to save her heroically. Gregor even had the presence of mind, afterwards, to go around to the local police and explain why he had been speeding and careening through stop signs. "It seems incredible," Lisa innocently told her husband, "that here she's nearly thirty and apparently has never been stung before, so nobody knew she would react this way. As a child I was always getting stung, weren't you?"

"I think Veronica," he said, "had a city upbringing."

"Still," Lisa said, hesitant in the face of his ready assertion, "that's no guarantee. There are parks."

Les, picturing Veronica in her house, in her bed, where an elongated pink-tinged pallor, like that in a Modigliani or a Fragonard, had been revealed to him, said, "She's a pretty indoor kind of person."

Lisa was not. Tennis, golf, hiking, and skiing kept her freckled the year round. Even her delft-blue irises were dotted, if you looked, with tan specks of melanin. She insisted, "Well, she nearly died," as if Les had been wandering from the point. His mind had been exploring the abysmal possibility of Veronica's beauty and high spirits being removed from the world by a chemical mischance. In her moment of need, had her care passed to her lover the previous summer, he might have proved less effective than Gregor, who was small and dark and spoke English if not with an accent with a studied precision, as if locking the sense of his words into a compact metal case. She found him repellent, Veronica had confessed—his fussiness, his dictatorial streak, the cold assertiveness in his touch—but Les, by breaking off their affair at the end of the summer, had possibly saved her life. In Gregor's shoes he might have panicked, doubted what was happening, and fatally failed to act. As it was, he saw gallingly, the incident would be rolled into the Horst family annals, as a pivotal and eternally ramifying moment—the time Mommy (and, as she would become, Grammy) was stung by a bee, and funny foreign-born Grampa resourcefully saved her life. Les was so jealous that he nearly bent over as if with a stomach cramp. Had he, sweet dreamy Les, been there, instead of scowling, practical-minded Gregor, her emergency would have acquired and forever retained a different poetry, more flattering to her, more congruent with a doomed summer love. For what was more majestically intimate even than sex but death? He imagined her motionless profile, gray with collapsed blood pressure, cradled in his arms.

Veronica had a favorite summer dress, with a ballerina neckline and three-quarter-length sleeves, of orange, orange distributed with a tie-dyed unevenness. It was not a color most women would wear, but it brought out the reckless gleam in her long straight hair and the green of her eyes. Remembering their affair, Les seemed to squint through a wash of this color, though it was no longer summer but September when they parted, the grass in the fields going to seed and the air noisy with cicadas. Veronica's eyes watered, her lower lip trembled as she listened to him explaining that he just couldn't face leaving Lisa and the kids, who were still almost babies, and they should break their relationship off while it was still secret, before things got messy, and all their lives lay scattered and ruined. Through her tears Veronica appraised him and determined that indeed he did not love her enough to rescue her from Gregor. He was not free enough, was how he preferred to phrase it. They wept together—his tears made a gleam on the skin of her shoulder within the wide oval of her neckline—and agreed that no one but them would ever know.

And yet, through the fall and winter and into the next summer, he felt cheated by this secrecy; their affair had been something wonderful he wanted known. He tried to rekindle her attention. She ignored his longing looks and rebuked his confused attempts to single her out in a crowd. Her green eyes glared, under the frown of her long reddish eyebrows. "Les dear," she said to him once when he cornered her late at a party, "did you ever hear the expression 'Shit or get off the pot'?"

"Well, I have now," he said, shocked and offended. Lisa would never have said such a thing, any more than she would have worn a splashy tie-dyed orange dress.

His concealed affair with Veronica burned within him like an untreated infection, and as the years went by it seemed that Veronica, too, suffered from it; she seemed never to have quite recovered from the bee sting. Weight loss, making her look gaunt and stringy, alternated with periods of puffiness and overweight. There were trips to the local hospital, about which Gregor was adamantly mysterious, and spells when Veronica was hidden within her house, suffering from complaints which her husband, showing up at parties by himself, refused to name. Les, in his inert, romantic way, imagined her, having in a fit of treacherous weakness confessed their affair to Gregor, being held captive by him. Or else regret over losing Les was gnawing at her delicate constitution. Her beauty did not greatly suffer from her frailty, but gained a new dimension from it, a ghostly glow, a poignance. After years of sunbathing—all wives did it back then—Veronica developed phototoxicity, and stayed out of the sun all summer. Her teeth, as her thirties wore on, gave her trouble, and the orthodontic and periodontal specialists she regularly consulted had their offices in the nearby middle-sized city, in a tall building across from the one in which Les worked as an investment adviser.

Once, he glimpsed her from his window as, preoccupied and solemn in a dark, wide-skirted cloth coat, she reported for treatment across the street. After that, he kept looking out his window for her, mourning the decade they had let slip by while married to other people. Lisa's outdoor bounce and freckled good nature had become somewhat butch; her hair, like her mother's, turned gray early. Gregor was rumored to be discontented and having affairs. Les imagined these betrayals as wounds Veronica was enduring, within the silent prison of her marriage. He still saw her at parties, but across the room, and, when he maneuvered close to her, she had little to say. During their affair, they had shared, along with sex, concerns about their children, and memories of their parents and upbringings. This sort of innocent exposure of another, eagerly apprehended life figures among the precious things lovers lose—a flow of confidences that, halted, builds up a pressure.

So when he spotted Veronica leaving the dentists' building, unmistakably her although he was ten stories high and she was bundled against the winter winds, he left his office without bothering with a topcoat and ambushed her on the sidewalk a half-block away.

"Lester! What on earth?" She put her mittened hands on her hips to mime exasperation. Christmas decorations were still in some shop windows, gathering dust, and tinsel rain from trashed evergreens glittered in the gutters.

"Let's have lunch," he begged. "Or is your mouth too full of Novocain?"

"He didn't use Novocain today," she primly told him. "It was just the fitting of a temporary crown."

The detail thrilled him. In the warmth of a booth in his favorite weekday lunch place, he marvelled at her presence across the table. She had reluctantly removed her dark wool overcoat, revealing a crimson cardigan and a necklace of pink costume pearls. "So how have you been these many years?" he asked.

"Why are we doing this?" she asked. "Don't the people in here all know you?"

They had arrived early, but the place was filling up, with noise and little sharp drafts as the door opened and closed. "They do and they don't," he said, "but what the hell, what's to be afraid of? You could be a client. You could be an old friend. Which you are, actually. How's your health?"

"Fine," she said, which he knew to be a lie.

But he went on, "And your children? I miss hearing about them—there was the rough-and-tumble one, and the sensitive shy one, who you couldn't stand some days."

"That was ages ago," Veronica said. "I can stand Jane now. She and her brother are both at boarding school."

"Remember how we used to have to work around them? Remember the time you sent Harry off to school even though he had a fever, because you and I had a date set up?"

"I had forgotten that. I'd prefer not to be reminded; it makes me ashamed now. We were foolish and heedless, and you were right to break it off. It's taken a while for me to understand that, but I do."

"Well, I don't. I was crazy to give you up. I exaggerated my own importance. Kids—mine are teen-agers now, too, and away at school, and I look at them and wonder if they ever gave a damn."

"Of course they did, Lester." She cast her eyes down, toward the cup of hot tea she had ordered, though he had pressed her to have, like him, an alcoholic drink. "You were right: don't make me say it again."

"Yeah, but now that I'm with you again, it feels desperately wrong."

"If you flirt with me, I'll have to leave." This threat provoked a long chain of thought in Veronica that led to her saying solemnly, "Gregor and I are getting a divorce."

"Oh no!" Les felt as if the air had thickened, pressing like pillows in his face. "Why?"

She shrugged, and grew very still over her cup of tea, like a card player guarding her hand. "He says I can't keep up with him any more."

"Really? What a selfish, narcissistic creep! Remember how you used to complain about his touch?"

She repeated the almost imperceptible shrug. "He's a typical man. More honest than most."

Les wondered, was this a dig at him? In their game of reopened possibilities, he didn't want to overplay his own hand. Rather than say nothing, he said, "Now that winter's here, you don't seem as pale as in summer. How are you doing with sunlight?"

"Since you ask, it makes me ache. I have lupus, they tell me. A mild form, whatever that means." Her grimace he took to be sarcastic.

"Well," Les said, "that's nice it's mild. You still look great to me." The waitress came back, and they hastily ordered, and passed the rest of the lunch uncomfortably, running out of the small talk, the innocent sharing, that for so long he had felt deprived of. The small talk had come, however, in bed, in the languid aftermath of erotic fulfillment. Veronica was less apt now, Les sensed, to be languid; she carried her wide-hipped, rangy body warily, as if it might detonate. There was something incandescent about her, like a filament forced full of current. Before the waitress could offer them dessert, she reached for her coat and told Les, "Now don't tell Lisa any of this. Some of it's still secret."

He protested, "I never tell her anything."

. . .

But he did tell her, eventually, that perhaps the time had come for them to divorce. His reacquaintance with Veronica—the present-day, more fragile and needy Veronica—filled him night and day with her image. In her pallor she had become the entryway to a kind of hospital radiance, a blur of healing, of old wounds repaired. Breaking off their affair had never sat right with him; now he would take care of her for the rest of her life. He saw himself bringing her broth in bed, driving her to tense appointments, becoming almost a doctor himself. The affair was not exactly resumed; their contacts were confined to her dental appointments, since risking anything more might imperil her legal status as a wronged wife. In these lunches and stray cocktails she more and more came to resemble the mistress he remembered: carefree in manner, lively and light-voiced in her conversation, with an edge that somehow cut through to his real self—the heroic, debonair self his dull and dutiful life concealed.

"But why?" Lisa asked, of the divorce he had threatened her with.

He could not confess Veronica's revival in his life, for that would entail confession of the earlier liaison. "Oh," he said, "I think we've pretty much done our work as a couple. I can't keep up with you, frankly. All your sports. You've become self-sufficient, maybe you always were. Think about it. Please. I'm not saying we should start with the lawyers tomorrow."

She was not fooled. Her blue eyes, their gold freckles magnified by small shells of tears, stared. "Does this have anything to do with Veronica and Gregor splitting up?"

"No, of course not, how could it? But they are showing how to do it—sensibly, with mutual respect and affection."

"I don't know about affection. People say it's shocking of him to leave her, when she's so sickly."

"Is she sickly?" He had thought that the bee sting had opened only his eyes to the extent of her vulnerability, her lovely old-fashioned faintingness.

"Oh, I think so," Lisa said, "though she puts up a good show. Veronica always did."

"See, that's it, show. That's how you think. That's what we've become, a show. All our married life, we've been a show."

"I never felt that. I must say, Les, this is all news to me. I'll need time."

"Of course, dear." There was no hurry; the Horsts were hitting snags, about money. The radiant portal would keep.

And Lisa, that good sport, did seem to adjust, day by day, as the house filled up with the musty feeling of impending abandonment. The children, peeking in on vacations from school, smelled the difference and took refuge in skiing trips to Utah or rock-climbing expeditions to Vermont. Lisa, on the contrary, seemed to become less and less active. Returning from work, Les would find her at home, listless, and when he asked about her day, she would reply, "I don't know where the time went. I didn't do anything, even housework. I have no energy."

One drizzly weekend in early spring, instead of going off to her usual Sunday-morning foursome in the indoor tennis facility, she cancelled and called Les into their bedroom. He had been sleeping in the guest room, which the children had noticed. "Don't worry, I'm not seducing you," Lisa said, lowering her nightie to expose her breasts, and lying back on the bed with not desire but a kind of laughing fear in her face. "Feel here."

Her fingers led his to the underside of her left breast. Instinctively, he pulled his hand back, and she blushed at this rejection and said, "Come on. I can't ask a child to do it, or a friend. You're all I've got. Tell me if you feel anything."

Years of faithful exercise and wearing a jogging bra had kept her body tone firm. Her nipples, the color of watered wine, were erect with their unceremonious exposure to air. "Not just under the skin," she coached him. "Down deeper. Inside."

He didn't know what he felt, in that dark knit of vein and gland. "A lump," she prompted further. "I felt it in the shower ten days ago and kept hoping it was my imagination."

"I . . . I don't know. There's a . . . an inconsistency, but it might be just a naturally dense place."

She put her hand on his and pressed his fingertips deeper. "There. Feel it?"

"Sort of. Does it hurt?"

"I'm not sure it's supposed to. Do the other in the same place. Is it different, or the same?"

He obeyed, shutting his eyes to concentrate on the comparison, trying to envision the interior nub, the dark invader. "Not the same, I think. I don't know; I can't tell, honey. You should get to a doctor."

"I'm scared to," Lisa confessed, and the blue of her eyes showed it, anxious and bright amid her fading freckles.

Les hung there, one hand still cupping her healthy right breast. It was soft, warm, and heavy. This was the bee sting, the intimacy he had coveted, legitimately his at last; but he felt befouled by things of the body and wanted merely to turn away, while knowing he could not.

The Accelerating Expansion of the Universe

Why should it bother Martin Fairchild? In his long, literate lifetime he had read of many revisions of cosmic theory. Edwin Hubble's discovery of a pervasive galactic red shift and therefore of universal expansion had occurred a few years before he was born; by the time of his young manhood, the theory of the Big Bang, with its overtones of Christian Creation by fiat—"Let there be light"—had prevailed over the rather more Buddhist steady-state theory claiming that space itself produced, out of nothingness, one hydrogen atom at a time. In recent decades, in astronomy as in finance, billions had replaced millions as the unit of measure: a billion galaxies, a billion stars in each. Ever stronger telescopes, including one suspended in space and named after Hubble, revealed a swarm of fuzzy ovals, each a Milky Way. Such revelations—stupefying for those who tried truly to conceive of the distances and time spans, the titanic amounts of brute matter accumulating, exploding, and dispersing throughout a not quite infinite vacancy seething with virtual particles—had held for Fairchild the far-fetched hope of a last turn: a culminating piece in the great skyey puzzle would vindicate Mankind's sensation of central importance and disclose an attentive mercy lurking behind the heavenly arrangements.

But the fact, discovered by two independent teams of researchers, seemed to be that deep space showed not only no relenting in the speed of the farthest galaxies but instead a detectable acceleration, so that an eventual dispersion of everything into absolute cold and darkness could be confidently predicted. We are riding an aimless explosion to nowhere. Only an invisible, malevolent anti-gravity, a so-called Dark Force, explained it. Why should Fairchild take it personally? The universe would by a generous margin outlive him—that had always been true. But he had somehow relied on eternity, on there being an eternity even if he wasn't invited to participate in it. The accelerating expansion of the universe imposed an ignominious finitude on the enclosing vastness. The old hypothetical structures—God, Paradise, the moral law within—now had utterly no base to stand on. Everything would melt away. He, though no mystic, had always taken a sneaky comfort in the idea of a universal pulse, an alternating Big Bang and Big Crunch, each time recasting all matter into an unimaginably small furnace, a sub-microscopic point of fresh beginning. Now this comfort was taken from him, and he drifted into a steady state—an estranging fever, scarcely detectable by those around him, of depression.

Fairchild had not hitherto really believed in his own aging. He could see in the mirror his multiplying white hairs, his deepening wrinkles, and feel his shortness of breath after exertion, his stiffness after sitting too long in a chair or a car; but these phenomena took place a safe distance from the center of his being. His inmost self felt essentially exempt from ruin.

His patient daily labors, with an ameliorating additive of pomp and prestige as his position at his firm improved, had accumulated an ample nest egg, enabling semiannual foreign travel with his wife. Their trips to Europe had gradually exhausted the more obvious tourist destinations—England, France, Italy, Greece, Scandinavia. She had never been to Spain, and he only once before, on a hurried student trip that had left little trace in his memory. After Madrid and the obligatory day flight to Bilbao to see Frank Gehry's titanium whale, they came south into the land where the Moors for centuries raised lemons, erected filigreed mosques, and sang love songs around the plashing fountains in the courtyards.

Seville seemed a little short of charm, or perhaps the Fairchilds were tired of being charmed. They were fresh from Granada and Córdoba. In every cathedral and palace there lurked a gloomy Christian boast that the Moors, with their superior refinement and religious tolerance, had been expelled. The Alcázar Palace and the Cathedral of Santa Maria de la Sede were both, it seemed to Fairchild, bigger than they needed to be, and the streets of the old ghetto, which held their hotel, were narrow and heavily trafficked by buzzing mopeds and rickety delivery trucks that ignored the pedestrians-only signs.

Late one afternoon, the aging couple, having done its duty by the Casa de Pilatos, emerged with some relief from the ghetto's quaint alleys onto a slightly broader thoroughfare. They had coffee at an outdoor table, and then headed back to their hotel. His sense of direction told him that the most direct route lay along a busy one-way street with a narrow sidewalk on one side. "You think?" his cautious wife asked. "Suppose I fall off into traffic?"

"Why would you fall off?" Fairchild scoffed. "I'll be right behind you."

It was true, the noisy stream of traffic did feel very close as they made their way single-file, Fairchild in the rear. Fiats and Vespas sped by, stirring the ubiquitous dust. He was watching his wife's feet, or thinking of his own, when a sudden sensation of pressure pushed him off-balance, and down; there was no resisting this inexplicable force. He fell sideways, twisting. In the midst of his plunge he saw, inches from his eyes, the porous new-shaven cheek of a dark-haired young man; the man was grimacing with some terrible effort, with some ordeal that he, too, was undergoing.

Then Fairchild hit the asphalt, face-down. His arms were pinioned by the relentless force at his back, and he foresaw that his forehead would strike the street's hard surface. No sooner had this thought been entertained by his brain than the sensation of a momentarily blinding blow on his brow told him that the worst was over, that he would survive.

Automobiles were braking behind him. He raised his head in time to see two men on a moped turn down a side street and, smartly leaning in unison, vanish. One of them had been his dark-haired companion in gravity's terrible grip. The weight on his back was still there, but it lifted, cautiously, and began to talk to him in a female voice, and Fairchild realized that the irresistible weight had been his wife's body. He lay some seconds longer on the street's abrasive, dirty surface, in a position that obscurely felt privileged, while he relished the apparent fact that his skull had taken the blow without causing him to surrender consciousness: he was one tough old *americano*, he thought, as if his consciousness had become a detached, appraising witness.

Bit by bit, his swirl of sensations was retrospectively clarified. By the time he got to his feet, with the help of several hands, he understood that his wife's shoulder bag had been snatched and the entangling strap had pulled her into him. The two of them had been welded together by the pressure as the dark-haired thief struggled to hold on to his prize without losing his seat on the speeding moped. Fairchild's thumped brain, he noted with satisfaction, was in excellent order, working very fast. But it had not been fast enough for him to reach up and pull his assailant down with him. He would have liked, very much, to have done that—to have dragged this criminal down to the dirty asphalt with him, and pulverized his smooth-shaven face with his fists.

His wife, Carol, had once been a nurse; she still quickened to emergencies. She was staring intently at his face. So, with less disguised alarm, were the several Spaniards who had gathered behind her. "I'm fine," he said to his wife. He addressed the Spaniards: "*Soy bueno. No problema.*"

His wife said softly, in her soothing emergency voice, "Darling, don't try to talk. Let's take off your jacket."

"My jacket?" A light-tan windbreaker, with a lining for warmth in the Spanish spring, it had been bought new for the trip. "Why?"

He wondered if he was supposed to be translating their exchanges to the gathered crowd. "*¿Por qué?*" he translated aloud.

"Keep calm," she told him levelly, as if he were crazed. "I'll help you, darling."

Fairchild was beginning to find her officious; but in moving his lips to protest he tasted something warm and salty. He realized, as a walker in the woods realizes that a tickly swarm of midges have enveloped his head, that he was bleeding into his own mouth. His face had met the asphalt on the right eyebrow, the crest of bone there—a blood-packed site, he knew from his old sports injuries. He saw the light: his wife, the eminently practical nurse, was worried that he would bleed on the new windbreaker. It had not been expensive, but it evidently outweighed his wound, his drama, his near-tragedy. As she gently peeled the coat from his shoulders, the crowd behind her, and the cab driver who had braked in time to avoid running over him, started to offer advice, of which the most prominent word was *policía*. "*Policía*, *policía*," they seemed to be chanting.

After removing his coat, Carol had picked his hip pocket, and now she handed him his own folded handkerchief and indicated that he should keep it pressed against his right orbital arch. On center stage amid the halted traffic, Fairchild stood tall; he gestured rather grandly with his free hand, like a matador disavowing a spectacular kill. "*Policía*," he pronounced scornfully, and, unable to come up with the Spanish for "What can they do?," expressed the opinion "*¡Policía—nada!*" From their alarmed faces, it could have been more happily put. Not long ago, under Franco, this had been a police state.

Traffic was beginning to honk; the cab driver needed to get on his way. This driver, wearing a wool jacket and tie in the formal, self-important European manner, was small and round-faced and visibly shaken by nearly running over an elderly American. His hand still held aloft, Fairchild told him, "*Muchas gracias, señor—vaya con Dios.*" The phrase had floated into his head from a Patti Page song popular when he was an adolescent. To the crowd he proclaimed, "*¡Adiós, ami-*

gos!" This, too, was no doubt inadequate, but what he wanted to say in final benediction materialized in his head only in French: "*Vous tous êtes très gentils.*"

Fairchild felt exhilarated, striding through the antique streets holding a bloody handkerchief to his eyebrow while his wife—undamaged, younger than he—trotted beside him, holding his jacket, which, for all her concern, bore only a single drop of blood, now dried. "That son of a bitch," he said, meaning the thief. "What all did you have in it?" he asked, meaning her shoulder bag.

"My wallet, without much money. The credit cards are the big nuisance. They can help me cancel them back at the hotel. If they have any hydrogen peroxide at the desk, I can get the blood out of the jacket. Lemon juice and salt might do."

"Will you stop focusing on my *blood*? You knew when you married me I had blood." Why be angry at her? *¿Por qué?* As if in apology, he said, "You always hear of things like this, but I never thought it would happen to me." He corrected himself: "To us." She was teaching him, this late in his life, feminist inclusiveness.

Carol in turn explained, "I was so concerned with staying on the sidewalk I guess I forgot to switch the bag to my inside shoulder. Now I keep thinking of everything that was in it. The Instamatic full of shots of the Alhambra. My favorite scarf—you can't get wool that lightweight any more. Marty, I feel sick. This is all just hitting me. The guidebook kept warning us about Gypsies. Did he look like a Gypsy to you? I never saw him."

"Boy, I did. His face was right next to mine for a second. He didn't wear an earring, just a very determined expression. I guess he thought you'd let go before you did."

"I couldn't believe somebody else wanted it," she said. "It was so sudden, you don't think. Thank you, by the way, for cushioning my fall. I didn't even skin my knees."

"Any time, my dear. That's rotten about your perfect scarf."

"He won't know what it was worth to me. He'll throw it away."

La policía were already at the hotel. How had they known? "The cab driver reported the accident," the smiling young clerk behind the desk explained. "Then the police called hotels in this area for a couple of your description." How much of a police state was this, still?

The policeman himself, a phlegmatic bland man in his forties—colorless, as if a policeman's experience had washed out of him all his natural tint and capacity for surprise—spoke no English; he didn't risk his dignity by venturing even a phrase. He glanced at Fairchild's clotted eyebrow and gave him a long bilingual form to fill out. Through the desk clerk, the policeman communicated an intention to take him away, though the victim protested, "*Es nada. ¡Nada!*" Mrs. Fairchild, the desk clerk translated with a pleased smile, was invited to come along.

In the back of the police car she confided, "The clerk was telling me while you were filling out the form about a woman who got thrown down and broke her hip, and in another incident a husband who tried to intervene and got stabbed and killed. So we were lucky."

"Good for us," Fairchild said, beginning to feel weary. His eyebrow hurt. The invigoration of shock was wearing off. They were being taken, he realized, out of the tourist region, into the real Seville, its ordinary neighborhoods and everyday institutions, its places for working and shopping, living and dying. They passed down streets of restaurants, past banks and a department store, all still bustling in the growing dark, at an hour when an American city would be shutting up shop. The silent policeman parked at what must be the hospital. The building had a six-story Beaux-Arts core, with a post-Franco modern wing. Within, all was brightly lit but with a milkier, subtler light than an American hospital would have employed. Such dramas as galvanize hospitals on American television were not occurring here. Instead, there was quiet in the halls. Most of the desks in sight were empty. No one seemed to speak English. Nor did the policeman offer anyone in his own language a long explanation of Fairchild's case—his abrupt crisis, his heroic survival.

Two uniformed women, possibly nuns, one in green and one in white, interviewed the victim. Fairchild pointed at his wound and explained, "*Dos hombres jovenes—Vespa, vroom, vrrrooom! Mi esposa*"—at a loss for words to describe how Carol had been tugged down, he pantomimed a grab at his own shoulder, then did a toppling motion with his forearm—"*la señora, boom! y me con la.*" The women nodded sympathetically, and went away, and eventually brought a man down the echoing hall. Feminist though he was becoming, Fairchild was relieved to see a man taking charge. The word *hidalgo* came to his mind; the man was a somebody. He was short and fair and squarish—a blond descendant of the Visigoths, with a toothbrush mustache and an air of courteous amusement. He was a doctor. He examined Fairchild's bloody eyebrow and gestured for him to sit on a high, sheeted bed. Fairchild liked his gestures, firm but unhurried, with an Iberian touch of ceremony.

The patient's comprehension of Spanish was improving; he understood that the doctor was asking the nurse for

Novocain, and that the nurse came back, rather breathlessly reporting that no Novocain could be found. The doctor urbanely shrugged, but his eyes declined to join his patient's in a wink at such female incompetence. When at last, after much distant chatter and clatter, the anesthetic was found, Fairchild lay back and shut his eyes. He felt a paper mask being lowered onto his face. In her solicitous nurse's voice Carol described in his ear what was happening to him: "Now, Marty, he has the needle, you're going to feel a pinch, he's injecting all around the gash, don't move your head suddenly. Now he has some gauze, he's going to wipe out your eyebrow, don't make that funny face, keep your face still."

Through his numbness Fairchild felt the tug of the stitches, and the latex-gloved fingertips lightly pressing on his brow. How kind this doctor, and the policeman, and this entire post-Fascist nation were! When the operation was over, he produced his wallet, holding credit cards and a pastel salad of euro bills, but his attempt at payment was waved away. Instead, a flamboyantly signed document, giving his wound an official status, was handed to him. A slight, ceremonious smile tweaked the toothbrush mustache. "One week," the doctor said, in his lone effort at English, "stitches out."

In a week, his black eye faded, Fairchild was back in the United States, where his own doctor, a youth no older than the Gypsy robber, marvelled that the stitches were silk. "In this country," he explained, "you never see silk stitches any more."

Why was this unlucky event—being mugged and injured in a foreign land—so pleasing to Fairchild? It was, he supposed, the element of contact. In his universe of accelerating expansion, he enjoyed less and less contact. Retired, he had lost contact with his old associates, full of sociable promises though their partings had been. His children were adult and far-flung, and the grandchildren within his reach had only polite interest in the stale treats—the moronic kiddie movies, the expeditions to cacophonous bowling alleys indelibly smelling of the last century's cigarettes—that he could offer. His old poker group, which used to crowd eight around a dining-room table, had increasing difficulty mustering the minimum five players, and his old golf foursome had been dispersed to infirmity and Florida if not to the grave. One partner remained who shared Fairchild's old-fashioned aversion to riding a golf cart and was willing to walk with him; then on a winter morning this friend's handsome photograph, twenty years out of date, popped up in the obituary section of the *Boston Globe*.

Other than the obituaries, newspapers had less and less in them that pertained to Fairchild—crucial sports contests, burning social issues, international crises all took place over a certain horizon. A curvature of concern left him out of it; he was islanded. Even his doctors and financial advisers, the caretakers of his old age, were increasingly difficult to reach, hiding behind a screen of recorded messages and secretaries whose hurried, immigrant accents were difficult for Fairchild to decipher. If a heart attack or a catastrophic downturn in the market were to overtake him, he would be left clutching the telephone while shimmering streams of Vivaldi or, even more insultingly, soupy instrumental arrangements of old Beatles standards filled the interminable wait for the next available service representative.

As opposed to this, there had been the Spanish doctor, his firm velvet touch on Fairchild's brow, and the member of the *policía* providing in stoical silence a tour of the real Seville, and the swarthy young mugger, not necessarily a Gypsy but distinctly dark, with shiny black hair *en brosse*, his face inches away and touchingly contorted in the work of retaining his loot. Everything in Spain had felt closer. There had been contact.

Mrs. Fairchild, meanwhile, led an ever busier American life, with her committees and bridge groups and book clubs and manicure appointments. She had joined the universal dispersion of which Fairchild felt himself at the center. As she went off one day, she assigned him a small task which, she patiently explained, "even he" could do. Last summer she had decided, against his advice, to have the two heavy tall doors opening into the living room removed. "I *hate* stuffy rooms," she told him, unstoppably. "Air! Light!" It made the house airier but (he pointed out in vain) harder to heat.

Too heavy for him to lift, the doors had been carried down to the barn by two young men and wrapped in a tarpaulin and leaned in a corner, against the remote possibility of their reinstallation some day, if not by the Fairchilds by the next owners—even the house, as his time in it dwindled, was flying from him. One of the doors had a blue doorknob, rare old cobalt glass, which Carol wanted to see installed where they could enjoy the sight of it. Could he possibly go down and take the knob off? "Really, Marty, a *child* could do it," she said.

The day was a clear one in February, with a chilly breeze. The barn was a relic of the horse-and-buggy era, with several stalls and mangers and a large central space the Fairchilds had slowly filled with things the couple didn't have the heart or the imagination to throw away. Their children had left bulky deposits of schoolbooks, flat-tired bicycles, defunct toys, unplayable 33⅓ rpm records. Dead ancestors persisted in the form of framed diplomas, garden tools, and musty trunks stuffed with clothes and letters more ancient than the barn itself.

After a frightening moment of senile blankness, Fairchild recalled the padlock combination. The creosoted barn doors creaked open. The interior, lit by high windows of dirty glass, held the expectant hush of an abandoned church. The two living-room doors leaned in their beige tarpaulin against a wall six feet behind an antique cherrywood corner cupboard that Fairchild had inherited when his mother died.

The imposing three-sided cupboard had been a presence in his childhood, a choice piece of Philadelphia cabinet-making and a looming proof of his family's pretensions to respectability. In a child's view it had emanated the grave mystery of ownership. To buy things, and then to have them all yours, and to place them safely on shelves, and to have the government with its laws and enforcers keep others from taking them, had struck him as a solemn privilege of grown-up life. He could still hardly bear to part with anything that was his. Even the oldest clothes might be used as cleaning rags, or an outfit for a very dirty job, dirtier than this one.

A section of the corner cupboard with two panelled doors formed the lower portion; upon it rested, with no attachment but gravity, a similar-sized unit whose single large door held nine panes of wavery old glass. The shelves behind the glass used to be loaded with rarely used family china, its gleaming ranks changelessly presiding in the dining room while Fairchild as a child played on the carpet and executed crayon drawings, much admired by his elders, at the dining table. When, after a long widowhood, his mother had died, the cupboard had seemed the most precious part of his inheritance, and he had saved it from auction and in a rented truck brought it up to Massachusetts from Pennsylvania. But none of his children had wanted it, or had room for it, and Carol, whose sense of décor, formed in hospitals, favored a clean and uncluttered look, didn't see that their house, a stately neo-colonial with more than its share of windows and radiators, had any place for it either. And so it had come to rest in the barn, waiting for someone to cherish it as Fairchild did and come take it away.

Fairchild loved it because its subtly irregular old panes reflected into his mind the wobbly ghosts of his grandparents and his mother and father and Uncle Wilbur, a New Jersey dairy farmer who once had taken out his penknife and jimmied open the corner cupboard's door during a summer visit. Uncle Wilbur had had an accent that Fairchild never heard any more, a soft mild wheeze formed, possibly, in patient conversation with animals. Fairchild's mother on that long-ago summer day (the air heavy with promise of a thunderstorm) had complained of being unable to retrieve something from the cupboard—the big porcelain soup tureen, perhaps, or the dessert dishes with scalloped edges, like glossy thick doilies. The door was stuck, swollen by the humidity. The New Jersey cousin's clever patience with his penknife had opened it and saved the day—that distant day—so that joyous exclamations arose from the visiting relatives seated expectantly around the table. It was a trivial incident magnified by family feeling; it touched Fairchild to realize that in the level run of his childhood days so small a thing would stick up and stay in his memory. Uncle Wilbur's knife-marks could still be seen on the edge of the beaded cherrywood. In New England's drier climate, the door swung open easily.

With the enshrined china auctioned off, along with most of the rest of the family possessions, Fairchild had sentimentally filled the cupboard with his mother's remaining treasures—a heavy pottery vase wearing a purplish-brown glaze, a thinner tubular one with a matte marbled pattern like that of endpapers in a *de luxe* book, several baskets woven of multicolored straw, a collection of possible arrowheads she had collected as a young farm girl, her father's hand-painted shaving mug with his name in gilt, porcelain figurines (an elf with polka-dot wings, a baby robin in its tinted nest), some sandstone "rose stones" acquired as souvenirs of her one trip west, with her husband, a year before she became a widow. In a small flat box, from the days when department stores packaged even small gifts in substantial boxes, she had saved the Sunday-school attendance badges and field-day ribbons that her only child had once been awarded.

Fairchild had even put into the cupboard her last pocketbook, a plump black one with its catch on the top. Its leather had mildewed since her death. A pocket inside it, he knew, still held her driver's license, her Social Security and Medicare cards, and a computer-generated reminder of a doctor's appointment scheduled for the week after she had, abruptly, died, rendering all these accoutrements of her existence useless. Souvenirs of a life of which Fairchild was the last caring witness, these remnants that he lacked the will to discard depressed him, deepening the depression from which even so modest a task as removing a blue doorknob from a disused door loomed like a mountain almost impossible to climb. Why bother? Everything decays and sinks and fails under the dominion of time and entropy.

Moving the tarpaulin to one side was difficult. The husky workmen—*dos hombres jovenes*—had wrapped the two living-room doors together and then leaned them so their weight pinned the covering top and bottom. The blue knob was on the inside, toward the wall. Fairchild had left his reading glasses up at the house, so he could not make out the head of the little screw that held the knob in place. The light, falling through the dirty high windows, was poor. He lifted the doors toward him, closer to what light there was. He seemed to make out, shifting his head to gain a clearer spot of vision, that there was no screw; in the hole where one should have been was something like a nailhead, that would have to be pulled with a needle-nosed pliers. He hadn't brought pliers.

Why was everything in life so difficult?

To see a little better, to get the blue knob a few inches farther into the open, he shifted the doors, in their encumbering wrap, toward him, so that they were precariously balanced in a vertical position, against his shoulder.

Suddenly he was being pressed, as he had been on that street in Seville, downward irresistibly, by a force he could not at first understand. Then he *did* understand: the doors were falling on him. Together the two substantial doors of oak pressed him flat, face-down, onto a pile of old pine boards that he, with thrift's absurd inertia, was saving. His knees scraped on the rough edges. Splinters gouged the side of his right hand. As his brain registered these injuries he felt the weight of the doors continue to fall, past him, over him; in the split second before it happened he knew what was going to happen: they would slam into the top half of the corner cupboard, and it would topple from its perch on the lower half, and all would be smashed and scattered—arrowheads and badges and vases and baskets and figurines and the nine panes of irreplaceable old wavery glass.

The crashing successive tumult, as he lay with shut eyes and stinging knees on the useless saved lumber, came in stages, bad followed by worse, worse by worst, and then by silence. Winter wind whispered in a high corner of the barn. A splinter of glass tardily let go and tinkled to the floor. All was destroyed, shattered, dispersed. Fairchild's brain, working as fast as a knitting machine, had in a split second seen it all coming. For that split second, he had not been depressed.

German Lessons

Boston had a patchy, disconsolate feel in those years, the mid-Seventies. Girls with long hair and long skirts still walked along Charles Street with bare feet, but the Sixties bloom was off; you found yourself worrying that these flower children would step on broken glass, or that parasites would penetrate their dirty soles, which were stained green from wandering on the grassy Common. The cultural revolution had become unclean.

Ed Trimble felt unclean and guilty. He had moved to the city alone, having left a family behind in New Hampshire. His wife and he ran a small real-estate firm in Peterborough, and Arlene made most of the sales. She had more gusto and social grace; she didn't let her real feelings about a property sour her pitch, as he did. He resented her superior success, and knew she could hold things together if he pulled out for a time. He needed space; things were up in the air. In this interim, with the begrimed conveniences of a city all about him, he saw a chance to fill some of his gaps. Guided by the

Yellow Pages, he enlisted in German lessons, at a so-called Language Institute in Cambridge.

The Institute turned out to be an ordinary wooden house north of Central Square, and the class a ragged handful of other gap-fillers, some of them not much younger than he, and the classroom a small basement room where an excess of fluorescent lighting blazed as if to overcome the smallness with brightness. Their teacher was Frau Mueller—Müller in Germany—and their textbook was *Deutsch als Fremdsprache*, a slender blue tome designed, as the multilingual cover announced, for speakers of any other language. It was illustrated with photographs that Ed found alienating—the people in them could have been Americans but for an edge of formality and the ubiquity of Mercedes cars. The men, even the auto mechanics, wore neckties, and the young women sported slightly outdated miniskirts and Jackie Kennedy hairdos, teased into glossy bulk. Ed's older brother had acquired a shrapnel wound and a lifelong limp in the Ardennes counteroffensive, and Ed rather resented the prim, bloodless prosperity revealed in these lesson illustrations. Now, while the U.S. was risking troops and going broke protecting what was left of the Deutschland from the Russians, these defeated Huns, sleek and smug, were wallowing in a picture-book capitalism.

Frau Mueller did not look like the well-groomed women in the photographs. Her hair, straw color fading to gray, had been pulled back into a streaky ponytail; stray strands fell untidily around her face. She dressed in the absent-minded Cambridge manner, adding woolly layers as the summer waned and autumn deepened into winter. To Ed she seemed much older than he, but perhaps the difference was as little as five years: she had just suffered more. Her nose came to a sharp tip reddened by perpetual sniffles; her thick spectacles magnified pale-lashed eyes that twinkled sometimes as if remembering a joke it would be too much trouble to explain.

Though *Deutsch als Fremdsprache* contained no English, Frau Mueller's accompanying guidance contained plenty of it, much of it focused on fine points of English grammar. Ed knew this was wrong; he had taken enough language courses—French, Spanish, both mostly forgotten—to know that the modern method, proven over and over, was immersion, no matter how painful at first for the students and the native speaker leading them. When they came to the German subjunctive, she informed the class, "Your English subjunctive fascinates me. It does not seem—how can I say this?—quite serious. When does one employ it? Give me examples."

"If I were king," Ed hesitantly offered.

"If any man sin," timidly chimed in a student called Andrea—quoting, Ed realized, the Book of Common Prayer.

Frau Mueller's eyes, twinkling, darted around her mostly silent little flock. "Ah," she triumphantly told them, "you must *think* for examples. If the subjunctive in English did not exist—if it exist not, would it be correct to say?—no one would miss it! No one would notice! That is not the case in German. We use it all the time. Not to use it would be a serious discourtesy. It would sound—can I use the word?—*pushy*. Germans are always being described as pushy, yes? I think it is fascinating, the looseness of English."

"*Aber—Englisch hat Regeln,*" Ed protested, hoping that that was the plural of *Regel*, and the accusative. The rest of the class looked at him as if he were crazy, trying to communicate in German.

"Ein Satz Regeln," Frau Mueller smiled. *"Aber es ist nur eine Kleinigkeit."*

Ed found German disagreeable and opaque; its closeness to English addled his mind. Reading, in the lesson "Im Restaurant," the fictional Herr Weber's polite request, *"Vielleicht haben Sie einen Tisch am Fenster?,"* he had to fight the impulse to make *Tisch* into "dish" and *Fenster* into "fender." He might have quit the class but for Andrea. In this disordered period of his life, she radiated, though well advanced into her thirties, a healing innocence. She was on the small side, with the wide-eyed, washed-out face of an aging child, her lips the same color as her cheeks and clear brow. As winter closed in, her delicate lips cracked and she kept applying a lip balm that made them, under the harsh fluorescent lights, gleam.

Frau Mueller not only spoke too much English, but when it came time for the class to examine the assigned German texts, she waved them aside as if their meaning was obvious to all. Little was obvious to Ed, including the differences between *noch* and *doch*. *Doch* seemed to be untranslatable, sheer padding, like the English word "well"—but the utility and sense of "well" were inexpressibly apparent. Andrea was less indignant than he, coming up against the language barrier. He and she began to sit side by side in class, and to arrive with lessons they had worked up together, either in the underfurnished two rooms he rented in the South End, or on the sofa or bed of Andrea's apartment, the third floor of a stately Cambridge house on Fayerweather Street. The genteel landlady was a professor's widow, hanging on beyond her means. Andrea shared the third floor with a female cellist who was often away, performing. She herself was a part-time librarian, on duty evenings at an East Cambridge branch of the city system. Her immurement in books, and her acquired skill at aurally deciphering what the library's minority patrons wanted, enabled her to see through the opacity of the German texts into a sphere of human meaning. He even once caught her, as they coped side by side with a set passage from Brecht, laughing at a joke that had leaped out at her. Feminine intuition: Arlene back in New Hampshire had possessed it also, but had used it less and less to anticipate his desires. When he and this new woman, an aging flower-child, a vegetarian, and a peacenik, made love, Andrea seemed a filmy extension of his wishes. Her gentle shyness merged with a knowingness, an experience of other partners, that slightly unnerved Ed. She had been, in a way that worked to his benefit, corrupted.

His and Andrea's becoming a kind of couple in German class, and their being somewhat older than the other students, won them an unlooked-for honor; before Christmas, as the first term was ending, Frau Mueller invited them to tea. "Only if you like," she said.

"You've used the subjunctive!" Ed told her.

She half-smiled—her smile was rarely more than half, diluted by a nagging wariness—and said, "I think it was merely the conditional."

She lived in one of three squat brick apartment buildings built on an old Kenmore Square industrial site; the complex had the small-windowed look of a modern prison, but lacked the barbed wire and guard towers. Ed and Andrea would not have gone, except that they did not know how to decline an invitation that clumsily crossed the American line between paid instruction and social friendship. "What do you say? *Nein, danke*?" Ed asked.

"You don't want to hurt her feelings," Andrea said. This excursion was a step for them, too, venturing forth for the first time to be entertained as a couple. For a present they took something that they considered, after much deliberation, to be uniquely American—a tin log cabin full of maple syrup. Though, without pancakes, did maple syrup make any sense?

They were taken unawares when a man, speaking in the thick accent of a stage German, responded over the security speaker at the entrance and then greeted them in the dark hall. "I am Hedwig's husband, Franz," he told them, pronouncing the name "Hettvig." "It is werry obliching of you to come." He, too, sensed something strange about the occasion, its awkward reaching-out.

Tea, it developed, was not offered, though cookies, sprinkled with red and green sugar in honor of the Christmas season, had been set out, along with some miniature fruit tarts still in their pleated wax-paper cups from the deli. Franz urged a beer, an imported Löwenbräu, upon Ed, and for Andrea, who did not drink alcohol or smoke or eat meat or fish—"nothing with a face" was her creed—he found a Coke in the back of the refrigerator. She did not drink caffeinated soft drinks, either, Ed knew, but with a docility that broke his heart she accepted this desperate offering from her host. Franz was plump but energetic, with thinning blond hair combed straight back on his skull; his scalp was dewy, and his shirt damp, as if in silent comment upon the overheated airlessness of this rented apartment.

In her husband's presence, an invisible burden seemed to slip from Frau Mueller. She became passive and betranced, sipping an amber drink that Franz quickly replenished when the ice cubes settled to the bottom. She seemed pleased to have the conversation focus on Franz. He was a photographer—weddings, graduations, bar and bat mitzvahs. "To the Orientals especially," Franz explained, "the photographer is more important than the minister. He *iss* the minister, in practical fact. He iss the Gott who says, 'Let sare be light,' and this passink event iss made—*Was ist 'ewig,' Liebchen?*"

"Eternal," Frau Mueller supplied, out of her smiling, drifting state.

The living room was configured like a basement: steps led up to a floor above, and the triangular space beneath the stairs was filled with stacks of magazines. Ed, who had taken the easy chair nearest the stairs, slowly saw that most of the saved magazines were *Playboy*s and *Penthouse*s and *Hustler*s. On his second Löwenbräu Ed felt empowered to remark upon this unusual domestic archive. His zealous host hopped up and placed a few in his hands, urging him to flip through. The glossy pages reminded Ed of a rose-grower's catalogue, so many vivid shades of pink and red, with the occasional purple and mauve of a black woman. Franz explained, "They use mirrors, to focus light upon"—he hesitated, glancing toward Andrea—"chust *that* spot."

Ed, too, glanced at Andrea, and was startled by the angelic beauty of her face, blankly gazing elsewhere in serene ignorance that the men were discussing mirrors focused on vaginas. She was a silverpoint beauty, all outline, transparent to the radiance beneath things: the sudden contrast, perhaps, with the dirty girls of *Penthouse*, their spread legs and forced leers, created the impression. She was so good, so abstemious that Ed saw, sinkingly, she could never be his. This glimpse of truth persisted when most of the details of the slightly mad tea party had faded.

The Muellers wanted, it seemed, to talk about themselves.

Of this couple, the man was the natural teacher, the natural sharer and salesman. Franz had been a young soldier in the Wehrmacht, and had ingratiated himself with the two great armies that had defeated his own. As a prisoner of war in the Soviet Union, he had learned enough Russian to make himself useful and win favored treatment in a harsh environment. Then, repatriated to the Western zone, he had learned the American version of English. He had acquired skills, photography being only one of them. Weekdays, he worked at MIT, as a lab technician. Hedwig and he had come to the United States nearly ten years ago, already linked by marriage.

If they ever described how they had met, or what dream had brought them to the United States, Ed, mellow on Löwenbräu, let it slip through his mind.

As her third tea-colored drink dwindled before her, Hedwig's languid passivity warmed into lax confidingness. She called Franz by a nickname—"*Affe*," and he responded with "*Affenkind.*" Monkey and baby monkey. She shocked Ed by referring, out of the blue, to Franz's "cute little heinie." The word "heinie" was one Ed had not heard since his childhood, and American women in the Seventies still kept to themselves any interest in men's derrières—the words "bum" and "butt" and "ass" were saved for, if ever, intimacy. He reasoned that the two Germans, childless, in strange and formerly hostile territory, would make much of their sexual bond. But here among the four of them it was as if, in their eagerness to achieve closeness, the couple were using sex as a stalking horse for darker confidences. These were real Germans, Ed told himself—the people his brother had fought against, not the "Dutch" who had come to this country to be farmers or brewers, and not the Jewish Germans who had come here to flee Hitler. These Germans had stayed where they were, and fought. They had fought hard.

Late in their little party, the early-December night tightening cozily around them, Hedwig announced, with a smile rather broader than her usual wary one, "I was a Hitler bitch." She meant that she had been, in her teens, with millions of others, a member of the BDM, the Bund Deutscher Mädel, the League of German Maidens. The matter had arisen from her description, fascinating to the Americans—Ed had been a boy during the war, and Andrea was not yet born—of the Führer's voice over the radio. "It was terrible," Hedwig said, picking her words with especial care, shutting her eyes as if to hear it again, "but exciting. A shrieking like an angry husband with his wife. He loves her, but she must shape up. Both of you know, of course, how in a German sentence the verb of a compound form must come at the end of a sentence, however lengthy; he was excused from that. Hitler was exempted from grammar. It was a mark of how far above us he was."

And Ed saw on her face a flicker of grammatical doubt, as she rechecked the last sentence in her head and could find nothing wrong with it, odd as it had sounded in her ears.

Two other shared occasions, on the scant social ground where Ed and Andrea and Franz and Hedwig met, remained, decades later, in Ed's spotty memory.

First, there was a bitterly cold January night in which the two couples and another, Luke and Susan, had gone out to eat together. Luke and Susan were hardly a couple, since Luke, a weedy slight youth with a pained squint, was generally assumed to be gay. He had come along as Susan's guest. In the class, where dwindled enrollment encouraged an even looser informality, Hedwig, digressing from the lesson on *weil*, *um zu*, and *damit*, had expressed a desire for more authentic Cantonese cuisine than the "mongrelized"—she pronounced the English word deliberately, in apparent ignorance of its bad historical connotations—fare offered as Chinese food. Susan, a large-framed, exuberant brunette given to sweeping pronouncements, had responded that she knew just the place, an unbelievably tiny family restaurant in Chinatown. It was agreed that after the next lesson—lessons occurred in the late afternoon, the students emerging from oppressive brightness into the January dark—Franz would pick the five of them up in his car, which turned out to be an early-Sixties Buick, proudly maintained. The Americans, climbing in, giggled at its largeness, its inner swaths of soft velour, reminiscent of their parents' more naïve, expansive America. Chinatown proved too cramped and crowded for the spacious car, and Franz finally took a chancy spot at a corner of Beach Street, his front bumper and knobby chrome grille nearly protruding into traffic.

The meal, deftly served in a smoky, clattering congestion by what seemed a pack of children in slippers, fell short of Susan's expectations, but no one else complained. The Tsingtao beer tickled Franz's palate, and he insisted, against feeble objections from his impecunious crew, on picking up the check. When, however, overfed and overheated and talking too loud, they all went back out into the freezing January night, the spot on Beach Street where Franz's car had been parked was empty. The nostalgic big Buick was gone.

Ed, at heart a country boy, assumed the worst: the car had been stolen; the loss was total and irremediable. If he were by himself, he could simply walk back to the South End, and he resentfully pictured the long trek, by taxi or the T, that he must endure to return Andrea to her Cambridge widow's house. The others, more city-smart, took a less dire view of the disappearance. Franz and Luke agreed that the car, illegally parked, had been towed by the police, and a call, from an imperfectly vandalized pay phone, with Luke doing the talking, confirmed that this was the case. The car was being held captive at the great fenced-in impoundment lot beyond the Berkeley Street overpass of the Massachusetts Turnpike, to be released upon payment of fine and fees. The Muellers offered to say good night on Beach Street right then and take a taxi to ransom their automobile, but the Americans would not hear of it. There were too many for a cab, so all walked together, their cheeks on fire with the cold, the mile to the dismal civic site.

Susan, in white earmuffs and a long striped scarf wound around her neck, led the parade. Her dark hair gleamed beneath the streetlights. Broken glass glittered all around. Andrea, it seemed to Ed, glowed in a religious rapture; the physical challenge of the trudge through the litter and the desolate urban margins of the Turnpike, with a group goal of redeeming a lost thing, spoke to her ascetic, coöperative spirit. As their brave parade moved through the blasted cityscape, its rubble and battered playground fencing and hard-frozen puddles, Ed kept thinking of bombed Berlin, and of cities Berlin had bombed, and of the black-and-white wartime movies that had communicated to his childhood an illicit exhilaration.

The episode was one of unequalled solidarity and spontaneous fun with the Germans. Franz had paid for their feast in cash, in those days before credit cards became universal tender, and found himself lacking the dollars that the heavy-lidded, implacable police clerk demanded from within his fortified and snugly heated shack. The others quickly made up the sum, raising their American voices as if to hide Franz's accent. The cop did not like the accent, or Franz's toadying manner, acquired in the postwar ruins. The cop suspected that his leg was being pulled; he was used to sullen hostility, not a cluster of tow-truck victims happily gabbling. The German students clambered into the liberated vintage sedan like schoolmates on an educational outing that has gone slightly, hilariously awry.

Second, there was the spring party, the end of German lessons. It took place not in the Muellers' dank ground-floor Kenmore Square apartment but in a new, more spacious one, on a fourth floor, in Boston, near the Massachusetts College of Art and, across the trolley tracks, dangerous Mission Hill. Out here, beyond the Museum of Fine Arts, the city had a rakish low-rent feeling, a bohemian swagger. The festivity was ambitious; all the students from both terms had been invited, with their significant others, plus associates in the photography studio where Franz worked and various other strays the Germans had rounded up. In this ungainly gathering Franz gamely bustled back and forth, transporting beers and other beverages, an adroit, cheerfully sweating factotum, while Hedwig seemed paralyzed and dazed by the extent of her hospitality.

A number of the female students had brought hors d'oeuvres—raw vegetables with a hummus dip, tepid cheese puffs—but as the hours went by these morsels evaporated, as did the initial abundance of good will and polite conversation. A table by the big bay window had been set with paper plates and napkins and cutlery, but where was the food? Frau Professor sat in a thronelike ladder-back chair while her guests circulated with less and less energy, and it came to Ed that he had no business being here, among these young and would-be young, these part-time students and half-baked culture workers. Spring was the liveliest time for real estate in Peterborough, and his lawn and garden would need tending. Andrea came up to him with her version of the same feeling. She had finally disengaged herself from an elegant black photographer's assistant, in torn jeans and a purple dashiki, who kept blowing some sort of smoke into her face. She was uncharacteristically querulous. "I'm starving. What's happening?" she said.

"Ask Hedwig."

"That would be rude, wouldn't it? We're guests. We take what comes." Ed heard in this the implication that he, too, in his city sojourn, had taken what came.

He stuck to the immediate topic. "But nothing is coming. Forthcoming."

"She doesn't move," Andrea plaintively agreed.

Over Andrea's shoulder Ed saw Frau Mueller still in her chair, smiling even though no one was talking to her, and it came to him that she was stoned. If not stoned on a controlled substance, then on a cumulative dose of being German, a Hitler bitch in a foreign land where the subjunctive was withering away and everything was mongrelized. America had worn her down. Or Hitler had left her, in a way slow to emerge, disabled. In a corner of the room, Franz, sweating, was on the telephone. What seemed another hour later, a Hispanic deliveryman came through the door bearing a baby-sized bundle wrapped in butcher paper. Hedwig made a helpless welcoming gesture by raising one arm and called, "Franz!" It was, rumors ran through the sagging party, a pork roast, and Franz was now placing it in the oven. Andrea said to Ed, "It'll take till midnight. Meat disgusts me. I want to go home."

"Me, too, *Liebchen.*" Ed had had one too many Löwenbräus.

"Would it be too rude to leave?"

"I don't think it'll be noticed."

"Should we say good-bye to the Muellers?"

"No. It'll hurt their feelings. Anyway, this whole party is a good-bye. *Verstehen Sie?*"

She looked up at him with her childlike face, her chalky eyes wide and her lower lip retracted beneath the upper, and understood. "*Ja,*" Andrea said. He sensed she was trying not to cry, but he lacked the energy to put his arms around her. The trouble with Andrea was that she made no resistance. There was not enough to push against. She had been a silverpoint outline.

Over the years, word filtered back to him, in New Hampshire, of the two Germans. Andrea wrote him several times at first, assuring him that his decision to return was a wise one—"Your dear uxorious heart never seemed to be in Boston." Luke and Susan sent annual Christmas cards. They had taken up living together, though they never announced a marriage. Franz and Hedwig, they wrote, had left New England for the Southwest, where they were swallowed up like raindrops in the desert. It was as if they had sought to lose themselves in the American landscape that least resembled damp, crowded, highly engineered Germany.

Word came through, in the Eighties, that they were divorced. Franz had moved to southern California, the capital of camerawork. But he was long out of photography and with his new wife had begun a catering service. Then, Susan's florid big handwriting confided, her cards to Hedwig were returned by the Tempe post office, and it seemed likely that without Franz to take care of her she had died. But an old photography associate of Franz's later told Luke, at a wedding in Brattleboro, that it was Franz who had died, of a heart attack. He had survived two armies but not the unhealthy diet in America.

In the late Nineties, Arlene began to agitate for foreign travel, before they became too old and lame a couple to manage it. At the turn of the century, they signed up for a cruise of the Elbe and then, by bus, three days in reunited Berlin. One of their young guides, slim and sharp-featured, with straw-colored hair, reminded Ed of Hedwig, with her wary half-smile and her faintly deranged seriousness. Her name was Greta. At the tour stop in Potsdam, she lectured their group of footsore, aging Americans too lengthily and dogmatically, insisting that Truman and Attlee had been *babies* in 1945, new to power, and at the mercy of canny Joe Stalin, so that a great chunk of Germany had been stolen and given to Poland. "They were *babies*," she repeated. Her English was almost flawless, and so fluent that the group tended to drift toward the other, less opinionated guide. Greta was what Hedwig might have been, had she had a grievance, a sense of having been wronged, instead of the opposite: Greta had grown up under East German Communism, lived by her wits in the capitalist economy fallen upon her, and was ready to fight, without apologies to anyone.

Though Ed listened carefully on all sides of him, on the street and at the opera house and in restaurants, he almost never recognized an expression or a phrase; it was as if he had never taken German lessons at all, except that a waitress in Wittenberg complimented him, in English, on his pronunciation when he read aloud to her his choices from the menu. "Werry goot German!" she said.

"Why, darling!" Arlene commented dryly beside him, nettled by the unexpected compliment. "I'm impressed."

"I was not, actually," he told her, remembering how Andrea with such dear sad expertise would fit her small but wiry and knowing body to his, "much of a student."

The Road Home

In his rented beige Nissan, in a soft but steady early November rain, David Kern exited from the Pennsylvania Turnpike at a new tollbooth and was shot into an alien, majestic swirl of overpass and underpass. For some alarming seconds, he had no idea where he was; the little village of Morgan's Forge—an inn, two churches, a feed store—which should have been on his left, had vanished behind a garish stretch of national franchises and retail outlets. The southern half of the county, a woodsy stretch of rural backwardness when, soon after the Second World War, his family, at his mother's instigation, had bought back the family farm, was now a haven for Philadelphians, who were snapping up the old stone farmhouses for weekend retreats. There were even, he had been told, daily commuters—over an hour each way, but for them it was somehow worth it. For his part, fifty years ago, Kern couldn't get out of the region fast enough.

He felt lost. Then a rusted, bullet-pierced road sign in the shape of a keystone, naming Route 14, oriented him, and he pressed on the accelerator with a young man's verve. He knew this road: the gradually rising straightaway, with Morgan's dam far below on the right; the steep downhill plunge, heralded by a sign advising trucks to shift to a low gear, toward the creek that curled around the roofless shell of the one-room schoolhouse his mother had attended as a child; the crumbling piece of asphalt, an earlier road, where his mother and he on June days used to set up a sign and a kitchen chair and sell strawberries, for forty cents a quart box, to the few cars that stopped; and then the sharp right turn, slowing you more than the car pressing behind you ever expected, onto the stony dirt lane, now macadamized, that led to what had been, for a time, his home.

Persistent small raindrops speckled his windshield. He drove between twin housing developments that had once been the Gengrich dairy farm and old Amos Schrack's orchard, and from the crest saw what had been his family's farm. The meadow, low land once drained by stone-lined ditches that had been dug by his grandfather and great-grandfather, was no longer mowed; instead, it was planted, by the new owner, in rows of evergreens and birches for sale to landscapers. Along its edge, quite buried in sumac and wild-raspberry canes, lay the road his mother used to walk, all by herself until joined by the Gengrich children down the road, on her way to the one-room schoolhouse. There had been a towering tulip poplar beside the meadow which had survived into Kern's middle age, as had his mother. She would tell him how, in warm weather, she would pause, in her solitary walk, beneath the tree's big, smooth, four-lobed leaves, grateful for the shade and for the birdsong—strong in the morning, subdued by late afternoon—in the branches.

His vivid image of her as a little girl, her hair braided and pinned so tight by her mother that her scalp hurt as she walked, in her checked dress and matching ribbons, down this sandy road between the fields, had been her creation, as she conjured up for him those days of country paradise, of trusting animals and hazy silence. She had wanted to infect him, her only child, with her primal happiness, so that when she died and he inherited the farm he would live on it. In the event, he had inherited it only to get rid of it quickly. The thirty acres on one side of the road, with the barn and house and chicken house, he sold to a second cousin, and the remaining fifty, fields and woods, he rented to the neighboring farmers, the Reichardts, thus keeping the green space free of development, as his mother would have wanted. He had inherited as well her childhood bird guide, a tattered oblong small book with a crumbling oilcloth cover and notes, pencilled in a careful adolescent hand, on the species—bluebirds, grackles, chimney swifts—that she had spotted on this farm. When he held her limp little guide in his hand, he felt her absorption in birds as pathos. One of her tales of herself recalled, with a trace of lingering grievance, how fiercely her mother had scolded her for climbing into a basket of freshly dry wash in imitation of a nesting bird.

The absentee owner of fifty acres, Kern felt guilty at the rarity of his visits. His career had taken him west. He had retired from teaching English at Macalester College, in St. Paul, and he and his wife, who hated the Midwestern cold, had moved to southern California. He had come East this time to attend an expenses-paid, three-day conference of educators in New York, where he had read a paper on the not inconsiderable contemporary relevance of Edmund Spenser. He drove past his old house with hardly a glance. The cousin had sold it, and then it had been sold again, to a Philadelphian, and renovated almost beyond recognition. The first time Kern had seen this house, he was thirteen, and a tenant farmer's children scurried off the half-collapsed porch and hid. Where sandstone steppingstones had once led the way across a lawn mostly crabgrass, a smooth circular driveway now enclosed a clump of shrubs in shades of green like a nursery display, crowded around a terra-cotta gargoyle. Kern's mother's many birdhouses, and her wind chimes on the back porch, were gone. She had maintained, with the earnestness with which she advanced her most fanciful theories, that this had always been a woman's house. She cited as proof the fact that its first owner was recorded, in 1816, as being a woman, named Mercy Landis. Nothing was known of her but her name on the old deed; she existed where history shaded into myth. And, in his mother's version of things, her own mother had made the farm profitable by driving the wagon to market in Alton, every Saturday, and by growing cigar-wrapper tobacco, in short supply during the First World War. Her husband invested the profits and sold the farm and moved to Olinger, an Alton suburb. Twenty years later his daughter used the family savings accumulated in the Second World War to buy the farm back, from an Alton hosiery-mill owner who had installed tenants and cows on the acres. It was hilltop land, not the rich valley soil where the Amish had their picture-book farms, and the magnate parted with it for four thousand dollars.

Kern felt the tracks of his ancestors all around him—generation after generation laboring, eating, walking, driving within this Pennsylvania county's bounds, laying down an invisible network of worn paths. Only he had escaped. Only he, of his boyhood household, now lived to witness how the region was changing, gradually consuming its older self, its landmarks disappearing one by one in the slow-motion tumult of decay and substitution as the newer generations made their own demands on the land.

He drove on, a quarter-mile, and pulled into the parking lot for the Reichardts' produce stand. Their farm, one of the few surviving in the neighborhood, prospered as the south of the county filled in with new customers. The Reichardts were pious people but not superstitious about keeping up with the times. Kern's annual rent check was printed by a computer; the simple shed that he remembered, with an awning and a few boards on sawhorses holding bushel baskets of peaches and apples, sweet corn and string beans, had sprouted freezers and cash registers and supermarket carts and a sizable section of imported gourmet delicacies. Young Tad Reichardt, who usually dealt with Kern on his rare visits, was off with his family for a week at Disney World. "He goes every year, down to Orlando," a girl at the cash register volunteered. "He says it's never the same trip—as the children get older, they see different things. His little girls have outgrown the princesses. Now, you live near Disneyland, I understand."

"Miles from it. Miles and miles. I've never been."

"Oh. Well, Mr. Reichardt got your postcard saying you were coming and said I was to fetch his father when you did." Though her hair was worn in a traditional white-net Mennonite cap, she pulled a cell phone from her apron pocket and deftly punched in numbers with her thumb, a trick all young people seem to have.

Kern protested, "There's no need to bother Enoch. I can see for myself. Things are going fine here."

"He's here," she announced into the tiny phone. Within a few minutes, a member of Kern's own generation, Enoch

Reichardt, appeared, damp with the rain and grinning widely. They had been boys together, on adjoining farms, but their attempts to play together had not been successful. Enoch, a year younger, had brought a softball and bat over to the Kerns' yard—the Reichardts had no yard, all the space between their buildings was used for equipment and animals—and David, newly a teen-ager and not yet used to his own strength, had hit the ball far over the barn, into the thorns and poison ivy past the dirt road, next to the tumble-down foundation of the old tobacco-drying shed. The road in those days, before it was macadamized and straightened, swung closer to the barn, to the broad dirt entrance ramp, and then dipped downhill to run along the meadow, past the tulip poplar. Though the boys searched for a scratchy, buggy twenty minutes, they never found the ball, and Enoch never came back to play.

Today, more than fifty years later, he seemed to bear no grudge, and Kern was happy to see someone nearly as old as he looking so well—stocky and tan, repelling the rain as if waxed. His grin showed straight white teeth. Enoch's teeth had been crooked and brown and must have pained him for years. He asked his visitor if he would like to see his fields, how they were being farmed.

"It's pretty wet out," Kern said. "I think I get the idea."

He had arranged to meet two old Olinger High classmates, with their spouses, at the Alton Country Club that evening, and was wearing a Burberry, a gray suit, and thin-soled black loafers bought at a Simi Valley mall.

Enoch's uncannily white smile broadened as he explained, "We'll go in my car. It'll take hardly a minute. There's some new ideas around since you were here last. My car's right outside. David, should I get you an umbrella?"

"Don't be silly," Kern said. "It's just a drizzle."

"Yes, well. That's the way I look at it," Enoch allowed. "But I know in California you don't see much rain."

His car was a reassuring relic—a black Ford sedan, with its chrome painted black. The former playmates slithered in. Not far along, on the edge of the enlarged parking lot, which even in this weather held a dozen customers' cars and vans, stood the first of the new ideas—a kind of Quonset hut of white plastic, upheld by arching ribs. "Remember how we used to grow strawberries?" Enoch asked.

"How could I forget?" Strawberries had been David's 4-H project, a means of making a few hundred dollars a summer toward his eventual college expenses. He and his mother standing along Route 14 selling them had humiliated him—she pretended not to understand why.

Enoch braked. "Would you like to take a look inside?"

David felt he had no choice, though the rain seemed to be intensifying and his Burberry was rain-resistant rather than rainproof. Enoch roughly, in his proud excitement, widened a gap in the plastic, and David peeked in. He saw strawberry plants up on several narrow troughs, four feet off the ground, so that the berries, ripe in November, hung down into sheer air like cherries, like Christmas ornaments. "Hydroponic," Enoch told him. "The plastic keeps the warmth in and allows for the solar effect; all the nutrients are trickled in from a hose. There's no dirt."

"No dirt," David numbly repeated.

"Remember how the berries would rest on the ground and pick up sand? And the turtles and snails would nibble at them before they could be picked?"

"And how your back would ache from straddling the row and bending over. The daddy longlegs would climb up your arms."

"No more," Enoch said, pleased that David remembered. "You pick these standing up. They bear all through the winter if we put in space heaters and growing lights."

"Amazing," Kern conceded, climbing back into the car after checking his new loafers for mud. Enoch wore thick yellow boots and a green slicker over denim bib overalls; he was one with the weather.

Enoch asked, "Would you like me to drive you over the big field?"

"Sure," David said. "If you won't get stuck."

"Oh, now, I don't think we'll get stuck," Enoch said slowly, as if to a child.

In farming the acreage, and in selling to people who drove here and picked the fruits and sweet corn themselves, the Reichardts had laid out little roads, firmed up with spalls to check erosion, between the crops. *Development*, David thought. His mother had dreaded it. Enoch drove, slightly skidding, among reserve lengths of PCP irrigation pipe, and dormant rows of strawberries grown through perforated black plastic, and several prefabricated shacks slapped up for the convenience of the summer trade. When the big field was under his mother's management and lay fallow in clover and wildflowers, David used to mow it through a long August day on their old John Deere tractor, which he could drive before he could drive a car. Bought second-hand and painted mule-gray, the machine had crawled over the terrain gently rocking, dragging behind it the roaring rotary blade in its rusted housing.

"Would you like to get out?" Enoch asked. The car had gone as far as it could. David looked down at his shoes, and solicitously considered of the crease in his suit pants. He had never been a guest at the Alton Country Club before.

"Sure," he said. He still owed Enoch that softball. They got out and stood together in the rain. A breeze made itself felt, at this high point of the hill. From here on a clear day you could see the tips of the tallest buildings in Alton, ten miles away. Today the city hid from sight. Kern's mother in her decline would talk pathetically of his building a house out here, for him and his family, when he came back some day to the county to live. She would be safely tucked in the Mercy Landis house, just out of sight. "You won't even know I'm there," she had promised.

As he feared, the red earth was as gummy as clay. Transferring his feet from one patch of old-fashioned hay mulch to the next, he watched his steps so carefully that he missed much of Enoch's friendly lecture on crop rotation, and on the ingenious new machines that planted peach saplings at scientifically determined intervals, and on new varieties of corn that didn't take so much nitrogen out of the soil. *Soil*, Kern thought, looking down. Ancestral soil, and to him it was just mud. He turned his attention upward, to the corner patch of woods that no farmer of these acres, for some good country reason, no doubt, had ever bothered to cut, de-stump, and plow.

Feeling his listener's attention wander, Enoch said, with what seemed a twinkle but might have been raindrops in his eyelashes, "Your mother used to talk about how some day you'd build a house up here."

David said, old as they both were, "Well, I may yet." He couldn't resist adding, with a wave over the irrigated and plasticized acres, "And make all this my big front yard."

On the way back, sure enough, the Ford began to slough and wallow in a stretch of puddles a short distance from the paved road. But Enoch downshifted and the black Ford slithered free, and Kern was spared having to get out, in his delicate clothes, and push.

He took away a gift, a paper bag of Enoch's fresh apples. Driving north on Route 14 toward Alton, he moved from his mother's territory into his father's. He and his father, a schoolteacher, had daily driven together in this same direction, away from the farm to the region of schools, of close-packed row houses, of urban pleasures.

Kern was staying the night at the Alton Motor Inn, in West Alton, but was in no hurry to get there, by way of the newly developed section of malls and highways sprung up in recent years. He turned off 14, past the Jewish cemetery and under the railroad bridge, into Alton, over a bridge that his father, out of work at the start of the Depression, had helped to build, setting paving stones and tamping them snug between the trolley tracks. He had remembered that summer as pure back-sore misery, and his son never crossed this bridge without imagining drops of his father's sweat as part of it, dried into the concrete. Kern's bloodlines had left not just rural traces in this county.

Alton was a dying city, but its occupants persisted in living. Its prime's ebb, which David located in his own boyhood but which his elders put earlier yet, before the Depression, had stranded a population that occupied the tightly built grid like sleepy end-of-summer wasps clustering in an old paper nest. Even in his boyhood the venerable industrial town had been prolific of what the child had thought of as throwaway men—working-class males whose craft or occupation had withered away and left them with nothing to do all day but smoke cigarettes and wait for a visit to the local bar to ripen into a permissable activity. Driving through south Alton,

Kern spotted them through the flapping windshield wipers, standing on tiny porches, watching the rain drip from the aluminum awnings and darken the composition sidings.

He drove on, into the wide central blocks of Weiser Street, where the trolley cars would clang and pass, where the shoppers and moviegoers would throng, and where David, during the war, when his parents still lived a trolley-car ride away, would methodically wander through all the five-and-tens, from Grant's and McCrory's up to Woolworth's and Kresge's, looking to enlarge his collection of Big Little Books. At a dime apiece, it was possible, even on a thirty-five-cent-a-week allowance, to accumulate a sizable hoard. The five-and-tens all wore a warm cloud of perfume and candy scent just inside the entrance doors, and some had pet shops, with canaries and parakeets and goldfish, at the back. Alton, it seemed to him then, offered for sale everything a person could ever want in life.

He had been told by Ned Miller, one of the few high-school classmates with whom he kept in touch, that Blankenbiller's Department Store was being torn down, to make way for a new bank. *A dying city,* Kern thought, *and they keep putting up banks.* In the old days you couldn't find a parking space on Weiser Street; now he slid into one without trouble on the Blankenbiller's side of the square. Not just the grand old department store, with its wrought-iron cage elevators and overhead pneumatic tubes for the whizzing brass canisters carrying change and receipts from a hidden treasury above, was being torn down; a row of buildings beside it, where Kern remembered shoes and office supplies and hardware being offered for sale, had vanished, baring walls whose sloppy mortar had never been meant to show and basement chambers, now filled with rubble, that had not seen daylight since their construction. Even in the rain, as daylight drained from the afternoon, dolefully creaking backhoes were pecking away at the rubble.

His mother had once explained to him how she had become fat: she blamed Blankenbiller's basement restaurant, where the apple or rhubarb or pecan pie à la mode had been irresistibly good, to top off a lunch when she was working in the Christmas season as an extra saleswoman. You got so tired, she explained, standing on your feet for ten hours; the ordeal had made her a food addict. Kern gazed down into the sodden, brick-strewn grave of his mother's slender figure, a figure he had glimpsed only as a toddler. It had been at Blankenbiller's that, one day when shopping, he had let go of his mother's hand and gotten lost, burbling to the floorwalker and wetting his pants.

One of the city's surplus men, curious as to what Kern was seeing, crept out from one of the few sheltering doorways left on this block of Weiser Street. Kern winced in fear of being asked for a handout; but the man mutely stared with him through the chain-link fence. Kern's father used to embarrass him, in the city, by talking to strangers; the more disreputable they appeared, the more enthusiastically his father seemed to regard them as potential sources of enlightenment. Kern had been a fastidious, touchy adolescent, but had slowly shed many of his inhibitions. Now he turned to the poorly clad, indifferently shaven stranger, and attempted conversation: "Some hole, huh?"

The man turned away, offended by such levity. He might have said "Yeah" or said nothing at all, Kern wasn't sure.

The Alton Motor Inn and Function Suites sat slightly north of the river, where Kern's mental map of the county gave out. North of Alton had always had a different, hostile flavor: the high-school kids were tougher, the industrial landmarks were bigger and darker, and the rich, who had made their fortunes off the dismal mills and quarries, lived on walled estates well back from the highways. The geography was a tangle to Kern; confusing new highways sliced through former villages and sped shoppers to malls that after a few decades were becoming shopworn. Just after his mother's death, without her to guide him, he had gotten lost on his way to the local airport to meet his children for the funeral. Though he now managed, after several wrong turns, to find the motor inn on its little rounded hill of asphalt, Kern was afraid he could not find, in the dark, in the rain, the Alton Country Club.

The girl at the front desk wore a mannish jacket and had had blotches of magenta dyed into her tufty hair. To her it was so obvious where the Alton Country Club was that a few stabs of her pencil at a miniature map and a hurried recitation of several route numbers satisfied her that Kern was as good as there. Uncomprehending, but afraid of appearing senile, he docilely nodded and went to his room. The room, its picture window overlooking the muffled traffic of a mysterious cloverleaf, seemed a safe cave. But his classmates, in deference to their age and frailty, had urged an early dinner hour, so, instead of lying down on one of the inviting twin beds and turning on television, he unpacked his toilet kit, brushed his teeth, changed his tie to a more festive, flowered one, and tried to clean his muddy loafers with a wad of moistened toilet paper. Out on the parking lot, the controls of the rented Nissan still seemed foreign, the dashboard miniaturized and dim. There was an invasive sweet smell in the car: Enoch's apples. How could he get them home on tomorrow's airplane? Did California admit alien apples? Blazing streams of other cars were hurrying home; the county was not so depleted as to lack a rush hour. He was due at six, in just fifteen minutes. Where had the time gone?

As Kern squinted to see road signs, the headlights behind him pressed mercilessly, and those coming at him wore troubling haloes of refraction. He had turned off at the route number that the girl at the hotel desk had written for him, but possibly in the wrong direction. Anonymous mills and storage tanks hulked on one side, with silhouetted conveyor belts and skeletal stairways; on the other side, after a distance, a restaurant in an old limestone house advertised itself with a discreet white sign, and, closed for the winter, a driving range and miniature-golf course hurtled by. None of this was exactly unfamiliar—ages ago he and some boisterous friends had played, he felt, on those miniature fairways, merrily putting small white balls through windmills and tunnels—yet nothing told him exactly where he was. He was being punished: he had lived his formative years in this county while disdaining to learn its geography, beyond the sections proximate to his ego and his immediate needs. Now, in revenge, the area manifested itself as a shapeless shadowy mire, experienced at a perilous speed.

Then a sweeping searchlight straight ahead declared, he realized, the presence of the Alton airport. It was down to about two flights a day yet kept its bright lights on. But it seemed to be, if he remembered the magenta-tinged hotel clerk's sketchy indications, on the wrong side of the highway. Kern was beginning to sweat. He would never get there. The highway surroundings were thinning into countryside—distant isolated house windows, darkened low stores for carpeting and auto parts. He wanted to scream. He needed to urinate. At last, the broad glow of a combination Getty gas and 7-Eleven appeared. The doughy woman behind the counter—the lone sentinel in a sea of darkness, wearing steel-rimmed granny glasses—seemed afraid of him, her only customer. He saw as if through her suspicious oval lenses his frantic expression and wrinkled Burberry and California-style necktie, splashily patterned in poinciana blossoms. When he explained his disorientation, her face hardened. She appeared offended that he could have gone so far astray. "Go back the way you came," she told him. "It's after the airport. You passed it."

"How far after?"

"Oh—a mile or so."

"On the right or the left?" These Pennsylvania people, it occurred to him, did not want out-of-staters to make themselves too much at home.

"On the left."

"Is there a sign or anything?"

The woman mulled this over, continuing to size him up and keeping one hand out of sight below the counter, probably on the button that would summon the police. "You'll see it," she grudgingly promised. "There's two big gateposts."

And Kern did, ten minutes later, see the gateposts, very faintly, on the other side of the road. They might have been ghosts—spectral apparitions between beats of the windshield wipers—but his only hope of refuge lay between them. It was the worst kind of highway, a two-lane wanting to be a three-lane. The streams of traffic behind him and coming toward him looked endless; he braked in the center of the road and, as halted headlights piled up in his rearview mirror, he took a breath and swerved into the oncoming lane. The first car coming at him gave a long blast of protest on its horn but braked enough to avoid the head-on collision that Kern's old heart had leaped up to greet.

He was in. A tiny sign in a flowerless flower bed named the club. An allée of horse-chestnut trees led him between two areas of darkness—golf-course fairways, he guessed. The clubhouse loomed, spottily lit. There was plenty of parking; it was a weekday night. Kern got out of the car. His eyes watered; his knees were trembling. The day's drizzle was letting up. He left his wet Burberry in the car. Ned Miller was waiting for him in the foyer. "We were getting worried," Ned said.

"I had trouble finding it," David told him, fervently gripping his old friend's hand. "Then when I finally found it I nearly got killed pulling in. The guy who had to brake gave me a huge blast."

"That's a bad left turn. You should have been coming from the other direction."

"I know, I know. Don't rub it in. I'll do better next time. Maybe." Ned said nothing; both men were thinking that there might not be a next time.

Ned had been, like Kern, a good student, but less erratically and noisily so. He spoke no more than he needed to, and talkative Kern, so excitable the words sometimes jammed together in a stutter, had realized that Ned was his best friend only when he realized that silence was the other boy's natural, companionable mode. Ned's head was full of unvoiced thoughts; they were for him a reservoir of strength. He had become a lawyer, a professional keeper of secrets.

The three other guests were seated at the table, their faces glamorously lit by glass-shaded candles. Ned's wife was Marjorie, a firm-textured, silver-haired graduate of a different high school, east of Alton. Kern's other classmate he had known as Sandra Bachmann, though she had long since married one of Ned's legal partners, Jeff Lang. It had been Ned's sly, considerate idea to include the Langs, since Kern had, at a safe distance, loved Sandra all through school. It had taken no great imagination to love her—she was conspicuously vivacious, an athlete and a singer as well as the class beauty, with smoky green eyes and glossy brown hair worn, in elementary school, in pigtails and then, in high school, in a page boy with bangs. He had heard from Ned that she had fallen prey to various physical ills. He wondered if the aluminum walker tucked over by the windows was hers. Even as he gratefully took the place they had saved for him at the table, beside Sandra, he observed that her face had been stiffened and distorted by some sort of stroke. Yet, since his love for her had been born in kindergarten, long before sex kicked in, it was impervious to bodily change.

In his happiness to be next to her, he gushed, "Sandra, I had the most terrible time getting here, not knowing where anything is any more. Not that I ever did. And my night vision isn't that great. All the headlights had this rainbowy hair on them. In my panic I pulled right into the path of an oncoming car, and even in that split second I was thinking, 'Well, stupid, you were born here, you might as well die here.' Was the traffic always this bad?"

She stared at him out of her stony, twisted face, and with a spasmodic motion lifted her hand toward his lips as if to touch them, to still them. "David," she said carefully, "I don't hear well. Speak more slowly, and let me watch your mouth." Her hair was sleekly swept back; he saw that the socket of her dainty ear was filled by a flesh-colored hearing aid. But her voice had kept its rich timbre. Contralto in pitch, it bore for him the intimate music of the regional accent, the Germanic consonants pressed from birth into his own ears. Sandra had never had to shout to get attention. Except for her bust, abruptly outthrust in the eighth grade, her physical attributes were precise rather than emphatic; she was like a photograph slightly reduced to achieve an extra sharpness. Her nose had a barely noticeable bump at the bridge and her mouth a slight, demure, enchanting overbite. Kern's lips tingled where Sandra had almost touched them.

He slowly mouthed, for her eyes, the words "It's won-derful to see you. I'm sor-ry I was late."

The general conversation sought its rhythm, and David, the returned prodigal, for a time was allowed the lead. The questions he asked, the details he remembered, arose from years that for him had the freshness and urgency of youthful memories but that for his friends were buried beneath a silt of decades, of thousands of days spent in this same territory, maturing, marrying, childbearing, burying parents, laboring, retiring. He called across the table to Ned, "Remember how our mothers used to take us out once a summer to the Goose Lake Amusement Park, at the end of the trolley line? They would sit there," he explained to the others, "side by side on a bench, while Ned and I went into the arcade and put pennies in these little paper peepshows that you cranked yourself—girls doing the hootchy-kootchy in petticoats, all very tame, in retrospect. What the kids nowadays see, my God."

Decades of teaching had left him perhaps too fluent. He evoked aloud the long-gone trolley cars—their slippery straw seats, the brass handles at the corners to switch the backs back and forth at the end of the line, the serious-faced conductor with the mechanical change-maker on his belt. "Like all those pre-electronic things, it was so in*gen*ious!"

"Every child had to have one," Ned supportively chimed in.

"Exactly!" David agreed. He recalled aloud Ned's old house—its abundance of toys, its basement playroom, its side yard big enough for fungo with a tennis ball, and the slate-floored screened side porch where they used to play Monopoly for hours at a stretch. Kern, a schoolteacher's son, had envied that house, and intended to praise it. But he got the name of Ned's pet Labrador slightly wrong, Blackie instead of Becky; Ned made the correction with an uncharacteristic, irritated quickness.

Monopoly made Kern think of the canasta craze in their junior and senior years, those rows and rows of cards laid out on their parents' dining-room tables, and asked if anybody could still remember the rules. Nobody volunteered. Marjorie Miller began to look glazed, and stated firmly that no one in her high school had played canasta; it never spread, she insisted, to her part of the county.

Deferential waiters, meanwhile, took orders and brought food. They kept calling Ned "Mr. Miller" and Sandra "Mrs. Lang"; only Kern went unnamed, the outsider. He had belonged to faculty clubs and golf clubs, far from here, but had he stayed he could never have made the Alton Country Club; there was no road up into it for a schoolteacher's son.

Feeling the fatigue of his day's adventures, he fell relatively silent, and his companions lapsed into local talk—the newest mayoral scandal in Alton, the hopeless condition of the downtown, the invasion of Hispanic drug dealers, the misfortunes (illnesses, business misjudgments, ill-advised second marriages) of mutual friends. Kern thought that Sandra kept up with the conversation pretty well, her calm gray-green eyes darting from mouth to mouth, her own lips opening in a frequent laugh. When she laughed, the gleeful pealing, a bit harsher than expected, echoed in Kern's head a chord first heard during recess at elementary school, on the paved play space around the old red brick building, strictly divided into boys' and girls' sections. Her voice, though not loud, could be heard above those of all the other girls at play. He must have been listening for it then.

The waiters—two of them, for this was a light night—stood ready, in their pleated shirts and striped bow ties, to take orders for dessert and coffee. The group looked toward David, and he said what he sensed they wanted to hear: "I don't need anything. It's late, for us old-timers." There was a babble of grateful agreement, and a prolonged fuss of gathering coats and umbrellas. Sandra used her walker, but as if it were a toy, swinging it jauntily ahead of her. Outside, the rain had quite stopped, and Kern could see off to the left a shadowy green, with its numbered flag still in the hole, ready for play once November relented.

On the glistening driveway, they shook hands and hugged good-bye. He and Sandra studied each other's faces a second, trying to decide between a kiss on the cheek or on the mouth; he decided on a cheek, but as it happened on the side of her face somewhat paralyzed. Backing off, he mouthed at her, "Take care. You're the best." Not sure the lamplight was strong enough for her to read his words, he added an absurd gesture: he gave her a thumbs-up, and then blushed. In his excitement he had drunk three glasses of wine.

Marjorie, hugging him with a disciplining firmness, said, "We're all in one car; you follow us. We don't want you getting lost again."

"Oh, I don't think I will. I just do the same thing backwards, more or less. Don't go out of your way. Ways."

"David. You follow us."

. . .

The four had come in a big midnight-blue SUV belonging to the Langs. Marjorie's silver hair flashed in the back seat; Sandra's tidy profile sank into shadow beside her. Women still rode in the back here. Jeff Lang's tail-lights led Kern down the long, hushed double row of horse chestnuts, over the mushy litter of fallen pods. At the highway, after a wait for all traffic to clear, the tail-lights turned left, away from the airport, then right at the restaurant in the limestone house. Almost immediately, they were moving down narrow city streets. He had been on the edge of Alton, all along. *What was I doing way out at the airport?* Kern asked himself.

This section of the city was strange to him. Lone pedestrians flitted warily across the rain-stained streets. The glowing windows of Laundromats, delicatessens, and corner taverns slid by like the unexpected illumined spectres and tableaux in the water ride at the Goose Lake Amusement Park. Many of the signs were in Spanish. The SUV, seeming almost to brush the parked cars on either side, led him first downhill, and then up. Continuing uphill, the street without transition became a strange bridge, high above the black river. It descended on the other side into blocks where tight-packed semi-detached houses were approached up long flights of concrete steps. The two-car caravan came to a traffic circle near a large parking lot, with a garish state-run liquor store on one side, and Kern at last knew where he was: in West Alton.

He and his mother used to transfer to the West Alton trolley from the stop in front of Blankenbiller's for his piano lessons with—yes, of course—Miss Schiffner. Thin, wan, wistful Miss Schiffner, perhaps once beautiful in her way, had he been old enough to notice. Concrete steps covered by green outdoor carpeting led up to her front parlor, where the piano, an upright, waited amid doilies and porcelain figurines and dusty plush. Its white and black keys were cold to the touch of his nervous hands. The trolley car at its stop—there had been no traffic circle then—would unfold a step with a harsh clack, and David, leaping down, would jar the sour lump of anticipation in his belly, knowing that he had not mastered his lesson. This was before their move to the country, the beginning of his exile. His mother was still a town dweller, still banking on civilization, handing over precious Depression dollars in gullible hopes of lifting her son up from the ruck. It was clear to him and must have been to Miss Schiffner that he was no little Mozart, standing on tiptoe to tap out his first minuet.

Jeff Lang's smug ruby tail-lights continued halfway around the traffic circle, passed the liquor store, and headed up Fourth Street, toward the old textile mills that had been reborn as discount outlets and then had gone empty again; the busloads of Baltimore bargain hunters now went instead to the newer outlets near Morgan's Forge. It came to Kern that behind him, one block over from Fourth Street, there used to be an all-night diner where he, a teen-ager in no hurry to get back to the farm, would go alone after dropping off his date at her house. After an Olinger High dance, he would go with a gang of others, all the girls wearing strapless taffeta dresses if it had been a prom, their naked shoulders gleaming in the booths. Each booth had its own little jukebox, with "Stardust" and "Begin the Beguine" and Russ Morgan's "So Tired" among the selections. If Kern went there now, he could get a piece of Dutch apple pie with a scoop of butter-pecan ice cream, to make up for the dessert he had missed.

He wanted to reverse his course, but the Langs' tail-lights

inexorably receded, waiting at every intersection for him to catch up. He couldn't believe it: they were going to lead him like some out-of-town moron right to the parking lot of the Alton Motor Inn. In his head he shouted furiously, *I know where I am now! I'm here.*

My Father's Tears

I SAW MY FATHER CRY only once. It was at the Alton train station, back when the trains still ran. I was on my way to Philadelphia—an hour's ride ending at the 30th Street terminal—to catch, at the Market Street station, the train that would return me to Boston and college. I was eager to go, for already my home and my parents had become somewhat unreal to me, and Harvard, with its courses and the hopes for my future they inspired and the girlfriend I had acquired in my sophomore year, had become more real every semester; it shocked me—threw me off track, as it were—to see that my father's eyes, as he shook my hand good-bye, glittered with tears.

I blamed it on our handshake: for eighteen years we had never had occasion for this social gesture, this manly contact, and we had groped our way into it only recently. He was taller than I, though I was not short, and I realized, his hand warm in mine while he tried to smile, that he had a different perspective than I. I was going somewhere, and he was seeing me go. I was growing in my own sense of myself, and to him I was getting smaller. He had loved me, it came to me as never before. It was something that had not needed to be said before, and now his tears were saying it. Before, in all the years and small adventures we had shared, there was the sensation, stemming from him, that life was a pickle, and he and I were, for a time, in the pickle together.

The old Alton station was his kind of place, savoring of transit and the furtive small pleasures of city life. I had bought my first pack of cigarettes here, with no protest from the man running the newsstand, though I was a young-looking fifteen. He simply gave me my change and a folder of matches advertising Sunshine Beer, from Alton's own brewery. Alton was a middle-sized industrial city that had been depressed ever since the textile mills began to slide south. In the meantime, with its orderly street grid and its hearty cuisine, it still supplied its citizens with traditional comforts and an illusion of well-being. I lit up a block from the station, as I remember, and even though I didn't know how to inhale my nerves took a hit; the sidewalk seemed to lift toward me and the whole world felt lighter. From that day forward I began to catch up, socially, with the more glamorous of my peers, who already smoked.

Even my stay-at-home mother, no traveller but a reader, had a connection to the station: it was the only place in the city where you could buy her favorite magazines, *Harper's* and *The New Yorker.* Like the stately Carnegie-endowed library two blocks down Franklin Street, it was a place you felt safe inside. Both had been built for eternity, when railroads and books looked to be with us forever. The station was a foursquare granite temple with marble floors, a high ceiling whose gilded coffers glinted through a coating of coal smoke. The tall-backed waiting benches were as dignified as church pews. The radiators clanked and the caramel-colored walls murmured as if giving back some of the human noise they absorbed day and night. The newsstand and coffee shop were usually busy, and the waiting room was always warm, as my father and I had discovered on more than one winter night. We had been commuters to the same high school, he as a teacher and I as student, in second-hand cars that on more than one occasion failed to start, or got stuck in a snow-storm. We would make our way to the one place sure to be open, the railroad station.

We did not foresee, that moment on the platform as the signal bells a half-mile down the tracks warned of my train's approach, that within a decade passenger service to Philadelphia would stop, and that eventually the station, like railroad stations all across the East, would be padlocked and boarded up. The fine old building stood on its empty acre of asphalt parking space like an oversized mausoleum. All the life it had once contained was sealed into silence, and for the rest of the century it ignominiously waited, in this city where progress had halted, to be razed.

But my father did foresee, the glitter in his eyes told me, that time consumes us—that the boy I had been was dying if not already dead, and we would have less and less to do with each other. My life had come out of his, and now I was stealing away with it. The train appeared, its engine, with its high steel wheels and long connecting rods and immense cylindrical boiler, out of all proportion to the little soft bodies it dragged along. I boarded it. My parents looked smaller, foreshortened. We waved sheepishly through the smirched glass. I opened my book—*The Complete Poetical Works of John Milton*—before Alton's gritty outskirts had fallen away.

At the end of that long day of travel, getting off not at Boston's South Station but at Back Bay, one stop earlier and closer to Cambridge, I was met by my girlfriend. How swanky that felt, to read Milton all day, the relatively colorless and hard-to-memorize pentameters of *Paradise Regained*, and, in sight of the other undergraduates disembarking, to be met and embraced on the platform by a girl—no, a woman—wearing a gray cloth coat, canvas tennis sneakers, and a ponytail. It must have been the spring break, because if Deb was greeting me the vacation had been too short for her to go back and forth to St. Louis, where her home was. Instead, she had been waiting a week for me to return. She tended to underdress in the long New England winter, while I wore the heavy winter coat, with buckled belt and fleecy lining, that my parents had bought me, to my embarrassment, to keep me from catching pneumonia way up in New England.

She told me, as we rode first the Green Line and then the Red back to Harvard Square, what had happened to her that week. There had been an unpredicted snow squall, whose sullied traces were still around us, and, at the restaurant where she waited on tables some evenings, she had been given, because she was the only college student, the assignment of adding up numbers in the basement while the other waitresses pocketed all the tips. She was angry to the point of tears about it. I told her what I could recall of my week in Pennsylvania, already faded in memory except for the detail lodged there like a glittering splinter—my father's tears. My own eyes itched and burned after a day of reading in a jiggling train; I had lifted them from my book only to marvel at the shining ocean as the train travelled the stretch of seaside track around New London.

. . .

In the years when we were newly married and still childless, Deb and I would spend a summer month with each set of parents. Her father was an eminent Unitarian minister, who preached in a gray neo-Gothic edifice built for eternity near the Washington University campus. Each June he moved his family from the roomy brick parsonage on Lindell Boulevard to an abandoned Vermont farmhouse he had bought in the Thirties for five hundred dollars. That June, Deb and I arrived before her father's parish duties permitted him and the rest of his family, a wife and two other daughters, to be there. The chilly solitude of the place, with basic cold-water plumbing but no electricity, high on a curving dirt road whose only visible other house, a half-mile away, was occupied by another Unitarian minister, reinforced my sense of having moved up, thanks to my bride, into a new, more elevated and spacious territory.

The lone bathroom was a long room, its plaster walls and wooden floor both bare, that was haunted by a small but intense rainbow, which moved around the walls as the sun in the course of the day glinted at a changing angle off the bevelled edge of the mirror on the medicine cabinet. When we troubled to heat up enough water on the kerosene stove for a daylight bath, the prismatically generated rainbow kept the bather company; it quivered and bobbed when footsteps or a breath of wind made the house tremble. To me this Ariel-like phenomenon was the magical child of Unitarian austerity, symbolic of the lofty attitude that sought out a primitive farmhouse as a relief from well-furnished urban comfort. It had to do, I knew, drawing upon my freshly installed education, with idealism, with Emerson and Thoreau, with self-reliance and taking Nature on Nature's own, exalted terms. A large side room in the house, well beyond the woodstove's narrow sphere of warmth, held a big loom frame that had come with the house, and an obsolete encyclopedia, and a set, with faded spines, of aged but rarely touched books entitled *The Master Works of World Philosophy.* When I broke precedent by taking one of the volumes down, its finely ridged cloth cover gave my fingers an unpleasant tingle. It was the volume containing selections from Emerson's essays. "Every natural fact is a symbol of some spiritual fact," I read, and "Everything is made of one hidden stuff," and "Every hero becomes a bore at last," and "We boil at different degrees."

Deb used this large room, and the vine-shaded stone porch outside, to paint her careful oils and pale watercolors. When the day was sunny, and heating the tub water in a kettle on the kerosene stove seemed too much trouble, we bathed in the mountain creek an easy walk from the house, in a pond whose dam her father had designed and built. I wanted to photograph her nude with my Brownie Hawkeye, but she primly declined. One day I sneaked a few snapshots anyway, from the old bridge, while she, with exclamations that drowned out the noise of the shutter, waded in and took the icy plunge.

It was in Vermont, before the others arrived, that, by our retrospective calculations, we conceived our first child, unintentionally but with no regrets. This microscopic event deep within my bride became allied in my mind with the little rainbow low on the bathroom wall, our pet imp of refraction.

Her father, when he arrived, was a father I wasn't used to. Mine, though he had sufficient survival skills, enacted the role of an underdog, a man whose every day, at school or elsewhere, proceeded through a series of scrapes and embarrassments. The car wouldn't start, the students wouldn't behave. He needed people, the aggravating rub of them, for stimulation. Reverend Whitworth liked Vermont because, compared with St. Louis, it had no people in it. He didn't leave his hill for weeks at a time, letting the rest of us drive the two miles of dirt road to the nearest settlement, where the grocery store, the hardware store, and the post office all occupied one building, with one proprietor, who also managed the local sawmill. We would come back with local gossip and a day-old newspaper, and my father-in-law would listen to our excited tales of the greater world with a tilted head and a slant smile that let us guess he wasn't hearing a word. He had things to do: he built stone walls, and refined the engineering of his dam, and took a daily nap, during which the rest of us were to be silent.

He was a handsome man, with a head of tightly wiry hair whose graying did not diminish its density, but he was frail inside from rheumatic fever in his Maine boyhood. Rural peace, the silence of woods, the sway and flicker of kerosene light as drafts blew on the flaming wick or as lamps were carried from room to room—these constituted his element, not city bustle and rub. During his hilltop vacation months, he moved among us—his wife, his three daughters, his son-in-law, his wife's spinster sister—like a planet exempt from the law of gravitational attraction.

His interactions came mostly with games, which he methodically tended to win—family croquet in the afternoons, family Hearts in the evening, in the merged auras of the woodstove and the mantle lamp on the table. This was a special lamp, which intensified and whitened the glow of a flame with a mantle, a kind of conical net of ash so delicate it could be broken by even a carelessly rough setting-down of the glass base on the table. Reverend Whitworth was ostentatiously careful in everything his hands did, and I resented this, with the implacable *ressentiment* of youth. I resented his fussy pipe-smoker's gestures as he tamped and lighted and puffed; I resented his strictly observed naps, his sterling blue eyes (which Deb had inherited), his untroubled Unitarianism. Somehow, in my part of Pennsylvania blue eyes were so rare as to be freakish—hazel was as far as irises ventured from the basic brown the immigrants from Wales and southern Germany had brought to the Schuylkill Valley.

As for Unitarianism, it seemed so milky, so smugly vague and evasive: an unimpeachably featureless dilution of the Christian religion as I had met it in its Lutheran form—the whole implausible, colorful, comforting tapestry of the Incarnation and the Magi, Christmas carols and Santa Claus, Adam and Eve, nakedness and the Tree of the Knowledge of Good and Evil, the serpent and the Fall, betrayal in the garden and Redemption on the Cross, "Why has thou forsaken me?" and Pilate washing his hands and Resurrection on the third day, posthumous suppers in an upper room and doubting Thomas and angels haunting the shadier margins of Jerusalem, the instructions to the disciples and Paul's being knocked from his donkey on the road to Damascus and the disciples talking in tongues, a practice at which the stolid churchgoers of Alton and its environs did draw the line. Our public-school day began with a Bible reading and the Lord's Prayer; our teachers and bankers and undertakers and mailmen all professed to be conventional Christians, and what was good enough for them should have been, I think I thought, good enough for Unitarians. I had been conditioned to feel that there could be no joy in life without religious faith, and if such faith demanded an intellectual sacrifice, so be it. I had read enough Kierkegaard and Barth and Unamuno to know about the leap of faith, and Reverend Whitworth was not making that leap; he was taking naps and building stone walls instead. In his bedroom I spotted a paperback Tillich—*The Courage to Be*, most likely—but I never caught him reading it, or *The Master Works of World Philosophy* either. The only time I felt him as a holy man was when, speaking with deliberate tenderness to one of his three daughters, he fell into a "thee" or "thou" from his Quaker boyhood.

He was to be brought low, all dignity shed, before he died. Alzheimer's didn't so much invade his brain as deepen the benign fuzziness and preoccupation that had always been there. At the memorial service for his wife, dead of cancer, he turned to me before the service began and said, with a kindly though puzzled smile, "Well, James, I don't quite know what's up, but I guess it will all come clear." He didn't realize that his wife of forty-five years was being memorialized.

With her gone, he deteriorated rapidly. At the nursing home where we finally took him, as he stood before the admission desk he began to whimper, and to jiggle up and down as if bouncing something in his pants, and I knew he needed to urinate, but I lacked the courage to lead him quickly to the lavatory and take his penis out of his fly for him, so he wet himself and the floor. I was, in those years just before my separation from Deb, the eldest son-in-law, the first mate, as it were, of the extended family, and was failing in my role, though still taking a certain pride in it. My father-in-law had always, curiously, from those first summers in Vermont, trusted me—trusted me first with his daughter's well-being, and then with helping him lift the stones into place on his wall, where I could have pinched one of his fingers or dropped a rock on his toes. For all of my *ressentiment*, I never did.

I loved him, in fact. As innocent of harm as my own father, he made fewer demands on those around him. A little silence during his nap does not seem, now, too much to ask, though at the time it irritated me. His theology, or lack of it, now seems one of the spacious views I enjoyed thanks to him. His was a cosmos from which the mists of superstition had almost cleared. His parish, there in the Gateway to the West, included university existentialists, and some of their hip philosophy buffed up his old-fashioned transcendentalist sermons, which he delivered in a mellow, musing voice. Though Unitarian, he was of the theist branch, Deb would tell me in bed, hoping to mediate between us. I wasn't, as I remember it, graceless enough to quarrel with him often, but he could not have been ignorant of my Harvard neo-orthodoxy, with its Eliotic undercurrent of panic.

In Vermont, my household task was to burn the day's wastepaper, in a can up the slope behind the house, toward the spring that supplied our cold water. One could look across twenty miles of wooded valley to the next ridge of the Green Mountains. With Reverend Whitworth's blessing, I had been admitted to a world of long views and icy swims and New England reticence. He was a transparently good man who took himself with a little Maine salt. It is easy to love people in memory; the hard thing is to love them when they are there in front of you.

Pennsylvania had its different tensions for Deb and me. We had gotten off to a bad start. The first time I brought her home to meet my parents, we disembarked at the wrong train station. The train from Philadelphia was a local. One of its stops was a hilly factory town seven miles from Alton, also along the Schuylkill and closer by a few miles to the country farmhouse to which we had moved, at my mother's instigation, after the war. We were among a handful of passengers to get off the train, and the platform in its tunnel of trees soon emptied. No one had come to meet us. My parents, in spite of arrangements clear in my own mind—I was trying to save them mileage—had gone to Alton.

Now I wonder how, in that era before cell phones, we managed to make contact. But in that same era even little railroad stations were still manned; perhaps the stationmaster telegraphed word of our plight to Alton and had my parents paged in the echoing great station. Or perhaps, by the mental telegraphy that used to operate in backward regions, they guessed the truth when we didn't disembark and simply drove to where we were. I was a young swain, and Deb, so securely in her element in St. Louis or Cambridge, seemed lost in my home territory. I kept failing to protect her from our primitive ways. Blamelessly, she kept doing things wrong.

Though we were not yet married, she had put some dirty socks and underwear of mine through her own laundry, and packed them, clean, in her suitcase. When my mother, helpfully hovering in the guest bedroom, noticed this transposition, she let loose one of her silent bursts of anger, a merciless succession of waves that dyed an angry red V on her forehead, between the eyebrows, and filled the little sandstone house to its corners, upstairs and down. The house of my childhood, in the town of Olinger, a mere trolley-car ride from Alton, had been a long narrow brick one, with a long backyard, so there were places to escape to when my mother was, in my father's tolerant phrase, "throwing an atmosphere." But in the new house we could all hear one another turn over in bed at night, and even the out-of-doors, buzzing with insects and seething with weeds, offered no escape from my mother's psychological heat. I had grown up with her aggrieved moods, turned on usually by adult conflicts out of my sight and hearing. She could maintain one for days until, coming home from school or a friend's house, I would find it miraculously lifted. Her temper was part of my growing up, like Pennsylvania mugginess and the hot spells that could kill old people in their stifling row houses and expand the steel tracks on the street enough to derail trolley cars.

Whispering, I tried to apologize for this climate to Deb, while my mother's sulk, which had frozen all our tongues during dinner, continued to emanate from her bedroom down into the living room. The click of her latch had reverberated above us like a thunderclap. "You didn't do anything wrong," I assured Deb, though in my heart I felt that offending my mother was wrong, a primal sin. I blamed Deb for mixing up my underwear with hers; she should have anticipated the issue, the implications. "It's the way she is."

"Well, she should wake up and get over it" was Deb's response, so loud I feared it could be heard upstairs. Amazed, I realized that she wasn't tuned as finely as I to the waves of my mother's anger. She wasn't built from birth to receive them.

Near the sofa where we sat, my father, dolefully correcting math papers in the rocking chair, said, "Mildred doesn't mean anything by it. It's her femininity acting up."

Femininity explained and justified everything for his sexist generation, but not for mine. I was mortified by this tension.

That same visit, perhaps, or later, Deb, thinking she was doing a good deed, on Sunday morning began to weed the patch of pansies my mother had planted near the back porch and then neglected. Deb stood uncomprehending, her feet sweetly bare in the soft soil, like Ingrid Bergman's in *Stromboli*, when I explained that around here nobody worked on Sundays; everybody went to church. "How silly," Deb said. "My father all summer does his walls and things on Sundays."

"He's a different denomination."

"Jim, I can't believe this. I really can't."

"*Sh-h-h.* She's inside, banging dishes around."

"Well, let her. They're her dishes."

"And we have to get ready for church."

"I didn't bring church clothes."

"Just put on shoes and the dress you wore down on the train."

"Shit I will. I'd look ridiculous. I'd rather stay here and weed. Your grandparents will be staying, won't they?"

"My grandmother. My grandfather goes. He reads the Bible every day on the sofa, haven't you noticed?"

"I didn't know there were places like this left in America."

"Well—"

My answer was going to be lame, she saw with those sterling blue eyes, so she interrupted. "I see now where you get your nonsense from, being so rude to Daddy."

I was scandalized but thrilled, perceiving that a defense against my mother was possible. In the event, Deb stayed with my grandmother, who was disabled and speechless with Parkinson's disease. My rudeness to Reverend Whitworth was revenged when, baptizing our first child, his first grandchild, in a thoroughly negotiated Unitarian family service in the house of her Lutheran grandparents, he made a benign little joke about the "holy water"—water fetched from our own spring, which was down below the house instead of, as in Vermont, up above it. My mother sulked for the rest of the day about that, and always spoke of Catherine, our first child, as "the baby who didn't get baptized." By the time the three other babies arrived, Deb and I had moved to Massachusetts, where we had met and courted, and joined the Congregational Church as a reasonable compromise.

We are surrounded by holy water; all water, our chemical mother, is holy. Flying from Boston to New York, my habit is to take a seat on the right-hand side of the plane, but the other day I sat on the left, and was rewarded, at that hour of mid-morning, by the sun's reflections on the waters of Connecticut—not just the rivers and the Sound, but little ponds and pools and glittering threads of water that for a few seconds hurled silver light skyward into my eyes. My father's tears for a moment had caught the light; that is how I saw them. When he was dead, Deb and I divorced. Why? It's hard to say. "We boil at different degrees," Emerson had said, and a woman came along who had my same boiling point. The snapshots I took of Deb naked, interestingly, Deb claimed as part of her just settlement. It seemed to me they were mine; I'd taken them. But she said her body was hers. It sounded like second-hand feminism, but I didn't argue.

After our divorce, my mother told me, of my father, "He worried about you two from the first time you brought her home. He didn't think she was feminine enough for you."

"He was big on femininity," I said, not knowing whether to believe her or not. The dead are so easy to misquote.

. . .

My reflex is always to come to Deb's defense, even though it was I who wanted the divorce. It shocks me, at my high-school class reunions, when my classmates bother to tell me how much they prefer my second wife. It is true, Sylvia really mixes it up with them, in a way that Deb shyly didn't. But, then, Deb assumed that they were part of my past, something I had put behind me but reunited with every five years or so, whereas Sylvia, knowing me in my old age, recognizes that I have never really left Pennsylvania, that it is where the self I value is stored, however infrequently I check on its condition. The most recent reunion, the fifty-fifth, might have depressed Deb—all these people in their early seventies, most of them still living in the county within a short drive of where they had been born, even in the same semi-detached houses where they had been raised. Some came in wheelchairs, and some were too sick to drive and were chauffeured to the reunion by their middle-aged children. The list of our deceased classmates on the back of the program grows longer; the class beauties have gone to fat or bony cronehood; the sports stars and non-athletes alike move about with the aid of pacemakers and plastic knees, retired and taking up space at an age when most of our fathers were considerately dead.

But we don't see ourselves that way, as lame and old. We see kindergarten children—the same round fresh faces, the same cup ears and long-lashed eyes. We hear the gleeful shrieking during elementary-school recess and the seductive saxophones and muted trumpets of the locally bred swing bands that serenaded the blue-lit gymnasium during high-school dances. We see in each other the enduring simplicities of a town rendered changeless by Depression and then by a world war whose bombs never reached us, though rationing and toy tanks and air-raid drills did. Old rivalries are rekindled and put aside; old romances flare for a moment and subside into the general warmth, the diffuse love. When the class secretary, dear Joan Edison, her luxuriant head of chestnut curls now whiter than bleached laundry, takes the microphone and runs us through a quiz on the old days—teachers' nicknames, the names of vanished luncheonettes and ice-cream parlors, the titles of our junior and senior class plays, the winner of the scrap drive in third grade—the answers are shouted out on all sides. Not one piece of trivia stumps us: we were there, together, then, and the spouses, Sylvia among them, good-naturedly applaud so much long-hoarded treasure of useless knowing.

These were not just my classmates; they had been my father's students, and they remembered him. He was several times the correct answer—"Mr. Werley!"—in Joan Edison's quiz. Cookie Behn, who had been deposited in our class by his failing grades and who, a year older than we, already had Alzheimer's, kept coming up to me before and after dinner, squinting as if at a strong light and huskily, ardently asking, "Your father, Jimbo—is he still with us?" He had forgotten the facts but remembered that saying "still alive," like the single word "dead," was somehow tactless.

"No, Cookie," I said each time. "He died in 1972, of his second heart attack." Oddly, it did not feel absurd to be calling a seventy-four-year-old man on a pronged cane "Cookie."

He nodded, his expression grave as well as, mildly, puzzled. "I'm sorry to hear that," he said.

"I'm sorry to tell you," I said, though my father would have been over a hundred and running up big bills in a nursing home. As it happened, his dying was less trouble to me than Reverend Whitworth's.

"And your mother, Jimbo?" Cookie persisted.

"She outlived him by seventeen years," I told him, curtly, as if I resented the fact. "She was a happy widow."

"She was a very dignified lady," he said slowly, nodding as if to agree with himself. It touched me that he was attempting to remember my mother, and that what he said was, after all, true enough of her in her relations with the outside world. She had been outwardly dignified and, in her youth, beautiful or, as she once put it to me during her increasingly frank long widowhood, "not quite beautiful."

My father had died when Deb and I were in Italy. We had gone there, with another couple in trouble, to see if we couldn't make the marriage "work." Our hotel in Florence was a small one with a peek at the Arno; returning from a bus trip to Fiesole—its little Roman stadium, its charming Etruscan museum built in the form of a first-century Ionic temple—we had impulsively decided, the four of us, to have an afternoon drink in the hotel's upstairs café, rather than return to the confinement of our rooms. The place, with its angled view of the Arno, was empty except for some Germans drinking beer in a corner, and some Italians standing up with espressos at the bar. If I heard the telephone ring at all, I assumed it had nothing to do with me. But the bartender came from behind the bar and walked over to me and said, "Signor Wer-lei? Call for you." Who could know I was here?

It was my mother, sounding very small and scratchy. "Jimmy? Were you having fun? I'm sorry to disturb you."

"I'm impressed you could find me."

"The operators helped," she explained.

"What's happened, Mother?"

"Your father's in the hospital. With his second heart attack."

"How bad is it?"

"Well, he sat up in the car as I drove him into Alton."

"Well, then, it isn't too bad."

There was a delay in her responses that I blamed on the transatlantic cable. She said at last, "I wouldn't be too sure of that." Except when we talked on the telephone, I never noticed what a distinct Pennsylvania accent my mother had. When we were face to face, her voice sounded as transparent, as free of any accent, as my own. She explained, "He woke up with this pressing feeling on his chest, and usually he ignores it. He didn't today. It's noon here now."

"So you want me to come back," I accused her. I knew my father wouldn't want me inconvenienced. The four of us had reservations for the Uffizi tomorrow.

She sighed; the cable under the ocean crackled. "Jimmy, I'm afraid you better. You and Deb, of course, unless she'd rather stay there and enjoy the art. Dr. Shirk doesn't like what he's hearing, and you know how hard to impress he usually is."

Open-heart surgery and angioplasty were not options then; there was little for doctors to do but listen with a stethoscope and prescribe nitroglycerin. The concierge told us when the next train to Rome was, and the other couple saw us to the Florence station—just beyond the Medici chapels, which Deb and I had always wanted to see, and were destined never to see together. In Rome, the taxi driver found us an airline office that was open. I will never forget the courtesy and patience with which that young airline clerk, in his schoolbook English, took our tickets to Boston the next week and converted them into tickets to Philadelphia the next day. More planes flew then, with more empty seats. We made an evening flight to London, and had to lay over for the night. On the side of Heathrow away from London there turned out to be a world of new, tall hotels for passengers in transit. We got into our room around midnight. I called my mother—it was suppertime in Pennsylvania—and learned that my father was dead. To my mother, it was news a number of hours old, and she described in weary retrospect her afternoon of sitting in the Alton hospital and receiving increasingly dire reports. She said, "Doc Shirk said he fought real hard at the end. It was ugly."

I hung up, and shared the news with Deb. She put her arms around me in the bed and told me, "Cry." Though I saw the opportunity, and the rightness of seizing it, I don't believe I did. My father's tears had used up mine.

Kinderszenen

Windows frame pictures of the world outside. A window overlooking the side porch shows the painted beaded porch boards and the curved backs of the wicker furniture and, beyond the porch edge, the bricks of the walk where it broadens beneath the grape arbor and the ragged gaps of sunlight and scenery between the grape leaves. Ants make mounds like coffee grounds between the bricks, and the grapevines attach themselves to the boards of the arbor with fine pale-green tendrils that spell letters of a sort: these are things Toby knows from being outside and looking directly. What he does not know and never thinks to ask is who built the arbor, whose idea was it, his grandparents' or that of the people who owned the house before them? He will never think to ask. He once began to collect tendril letters—A, B, C—to make the whole alphabet but never got through D.

When Daddy flips a cigarette off the porch in the evening from sitting on a wicker chair with the other grown-ups in a row, its red star traces lopsided loops before shattering into sparks on the bricks. The grapes make a mess on the bricks in the fall; nobody ever thinks to pick them up when they fall. The panes in the window have bubbles in them, like hollow teardrops, that warp the edges of things when Toby slightly shifts his head, a little like the way that bad boys hold a magnifying glass above a scurrying brown ant until it stops moving and shrivels up with a snap you almost hear, feeling it within yourself.

The thin glass divides the world outside, which is ordinary, from inside the house, where something is out of the ordinary and feels sad and wrong. The assumption that the town is an ordinary one and just like many another is in the air, along with fireflies in summer and snowflakes in winter. Toby sees nothing ordinary about it. It is a tiny piece of the world but the piece nearest him. In his heart he knows that it is the best town in the world, and he the most important person, though he would never say that to the grown-ups he lives with. There are four—Mother, Daddy, Grandfather, and Grandmother—the same way the house has four sides.

On the side with the porch and the grape arbor, toward the alley that runs behind the square-trimmed hedge, where bigger boys walk along, talking loudly and rudely on the way to the school grounds and the baseball field, there is a side yard. Toby's mother and grandmother preside above this fussy, complicated area, a showplace of flower beds and flowering bushes maintained for the neighbors in case they walk by and look in over the hedge. The bushes need to be clipped and to have their lower branches held up while Mother, red-faced and almost angry, pushes the lawnmower, with its noisy scissoring, underneath to get at the secret grass growing there. She calls this job "holding up the bushes' skirts," which has a naughty sound to it that nevertheless doesn't make it fun.

She calls Toby outdoors to do it, away from his toys and his children's books and his pretending things to himself. The stiff branches poke his arms and face and some have little thorns that scratch, it seems on purpose. If he isn't careful he could lose an eye. His mother doesn't care about that; she is always working in the garden in pants with dirt-stained knees. Toby likes her better when she dresses up to go to the city on the trolley car, in a brown skirt and coat and a little hat tilted on her head, walking down not the alley but the street at the front of the house, along the sidewalk under the horse-chestnut trees, to the avenue where the trolley runs.

Across the alley is the vacant lot where the bigger children in summer have noisy games, with a lot of shouting and tumbling down into the grass, grass so tall it goes to seed at the top and at the bottom never loses the dampness of dew. Beyond this shaggy lot, houses stretch one after the other to a farm where the pig pen smells terrible. Some of the houses are tucked back from the sidewalk, like Toby's own—"out of harm's way," as Grandfather likes to say, twiddling his cigar on the sofa and putting on that foxy sly look that irritates Mother so. She says he should smoke his cigars only outdoors. Most of the houses along the street have just a little piece of grass in front of their porches, and many are really two houses, with two different house numbers and shades of paint, joined in the middle, so each has windows only on three sides, unlike the nice long white house Toby lives in.

The other side yard is toward the Eichelbergers', an elderly couple of which Mr. always wears a creased gray hat and Mrs. has a goiter hanging under her chin. Toby is afraid of the narrow gloomy yard in their direction and hates even to see it out of a window. Mr. and Mrs. Eichelberger always seem to be creeping about together, murmuring together, poking at things. Mother says their tragedy is they never had any children. Toby is an only child and so is his mother, so he escaped into life by the narrowest of chances.

People call his house white but in fact it is yellowy—"cream," he has heard his mother say. Cream, with green wooden trim, including the windows. In crayoning at elementary school a picture of the house where he lives, he discovered that green and yellow go together in a way some colors don't. Black and orange also go together, as at Halloween, and purple and gold at Easter, and red and green at Christmas. Red, white, and blue together in the American flag are like three notes on a brass trumpet. Discovering such harmonies excites him, more than it does other children.

His playmates, when he has them, come to him through the side yard toward the alley, by the little brick walk leading in past the pansy bed from the gap in the hedge. The gap used to have a heavy green-painted gate that creaked and clanged until eventually Grandfather gave it to the scrap drive for the war. It was rotten with rust anyway, he said, and he was sick of painting it. Wilma Dobrinksi, who is a year ahead of Toby at school and tall for her age in any case, peeks in at the gap to see if he is in the yard or on the porch, so she doesn't have to knock on the side door and face Grandmother in the kitchen. Grandmother makes her feel unwelcome. Yet Wilma is the best friend he has. The only friend, in a way. She takes all his suggestions for games and activities. Sometimes on the side porch they turn the wicker chairs upside down and pretend they are caves in which they are hiding from Indians or bandits. Or they cut out and color paper apples and pears and bananas and set them up in an empty orange crate to sell to imaginary customers.

Wilma likes his back yard, its lush lawn and abundance of trees compared to her own. Hers is beaten bare of grass by all her family and has a cross dog tied at the lower end. The dog lunged at Toby once, yanking his chain and his snarl showing horrible blue gums. Toby tries never to play at the Dobrinski house, which is small inside, and doesn't have much plumbing. Mrs. Dobrinski gives Wilma a bath by standing her naked on a chair in the kitchen and wiping her all over with a washcloth wet in a soapy basin. Toby knows this because he once peeked through a crack where the kitchen door didn't close completely, until Mrs. Dobrinski announced out loud that he wasn't being very nice. How had she seen him peeking? Had his spying eye gleamed in the crack? Girls, he observed, had bottoms like he did but in front there was something different, hardly anything, a little dent.

For some odd reason there are no boys near his age in the neighborhood, this side of the street, which he is not allowed to cross by himself. A kind of tough boy, Warren Frye, in Wilma's grade at school, lives in the other direction, down the alley, where it turns along the school grounds and becomes a street, with a row of houses on one side. He comes up to Toby's yard from the lower end, past the chicken house beside the vegetable garden. Grandmother doesn't like him. She doesn't care for his "people." She has known the Fryes since she herself was a child, way before Toby was born. He doesn't like to think about that strange deep empty period of time.

One day when Warren and Toby were wrestling on the linoleum kitchen floor—fighting because Warren had been treating Toby's toys too roughly and then teasing Toby for being too fussy about it, as if the toys had feelings, which they don't and which he said was sissy to imagine—Toby sneakily tripped him so his head went into the radiator spines and bled through his hair as if he might die. Toby was terrified. Grandmother made a nice tidy bandage for Warren out of a dust rag and sent him home still bleeding, and though Warren came back the next day already pretty much healed, he never did return the dust rag. To hear Grandmother tell it there had never been a dust rag like it for excellence. By not dying, Warren had cheated her.

Grandmother doesn't like Wilma's people either. What she doesn't like has something to do with how many brothers and sisters Wilma has and with money, though from what Toby overhears in the house Grandfather doesn't have his money any more; it was eaten up in the stock-market crash. What money they live on Daddy earns being a schoolteacher and is kept in a little red-and-white tin box saying Recipes on top of the icebox. The grown-ups dip into it when they go off shopping, Grandfather to Hen Geiger's little front-room grocery store a few houses up from Wilma's house, with floorboards so worn the nail heads shine, and Mother and Grandmother up the hill two blocks to Pep Sheaffer's bigger store, which has more kinds of ice cream and meat so fresh it oozes blood onto the butcher block, all crisscrossed with marks of the cleaver. Pep has a refrigerator he walks into without bending over and comes out of breathing the smoke your breath makes in January. When Toby got big enough to move a kitchen chair to the icebox and stand on it he was allowed to dip into the Recipe box too and take out a nickel for a Tastykake or a jelly-filled doughnut at Hen Geiger's on his way back to school after lunch. He loves eating while he is walking along instead of sitting down and being told to have good manners. Because there are five of them he sits at the corner of the little kitchen table and it pokes him in the stomach.

There is the alley, the street, and the avenue, where the

trolley cars run and the elementary-school building stands on its asphalt lake. As he walks down the street toward the avenue the houses he passes get smaller, their porches lower to the ground, without railings. Grandmother complains about "people" but it seems to Toby that these are the people his family lives among and they should make do with them. These are the people of his life.

The side yard is too crowded with bushes and flower beds to play in, except for hide-and-seek. But the back yard stretches all the way to the chicken house and the garage for the green Model A Ford in the days when Grandfather had a car. Toby remembers the car before they sold it, sitting squeezed in the back seat between his parents. His mother was somehow angry, giving off heat. Near the fenced-in chicken yard is the burning barrel where he is allowed to hold a match to the previous day's newspaper and the other paper trash, including magazines that won't burn up unless you poke them, separating the pages. The barrel has flaps cut near the bottom, because fire needs oxygen. Table scraps don't burn, and go to the chickens.

Above the burning barrel, nearer the house, is the vegetable garden. Grandfather spades it in the spring, and all summer the rows that come up must be hoed and weeded. Daddy is exempted from such farmers' labor, but not Toby. The weeds between the rows of lima beans and beets and carrots and kohlrabi have to be pulled and carefully laid flat, otherwise they will take root again. Until it dries, the hoed earth is the same dark damp color it is when Grandfather turns the soil in the spring. In the fall Mother and Grandmother put up tomatoes and sliced peaches and rhubarb in Mason jars, filling the kitchen with clouds of steam. The jars are sealed with red rubber rings that are good to play indoor quoits with. Each ring has a little tab that just fits your finger to impart spin.

The way the weeds lie helpless in the sun and then shrivel seems cruel to Toby, but, then, he didn't ask them to grow there. There is a plan and a purpose to things. At school Miss Kendall, who teaches third grade, told the class that grass was green because green was the most soothing color for the eyes. God designed it that way. If everything was red or yellow, she explained, people would go crazy with there being too much of it. The same with the sky being blue, though even so sometimes when Toby looks straight up his eyes wince as if overwhelmed out of all that incandescent blue, and if he catches the sun in his glance a circular ghost stays throbbing in his vision for minutes. God made the world for Mankind, Miss Kendall says.

The back yard slopes from the brick walk along the porch and the wooden cellar door down to the vegetable gardens through a breadth of grass where Daddy, the sleeves of his white shirt rolled up past his elbows, pushes the lawnmower on Saturdays. After dinner they move porch chairs out to the top of the yard and sit as the fireflies come out, Grandfather smoking his cigar and Mother not complaining. It keeps the mosquitoes away, her father explains to her. He speaks to her in a rumbling, friendly way. She is his daughter. "Lois," he calls her. It is a strange name, two syllables, like "Toby," and the same number of letters, and enough like it so that it seems his came out of hers, as he is supposed to have come out of her. And as she came out of Grandmother, whose name is Elizabeth, which in a way has Lois in it. Picturing all this makes Toby sleepy.

After school Wilma and Warren Frye, before he stopped

coming, and some others from the neighborhood, mostly girls, sometimes come to play in the back yard, climbing the trees or swinging on the swing Grandfather once hung on a low branch of the English-walnut tree for Toby when he was smaller. The swing gets quickly boring, the ropes being babyishly short for him now, but there are many trees—the peach trees with their long pointy deeply creased leaves, and the leaning cherry trees with their ringed bark like stacks of black coins, and the maples whose winged seeds you can split and stick on your nose, and the English walnut whose lowest branch is shiny from being climbed on. From tree to tree the children race, squealing in their versions of baseball and dodge ball, where when the person who has the ball yells "Freeze" everybody must stop, even off-balance in mid-step.

In his element, proud, Toby leads them to the stone birdbath that rocks a little on its pedestal, spilling some water onto the girls' shoes, and to the Japanese-beetle traps on their grape arbor, loudly buzzing with the beetles' angry dying, and the broad lilies-of-the-valley bed where it is against the rules to look for a lost ball, though what else can they do, treading on tiptoe to minimize the damage to flowers that they flatten as they search?

This lilies-of-the-valley bed is dizzyingly fragrant when the little white bells on their arched stems are in bloom. Once Toby stood on its edge persistently worrying at a loose front tooth with his tongue and fingers until finally it came out, with a fleck of blood at its rubbery root. He carried the tooth back into the house to win praise from the grown-ups, for growing. He wants to cheer them up. They give off a scent of having lived so long they are stuck where they are for good, as if with a disease he doesn't want to catch. His mother is not pleased by the tooth, worrying that because he forced it out the next one will come in crooked. She had told him that what he had were baby teeth and that stronger, bigger teeth would come in when they fell out. This knowledge hung over him as he stood there worrying at the tooth, adding to the pressure that hangs invisibly over the town, especially over the vacant lot next door.

The grown-up sadness he feels around him is thickest in the smaller side yard, the neglected one toward the Eichelbergers'. The houses cast a constant shadow between them, and green moss grows in the gloom beneath the hydrangea bushes. These bushes produce blossoms as big as a person's head but are almost the only flowering things here, as opposed to the other, sunny side. There is on this shadowy side (its lawn faintly spongy underfoot) the stillness of things Toby doesn't like to think about—church, and deep woods, and cemeteries where a single potted plant has been left in memory of someone but, itself forgotten, has long dried out and died. The Eichelbergers' house looms close, and the child has the fear that Mr. will somehow pounce, though in fact the stooped stout old man, in his baggy gray sweater with gray pearl buttons down the front, slightly smiles on the rare occasions when his and Toby's eyes meet across the property line.

All by himself on this side of the house, Toby becomes more frightened than when alone elsewhere in the yard. The house has fewer windows on this side, so there is less chance of Mother or Grandmother glancing out and seeing him to check on his safety. He might almost be on the moon. Though there is a long clear space here for a game of catch, he and Wilma never stay at it long. If the ball gets loose and goes into the Eichelbergers' peonies next to their house, the pair of them—Mr. in his greasy gray hat and then Mrs. with the apron she always wears and her horrible goiter—might come out and catch him retrieving the ball and, after giving him a good shaking, pen him into their cellar, among the cobwebby shelves of sealed fruit staring out and the skeletons of other caught children. Already the Eichelbergers, he has overheard, have complained to Grandfather about children making noise when they are trying to nap.

And yet, safe inside his own house, his grandfather's house, Toby looks out one of the few windows in that direction and feels sorry for the side yard, it looks so unused and unvisited. It is as still as the toadless terrarium at elementary school. It brims with the adult sadness he feels at his back, in his family.

What is the sadness about? Money, Toby guesses. They never spend any without Daddy worrying. When the coal truck comes and backs up over the curb on thick wooden triangles carried along for just that purpose and the long chutes, polished bright by sliding anthracite, telescope out of the truck's body into the little cellar window under the front porch, and the whole house trembles and fills with the racket of coal roaring into the bin, Toby feels the wonder of all the world's arrangements for his happiness, where Daddy feels money sliding away. He is usually at work, teaching unruly students, but when he is at home he looks worried, wringing his hands in a way Mother calls "womanish." They are a man's hands, square and freckled with raised warts on the backs, but they do perform a scrubbing, wringing motion like women's housework as Daddy tries to rub away the worry inside him. He sometimes says of himself that he has "the jitters" and "the blues." He calls Toby "Young America" and, when Toby is bored or complaining, announces to an unseen audience, "The kid has the wim-wams."

The sadness accumulates toward the back of the house, in the kitchen, farthest from the street and its daily traffic. The linoleum floor with its design worn off where feet walk most, and the old slate sink smelling like well-water, and the long-nosed copper faucets turning green, and the oilcloth that covers the little table where the corner pokes him in the stomach and they eat with bone-handled knives and forks—it all looks tired and old-fashioned, compared to the kitchens some of his playmates have. Not Wilma Dobrinski's people, but the Nagel twins three doors up from there, and some of the houses across the street, which sit higher than the houses on this side, above retaining walls and flights of cement stairs so long the mailman takes a shortcut along the porches by stepping over the low hedges—these ordinary houses have purring electric refrigerators instead of iceboxes dripping water into a tin tray, and toasters that plug in and pop up the toast instead of simply sitting on a smelly old gas stove, above the dirty burner with its little purple flames like dog teats.

And at Christmas, other front parlors, where people passing on the sidewalk can look in and see, hold in their windows, like illustrations in a magazine, long-needled evergreens drenched in tinsel's silver rain and bearing as thick as holly berries thin-skinned hollow ornaments sprinkled with glitter. Mother favors keeping the tree natural, and her ornaments, as simple as the glass eggs that trick a chicken into laying, emerge from a few boxes in the attic, where each is thriftily nested in tissue, in its own little cardboard square. The Nagel twins say their uncle in Alton buys new ornaments every year, all blue or red or on a "theme," like a department store. Toby doesn't want that; he just wants to be ordinary, and to have an ordinary amount of money.

Toby is not always good. He is timid and obeys rules but harbors dark things inside. His grandparents' house reaches around him with cobwebby corners and left-over spaces and even entire locked rooms where things not of this world, monsters and ghosts, have room to lurk and breathe. The five human lives in the house are not enough to crowd out these menaces, to oust the terrors in the coal-dark cellar and in the attic with its aromas of mothballs and cedar chests. Deep under the eaves the attic holds folded old carpets and fancy dishes with piecrust edges and kerosene lamps and knobby trunks that will never travel again and cloth-covered albums full of his grandparents' "people," ancestors long dead but with button-bright eyes staring right at him when he opens an album's thick gilt-edged pages. The men have mustaches and hair parted in the middle. The women have hair pulled tight back and layered stiff clothes of different shades of black. Throughout the house Toby is aware of little-used closets and creepy spaces under the bed. He avoids a back stairs whose doors are never unlatched, as if a mummy or a maniac is locked in there.

He rarely goes into his grandparents' room, and when he does there is a smell, an old people's smell, parched and sweet. Right at the heart of the house a certain space frightens him: the front stairs climb to a landing from which little sets of two steps lead one way to his grandparents' room and, in the opposite way, to his parents' room, and then a third way into the upstairs bathroom. When he does toidy in the bathroom, he is frightened by the door that closes behind him; something might be waiting for him behind the door when he comes out, so he makes Grandmother wait there, sitting on the little steps, to protect him. It is her duty because like Toby she is aware of the ghosts in the house. He has caught his belief in them from her.

One time when he came out of the bathroom she had fallen asleep on the steps, her wire-rimmed glasses tipped on her sharp small nose and her false teeth slipping down in a frightening way, and Toby was furious to find she wasn't awake protecting him. He leaped up and pounded on her hunched bony back as she tried to stand. She softly grunted as his fists hit. Her long gray hair seemed to fly out in every direction from her head. He knew he was being bad but knew she wouldn't tell Mother, and even if she did Mother would understand his being upset. Her mother annoyed her too.

The worst thing he does is torture his toys. His teddy bear, pale woolly Bruno, once lost one glass eye, the tempting brown of a horehound drop, to Toby's infant fingers, in the time before he can remember. The baby he once was had pulled it out on its wire stem and then forgot where it went. Now that he is older he likes to pull out the remaining eye, and gloat at Bruno for being blind, and then have mercy and kiss the woolly blank place and stick the eye back in. If he loses this eye they will have to throw Bruno away, to where he will lie in total darkness not seeing anything.

By saving pennies and begging for presents Toby has collected rubber dolls of Disney characters—a black-limbed Mickey with a hollow head that comes off, leaving a neck with a rim like the top of a bottle, and a Donald with a solid fat white bottom that weighs pleasantly in Toby's hand, and a Pinocchio who isn't as satisfactory, with his knobby knees and goody-goody, pink-cheeked, blue-eyed boy's face without the long nose you get by telling lies. In the stretch of bare floor beside the dining-room carpet he lines them up and bowls them down like tenpins, with a dirty softball. The hardest to knock over is a chocolate-brown Ferdinand the Bull, dense and short-legged. When he is playing this game just by himself, not with Wilma, as he sets them up again he threatens them with what he will do to them if they don't obey him and fall down.

Once, Toby got carried away with a single-edged Treet

razor blade he used for cutting cardboard into shapes, holding the edge against Donald's long white throat to get him to confess, and to show he was serious went deeper than he had meant to, so that now when he bends Donald's head back a second mouth opens in his throat, below the yellow beak. This evidence of his own cruelty shames Toby to see—each time he tips Donald's head back, the cut widens by a few molecules—but, then, he doesn't step on ants like a lot of boys and even girls do, showing off for boys, or go fishing out by the dam and put worms and grasshoppers on hooks. He doesn't see how people can do it, torture like that.

After Pearl Harbor, the United States is at war and violence has taken over the world. There are mock air raids in town. They have to turn off all the lights and sit, he and Mother and Grandfather and Grandmother, in the windowless landing that has always slightly frightened him anyway. Daddy is out in the dark with a flashlight, being an air-raid warden. While they are sitting there on the steps trying not to breathe, an airplane goes over, high above their roof. Toby knows that it will drop a bomb and they will all be obliterated. That is a new word in the paper, "obliterated," along with "Blitzkrieg" and "unconditional surrender." Incredibly, in England and in China children are among the obliterated. The saw-toothed drone of the airplane slowly recedes. Toby's life goes on. Elsewhere, millions die.

When he strips a tin can of its paper labels and removes the top and bottom and bends them in and, on the cement floor of the chicken house, jumps to flatten the shining cylinder, it is like jumping on the face of a Jap or a Kraut. Chicken-dung dust rises from the cement with each impact. Mother doesn't understand fighting—that you have to do it sometimes. On the walk back from fourth grade, the fifth-grade boys pick on Toby because he is still wearing knickers, or is a schoolteacher's son, or lives in a big white house, or raises his hand too much in class. They know this even though they aren't in class with him; he just has the annoying air of a boy with too many answers. Kids sneer to him, "You think you're much," when all he wants is to blend in, to be an ordinary boy.

Boys from the ordinary world keep attacking him. One time, one of the fifth-graders, Ricky Seitz, and Toby wrestled to a sort of standstill on the weedy asphalt behind the Acme's loading porch, except that Toby was on the bottom and emerged with a bloody nose. When he came in the front door, his mother saw the bloody nose and in a minute was on the phone—to the Seitzes and then to the principal of the elementary school. The telephone stands next to the Philco radio on a little table like a thick-stemmed black daffodil of Bakelite.

An even more humiliating intervention of his mother's once occurred on the softball field. The field is two minutes' walk away, across the alley and along a little stand of corn, from the lower end of his yard, through the narrow space between the chicken house and the empty garage. Mother complains that this space smells of urine, and blames the men of the house, including Toby. It makes her wild just to think about it. "What's the point of having indoor toilets?" she asks, getting red in the face. Still, Toby keeps doing it. Just being in this space between the two walls, the chicken house's asbestos shingles and the old garage's wooden clapboards with the red paint flaking off, makes him need to go wee-wee.

Daddy walks this way to the high school every day, wearing a coat and tie, out past the buzzing Japanese-beetle traps, down between the yard and the asparagus bed, out through the lower hedge. Mother almost never comes down here. She avoids the school grounds; that is part of what made what happened so shocking. It involved Warren Frye—Warren Frye of the bleeding head, who never came to the house any more and possibly resented Toby's being here in the territory of the lower alley, where Warren lives in a tight row of asphalt-shingled houses. Behind the backstop of the softball game—not a school game, a league game, on a Saturday, with players graduated from high school and an older crowd of spectators—Warren pushed Toby, and Toby pushed back, and soon they were tussling on the dirt, before a small standing crowd that included Daddy.

Daddy was just standing there, his shirtsleeves rolled up, his combed head high, trying to forget his worries and watch the game, trying to blend in. Perhaps, teaching school all week, he was enjoying not having to enforce any discipline, letting nature take its course, ignoring the child's fight in front of him and the crowd around him, which was noticing and loudly beginning to take sides. Toby was getting slightly the worse of the tussle—Warren had had a growth spurt, in the thickness dimension—and tears of fury were spouting in Toby's eyes when his mother appeared.

She was just suddenly there, his tall young mother, seizing Warren by the hair and slapping him in the face, as smart a sound as a baseball being hit. Then, not missing a beat, holding Toby tightly by the hand, she wheeled and with the same amazing accuracy reached out and slapped Daddy in the face, for just standing there and letting nature take its course.

She pulled Toby home. He was blinded by his tears and burbled protests, while the part of his brain not dissolved in shame tries to figure out how she had known to appear. She must have heard crowd noise from inside the yard, and then somehow seen, out across the lower hedge, him and Warren tussling in the dirt. Why, Toby wonders at the center of this scene (the softball field fading behind them, the white house and side porch and grape arbor drawing closer, the asparagus bed on their left already beginning to turn frothy and go to seed, his tears warping everything like bubbles in window-panes), does he have to be the one with a mother living so close to the school grounds, a mother so magical and fierce and unwilling to let nature take its course? His arm feels pulled from its socket. He begins to resign himself to the fact that with such a mother he can never be an ordinary, every-day boy.

The Apparition

Her appearance startled Milford when she stopped his wife on the hotel stairs, to ask a question. There was a flushed urgency, a near-breathlessness, to the question: "Have you been to the hairdresser yet?"

"No, not yet," Jean answered, startled to be abruptly accosted, though, since they were all members of a thirty-person museum-sponsored tour of the temples of southern India, in theory they were all comrades in adventure. It was so early in the tour that the Milfords hadn't yet thoroughly worked out the other couples, but he recognized this woman on the stairs as paired with a bespectacled, short, sharp-nosed man in a blue blazer, the two of them hanging back a bit shyly at the get-acquainted cocktail party beside the hotel swimming pool. Somewhere in their early forties, by Milford's estimate, they were among the youngest people on the tour, whereas the Milfords, in their early seventies, were among the oldest. Yet age differences, and differences of wealth and class, were compressed to insignificance by the felt presence of the alien subcontinent all around them. "How was she?" Jean asked, abandoning her usual reserve. There was, Milford had often noticed, a heated camaraderie among women when they touched on the technology of beauty. Already, he saw them as sisters of a sort.

"Horrible," came the swift, nearly breathless answer. "She didn't understand my hair at all. It's too *curly.*" The word was pronounced as a spondee—*cur-lee.* The woman, wearing her own, more snugly cut blue blazer, spoke with a faint strangeness—not an accent exactly but with her mouth held a little numbly, a bit frozen in the words' aftermath, as if whatever she said slightly astonished her. Her hair, now that he looked, was indeed remarkably curly, bronze in color and so thick and springy it seemed to be fighting to expel the several tortoiseshell barrettes that held it close to her head.

Milford, standing lower on the curved stairs, his feet arrested on two different steps, recalled an earlier glimpse of this apparition, also on steps. Those on the tour not too distinctly infirm were climbing the six hundred fourteen steps carved into a stone mountain, Vindhyagiri Hill, at whose summit stood a monumental Jain statue, a giant representation of a fabled sage, Bahubali, who had stood immobile for so many days and months that (legend claimed) vines had grown over his body. At the beginning of the climb Milford had been shocked by his first sight of a live "sky-clad" holy man. The naked man moved upward, one deliberate step at a time, with ceremonial pauses for chanting and shaking his wrist bells. His stocky, even paunchy body was tanned an oily coffee brown unbroken but by patches of gray hair on his chest and elsewhere. The ugliness of such an aging male body disturbed Milford. Did the holy man proceed up and down the stairs all day long? Wasn't there any law in India against indecent exposure? Or was it legal on sacred sites, in the vicinity of a giant nude statue whose penis, the guidebook calculated, was six feet long? Preoccupied by these questions, Milford felt himself being passed. A body brushed past his. He was being passed by a youngish woman in khaki slacks and white running shoes and a yellow baseball hat tipped rakishly forward on her head, as if her hair were too bulky, too springy, to fit into it. Without effort, it seemed to the gasping Milford, she moved upward and out of sight, amid the many other ascending pilgrims at Sravanabelgola. By the time he had made it all the way to the shrine at the top, out of which the huge effigy, symmetrical and serene, protruded like a jack-in-the-box, she had disappeared.

"But she shouldn't have trouble with *your* hair, it's so *straight*," the woman was telling Jean, with that terminal emphasis, her lips ajar as if there was something about straight hair that left her stunned. "I'd love to have straight hair," she did add, and thrust out a shapely, heavily ringed hand for Jean to take. "I'm Lorena. Lorena Billings," she said.

"I know." Jean smiled. "I'm Jean Milford, and this is my husband, Henry."

He wondered if Jean was lying, or if she had really known. Women lied, often for no other reason than simple politeness or the wish to round out a story, but, then, they did retain details that slipped by men. He had already forgotten the apparition's name. Taking her hand—startlingly warm and moist—he said, to cover his betranced confusion, "You passed me on the Jain steps yesterday. Breezed right up by me—I was impressed. You must be in great shape."

"No," was the thoughtful, unsmiling response, as she looked at him for the first time. Her brown eyes were a surprisingly pale shade, almost amber. "I just wanted to get it over with quickly, before I lost heart."

"Did you really know her name?" Milford asked his wife when the other woman had gone off, with her horrible haircut. It had looked pretty good to him, actually. With hair that curly, always retracting into itself, how could a hairdresser go wrong?

"Of course," Jean told him. "I looked over the list they gave us when we signed on to the tour and tried to match up names and faces. You would get much more out of these trips, Henry, if you did some homework."

She had been a schoolteacher in her early twenties, before he had met her, but he had a clear enough vision of her standing in front of the second- or third-graders, slender and quick and perfectly groomed, demanding with her level, insistent voice their full attention, and rewarding them at the end of each class with her brilliant, gracious smile. She would have subdued those children to her own sense of a proper education, and she was still working to subdue her husband. Sometimes, when he sought to evade one of her helpful lectures to him and sidle past, she would sidestep and block his way, insisting, with a blue-eyed stare, "*Look* at me!"

He said, kiddingly, kidding being another form of evasion, "I prefer the immersion method—to let it all wash over me, unmuddied by preconceptions."

"That's *so* sloppy," Jean said, endearingly enough. Physically she and the apparition were both, Milford supposed, his "type"—women of medium height with a certain solid amplitude, not fat but sufficiently wide in the hips to signal a flair for childbirth; women whose frontal presentation makes men want to give them babies. His and Jean's babies were themselves of baby-making age, and even, in the case of their two older daughters, beyond it. Yet the primordial instinct was still alive in him: he wanted to make this apparition the mother of his child.

Lorena Billings's body differed from Jean's not only by thirty years' less use but by being expensively toned. Though open to dowdy, education-minded New Englanders like the Milfords, the tour was basically composed of Upper East Side New Yorkers. They seemed all to know one another, as if the metropolis were a village skimmed from penthouses and museum boards, and their overheard talk dealt with, among other cherished caretakers of their well-being, personal trainers.

Much of the conversation among the women was in Spanish. The tour group included a strange number of wives from Latin America—remnants of an old wave of fashion, Henry surmised, in trophy mates. Lorena was one of them, the child of an adventurous American mining engineer and a Chilean banker's daughter. This explained her charming, intent way of speaking—English was not her mother tongue, the language of her heart, though she had been sent off while young to American schools and spoke the acquired language fluently. She even spoke it with a pinch of New York accent, that impatient nasal twang so useful, in her husband's mouth, for announcing rapid appraisals. Ian Billings was a lawyer, with unspoken depths of inherited, extra-legal resources lending his assertions a casual weight. Milford took what comfort he could, as their trip wore on and as acquaintance among the tourists deepened, in the observation that Billings had the thin skin and pink flush of a candidate for an early heart attack. He was no taller than his wife. In talking to Lorena, lanky Milford felt himself towering as if literally mounted on Proust's figurative stilts of time. He was plenty old enough, if he thought about it, to be her father, but in the society of the tour bus—a kind of school bus, with the discipline problems in the back and the brown-nosers up front next to the lecturers—they were all in the same grade.

Dusty villages and green rice fields flowed past the windows of the bus. Vendors and mendicants clustered at the door whenever the bus stopped. Temple followed temple, merging in Milford's mind into one dismal labyrinth of dimly lit corridors smelling of rotting food—offerings to gods who weren't having any. At the end of some especially long and dark corridors stood the *linga*, a rounded phallic symbol periodically garlanded and anointed with oil and ghee. In especially well-staffed temples, robed priests guarded the *linga* and stared expectantly at the tourists.

Milford was not good at Hinduism. He kept confusing Vishnu and Shiva, missing the subtle carved differences in hairstyle that distinguished them. He kept forgetting whose consort was lovely Lakshmi, goddess of wealth and good fortune, and whose consort was Parvati/Durga/Kali, daughter of the Himalayas, goddess of strength, warfare, destruction, and renewal. Jean and Ian struck up an alliance, a conspiracy of star students, comparing notes and memorizing lists of primary and secondary deities and their interrelations and of the eminently forgettable long names of the temples nested in their various dirty, clamorous cities, among their endless one-man shops and mutilated beggars and heartbreakingly hopeful, wiry, grinning brown children.

While their consorts matched notebooks and one-upped each other with snatches of Hindi and Sanskrit, Henry and Lorena were thrown into a default alliance of willful ignorance. They became, with sideways glances and half-smiles, connoisseurs of irrelevant details—the tour leader's increasing vexation with aggressive Japanese and Korean groups; the dead-on mimicry by Indian officials and maître d's of an obsolete imperial Englishness, bluff and haughty; a startlingly specific sex act included in a time-worn temple frieze; a lonely bouquet of withering flowers at the base of an out-of-the-way shrine to Parvati, goddess of (among much else) fertility.

In the bat-cave recesses of the larger temples, wild-eyed Brahman priests appeared, selling blessings to the tourists. The tourists learned how to put their hands together in offering their *namaste*, and how to bow their heads and receive a stab of bright henna or oily ash on the center of their foreheads. Lorena, it seemed to Milford, retained the fresh mark all day, a third eye above her two topaz-colored own. She had an aptitude for being blessed. In several of the larger and busier temples, a tethered elephant had been trained to receive a piece of paper currency in the prehensile, three-lobed end of its trunk, and to swing the trunk backwards to pass the note to the trainer's hand, and then to lower the pink termination of its uncanny and docile proboscis upon the head of the donor for a moment. At every opportunity, Lorena submitted to this routine, her eyes piously closed, her canary-yellow baseball cap tipped jauntily forward on the dense mass of her curls. The cap, Milford supposed, served as something of a prophylaxis, but it was with a wide-eyed merriment that after one such blessing she complained to Henry, "He spit at me! Right in my face!"

Wanting to feel an elephant's blessing as she felt it, he submitted to one, for the price of a pink ten-rupee note bearing the image of Gandhi, and did feel, on the top of his head, a fumbling tenderness, a rubbery heaviness intelligently moderated, as if by an overworked god.

. . .

He did not want to draw too close to Lorena. At his age he preferred to observe at a safe distance, to embrace her with a wry sideways attention. She was beyond his means in every way. On the one occasion when, in the informal rotation of the couples and widowed singles and gay bachelors whereby the tour group sought to vary the round of thrice-daily meals, the Milfords and the Billingses shared a dinner table, the younger couple radiated an aura of expenditure, as their conversation revealed details of second homes in Southampton, Long Island, and Dorset, Vermont, not to mention a Miami apartment and annual trips back to Chile. Though to the Milfords they seemed youthful, they were old enough to be much concerned with their children's admissions to preferred day schools and, eventually, Ivy League colleges. Like the solar beads that wink through the moon's mountain valleys during a total eclipse, an undeclared fortune twinkled in their humorous offhand complaints about the unbridled expenditures of nouveau-riche condo boards and the levies that New York City, in taxes and charities, extracts from its fortunate on behalf of its omnipresent poor.

Not that the Billingses were anything but pleasant and tactful with the elderly New England provincials. Milford observed that Lorena warmed in her husband's presence, her eyes and voice taking on a cosmopolitan quickness and gleam as she touched on plays, fashions, art exhibits, and Manhattan architectural disputes of which, she slowly realized, the Milfords knew almost nothing—only what had been laggardly reported in the *Boston Globe*. Her mouth lapsed into that frozen, uncertain look with which she had addressed the strangers on the stairs; but then she decided, with an inaudible click, that the Milfords were happy to bask in a reflected glitter, and talked on.

Billings, Henry saw with a vicarious husbandly pride, permitted her to be herself, to display herself. Her expanding curls softly bobbed, the faint formality of her English melted into brassy New York diphthongs. "People keep telling us Jap is so wonderful, but—no doubt it's my stupidity—I find his post-Pop stuff to be so *dry*, so—so *difundido*. But then we don't *own* any of him, except for a few prints Ian picked up when he was still doing the alphabet and numbers. Compare him, say, with Botero, who's just done a super series of drawings on the American atrocities at Abu Ghraib—utterly savage, like nothing else he's ever done. They absolutely rank with Goya, *Los desastres de la guerra*." When she dropped into Spanish, a truer self leaped forth, sharp edges and trilled "*r*"s, her voice a bit deeper, on bedrock.

Billings, more aware than she of a range of conservative opinion outside Manhattan, where the phrase "American atrocities" might possibly grate, readjusted his rimless glasses on his sharp-tipped nose. Almost inaudibly, he cleared his throat. These delicate alterations registered with his wife. Her lips took on their numb look, and she slightly changed the subject. "Did either of you happen to be in the city when they had these big fat Botero people in bronze all up and down Park Avenue? That center strip has never looked so good, even in tulip season. The statues *shone*—is that the word?—in the sun. They were noble, and ridiculous, and everything all at once!"

"Terrific," Milford said, meaning her entire presentation.

"I never saw them," Jean coolly interposed, "but I read about them, somewhere. Where was it, Henry? *Time?* But I never see *Time*, do I, except in the dentist's office? Oh dear," she added, sensing her husband's displeasure at her interruption, "we're such bumpkins."

Afterwards, when the Milfords were alone, Jean said, "They were very sweet, indulging us."

"I was fascinated," Milford told her, "by her husband's face. It's so minimal, like one of those happy faces. He gives away absolutely nothing."

"He's a lawyer, dear."

Milford had been a professor, teaching statistics and probabilities at a small but choice business school in Wellesley. It surprised him, upon retirement, to find how little he cared about his subject once he no longer had to teach it to classrooms of future profiteers. His teaching had been dutiful, and so now was his tourism. The world's wonders seemed weary to him, overwhelmed by the mobs that came to see them. The tour's head lecturer, too, after two weeks of shouting to make himself heard above the echoing hubbub of temples and the shuffling distractions of museums, seemed to be losing interest and looking forward to his next tour, of German castles. The experienced travellers on the tour explained to the Milfords that everything was simpler and more concentrated on the Rhine; you stayed in your cabin in the boat, instead of hopping by bus all over southern India and constantly packing and repacking.

As the tour leader's passion slackened, his native assistant, Shanta Subbulakshmi, a short, dark woman from Madurai and the warrior caste, took the microphone in the bus and spoke, shyly yet fluently, of herself—her parents' unusual determination that she pursue an education, the ornate etiquette (the advance scouts, the ceremonial visitations, the seclusion of bride and groom from each other) of her arranged marriage. She spoke of the way the roads of Tamil Nadu used to run, when she was a girl, through the emerald green of rice fields, field after field, before the advent of industrial parks and a ruthless widening of the dusty, pitted roads. "The roads are deplorable," she said. She made the only case for Hinduism that Milford had ever heard. "Unlike Buddhism and Catholic Christianity," Shanta explained in her strict, lilting English, "Hinduism does not exalt celibate monks. It teaches that life has stages, and each stage is holy. It says that sexuality is part of life, and business also—a man earns a living for his family, and this fulfills his duty to society. In the last stage of life he is permitted to leave his family and business and become a seeker after God and life's ultimate meaning. But the middle stages, the worldly stages, are holy also. Thus Hinduism allows for life's full expression, whereas Buddhism teaches renunciation and detachment. Hinduism is the oldest of religions still widely practiced, and also the most modern, in that nothing is alien to it. There are no Hindu disbelievers. Even our particle physicists and computer programmers are good Hindus."

Shanta helped the women of the tour dress in saris for the farewell dinner. The saris had been acquired in little shopping sprees squeezed between the long bus rides (some along a coast swept as bare as a desert by last year's tsunami) and the great temples—dingy mazes surmounted by towering polychrome pyramids of gods, gods upon gods, their popping eyes and protruding tongues and multiplied arms signifying divine energy.

Jean, a thrifty New Englander, reasoned that she would never have another occasion for wearing a sari, and showed up in her best pantsuit. "These clothes people buy on vacation in a kind of frenzy of being there," she said, "look so flimsy and tawdry back in the real world. They just collect dust in the back of the closet."

The luxurious New York wives, however, wore saris; their silks and sateen glimmered in the firelight of the lawn torches while their excited voices shot Spanish compliments back and forth beneath the palms.

"*¡Qué bonita!*"

"*¡Tú eres una India! ¡De verdad!*"

But in truth the costumes did not flatter most of the women: the fashionably thin appeared scrawny and starved, and those with more flesh seemed uneasy in their wrappings, as if something might at any moment pop loose. Milford would not have thought that a garment consisting only of an underblouse and a few square yards of cloth could fail to fit anybody, but the women by torchlight resembled a cluster of hotel guests who, chased by a fire alarm into the street, had in their haste grabbed gaudy sheets to cover themselves.

Except for Lorena: this bronze-haired, Americanized Latina looked in Milford's eyes as if she had been born to wear a sari, or at least this particular one, its pale-green border framing a ruddy, mysterious pattern that suggested in the flickering light rosy thumbprints. Her eyes seemed nearly golden. He had come up to her intending to say something jovial and flattering about her costume, but was struck dumb by how, with a kind of shameless modesty, she had given the tucked and folded cloth her shape—the inviting pelvic width, the exercise-flattened abdomen.

His voice came out croaky: "Terrific," he said.

She seemed uncomfortable, ambushed by this new version of her own beauty. Her shoulders defensively cupped inward and, in a plaintive New York whine, she asked, "You like it?"

Milford's stricken voice regained a little strength and smoothness. "I adore it," he told her, adding, kiddingly, "*De verdad.*"

He offered to move past her, releasing her to the company of her Upper East Side friends, but—a misstep on the uneven lawn, possibly—she moved sideways, blocking his way, just as Jean sometimes did, as a way of saying, "*Look* at me!" Lorena asked, "Do you and Jean ever get to New York?"

"We used to, but now almost never," he told her, wanting to flee this apparition.

When, with the night's torch-lit farewells jangling in his veins, Milford lay in bed face-down beside his sleeping wife, he seemed again to be confronting Lorena, body to body. A few nights before, the entire tour, but for its oldest and frailest members, had been taken to a giant city temple where, each night, a group of bare-chested, sweating priests carried a small bronze statue of Parvati, clad in wreaths of flowers, out of its sanctuary and through the temple corridors to stay until morning with the goddess's consort, Lord Shiva. The bronze statue, much less than life-size, was carried in a curtained palanquin, so there was nothing to see but the four Brahman priests shouldering the poles, and the other priests accompanying the procession with drums and shouts and a blood-curdling long trumpeting. The priests trotted, not walked, except when they halted for a serenade to the hidden goddess. The trumpet riffed in an orgasmic rapture that reminded Milford uncannily of, on a younger continent, jazz. The mob of sensation-seeking tourists and God-seeking Hindus jostled and stampeded in the fast-moving procession's wake; flashbulbs kept flashing and Ian Billings, his arm uplifted like the Statue of Liberty's, was videotaping the proceedings with a digital camera whose intensely glowing little screen projected what the camera saw—bouncing bodies, bobbing heads, the curtained palanquin—and betrayed, above the thundering pack, his and his own consort's whereabouts.

Milford followed at a timid, elderly distance, but his height enabled him to see, at the intervals when the procession halted and drummed and trumpeted as if to renew its supernatural sanction, the circling, sweating, blank-faced priests. One of them looked anomalously fair, grimacing and squinting through the smoke of incense in a skeptical modern manner—a convert, perhaps, except that Hinduism, in its aloof hundreds of millions, accepted no converts. The procession, after one last noisy pause, hurried down the corridor to Shiva's sanctuary, where non-Hindus were forbidden to follow.

Sleepless on the verge of departure, Milford saw that this had been truth, earthly and transcendent truth, one body's adoration of another, hidden Shivas and Parvatis united amid the squalor and confusion of happenstance, of karma. He rejoiced to be tasting lust's folly once more, though the dark shape he was lying upon, fitted to him exactly, was that of his body in its grave.

Blue Light

The dermatologist was a tall and intelligent fair-haired man who gave the impression that of all the things that exist in the world the one that interested him least was human skin. Twice a year he inspected Fritz Fleischer's epidermis—plagued by psoriasis in childhood, then by sun damage in old age—glancingly, barely concealing his distaste. Nevertheless, he kept up with the latest developments in the field. "There's a new technology," he said, "that flushes out precancerous cells. Before they turn cancerous. It might do well on your face. Blue light."

He spoke with a halting diffidence, while averting his eyes from the sight of his nearly nude patient.

"Blue light?" Fleischer echoed.

"The same sort ordinary light bulbs give off. No UVA, no infrared. Blue, only brighter. The skin is cleansed with acetone and then painted with delta-aminolevulinic acid. ALA. It sinks in and makes the cells respond. They shatter. It destroys them." A certain enthusiasm had entered his voice. His bills listed "destruction of lesion" and then some outrageous charge—two hundred ninety dollars, say—for spraying a spot with two seconds' worth of liquid nitrogen.

"Destroys them?"

"The bad ones," the dermatologist insisted, defensively.

"The immature ones?"

Fleischer had learned the term from his previous dermatologist, an older man who, before he in rapid succession retired and died, used to talk lingeringly, lovingly, about skin, tilting back in his swivel chair and closing his eyes as if peering into a mental microscope. Pre-cancerous cells, he explained, have simply failed to mature, and the reactive ointments—Efudex, Dovonex, Aldara—that he prescribed helped them to mature. "Maturing" seemed to be a euphemism for death—an unsightly convulsion of cells that faded away eventually, but not before making the patient look as spotty and insecure as a teen-ager. In his mental microscope Fleischer's former doctor had foreseen a bright future when the molecular secrets of skin lay all exposed for manipulation and cure.

The old healer's successor resisted the word "immature," with its implied teleology. "The damaged ones," he clarified. He manifested a faint, hurried enthusiasm: "You'd be a new man. Look ten years younger."

"A new man?" Fleischer barked out a greedy laugh at the thought, and the other man winced at the sight of the patient's oral membranes. "I'll give it a try."

The dermatologist bleakly nodded. "Let Sheela set it up. Mondays and Thursdays are the days we do it. Sixteen minutes and three-quarters—that's the exposure time. Seems an odd time, but that's what's been worked out. Less doesn't do the job, and more doesn't seem to add anything. Good luck, Mr. Fleischer." While Fleisher was still drawing breath to thank him, the tall, fair man loped around a corner of the hospital's labyrinthine dermatology department and vanished.

Sheela wore a sari, advertising the department's diversity. She was short, with the round teeth of a child and a skin of smooth Dravidian darkness. Towering awkwardly above her, Fleischer felt disgustingly mottled and leprously pale. "How undressed should I get?"

"Not one bit," she told him in her merry lilt. "Today concerns just your face." Using swabs of cotton that felt like a kitten's paws, she stroked Fleischer's face with one colorless fluid and then with another. Her nostril-bead glinted in his peripheral vision as she worked, moving around him as nimbly as an elephant trainer. "Now," she announced, "you must wait an hour, for the skin to absorb. Please sit with a magazine." There were others sitting and waiting, men and women mostly as elderly as he, all of a Northern European paleness and pinkness, but with nothing conspicuously wrong with what of their skins he could see. We are all, Fleischer thought, victims of the same advertisements, the same airbrushed photos of twenty-year-old models, the same absurd American dreams of self-perfection. A new man, my foot.

He picked up a tattered month-old edition of *People* and read of celebrities getting divorced, getting pregnant, confessing to unhappy childhoods, adopting an African orphan. He had never heard of most of these beautiful people, but, then, he had been long locked into the financial world, poring over *The Wall Street Journal* and its columns of figures, its rumors of collapse and merger. Now that he was retired from his Boston firm, he had begun to reread the classics of his college years—Dickens, Dostoevsky—and discovered that his callow initial impression that they were windy and boring was, surprisingly often, reinforced, with the difference that now he was under no academic obligation to finish the book. He spent an hour a day walking, with other retirees, the sidewalk above the littered beach, lined with condominiums, from which the sepia skyscrapers of Boston could be seen like a low cloud in the distance. He watched his investments. He feebly tried to keep in touch with his three adult children, and their children.

The blue-light device proved to be less elaborate than he had imagined. A thick large horseshoe-shape, it half-encircled his head and bathed his face in a humming brightness. His eyes were covered with small cup-shaped goggles; Sheela's voice kept him company in his blindness. "People tell me," she said, "the worst prickling is the first five minutes, and then the discomfort diminishes."

Fleischer had lived near a beach for much of his life, and, aware of no remedy for psoriasis but raw solar rays, had done more than his share of sunbathing—lying in the sheltering dunes in the windy spring, and floating face-up in the soupy sea of high summer with bright buttons and sequins of reflected sun glittering and bouncing all around him, and in the cool fall courting the last slant, dimming rays. Now, compressed into seconds, the sensations of those prolonged exposures were revived and ferociously intensified. Light pressed through the substance of the goggles and his eyelids to register red on his retinas. Needles of heat were thrust deep into his face. He could feel, at the tip of each, immature cells bursting like tiny firecrackers.

Sheela poured her lilting voice over his pain: "You've done two minutes. How is it?"

"Thrilling," Fleischer said.

"I can switch the machine off at any time, and resume after a break," she said. "Many patients are grateful."

"No, let's keep at it." Fleischer liked talking while blinded; his conversational partner, unseen, filled the room, giving the inescapable radiance a voice.

"My offer is good at any time," she continued. "Many patients discover they cannot stand the sensations."

"Tell me," Fleischer said, as the fire consuming his cheeks and brow boiled deeper beneath his skin, "about Hinduism. Does it have a God, or not?"

"It has a large number of gods."

"I mean," Fleischer said, as if his agony gave him the rights of a seeker—as if being blinded made him a seer—"beyond all that, Shiva and Shakti and so on, an overarching God—a Ground of Being, as it were." In his mind's eye the needles of light dug in like talons, each tipped with poison.

"We call that Brahman," Sheela's disembodied voice responded. "Not to be confused with Brahma. Brahma, with Vishnu and Shiva, is a major deity, though he has not generated the legends and temples of the other two. People do not love Brahma as they love the other two. But behind them is Brahman. He is what you might call Godhead, beyond describing. He is closest to your Christian concept of God. You have gone now more than six minutes. Almost halfway."

"Does anybody believe in Him? In It?"

"Numerous millions," Sheela assured him, her soft voice stiffening a little. "There are no disbelieving Hindus."

"Does He ask you to feel guilty?" Cell after cell, it seemed to Fleischer, was igniting within him, one microscopic sun after another.

Her voice became merry again. "No, we are not like Americans. We are still too poor for guilt. I do not mean to be flippant. Each Hindu feels set down in a certain earthly place, and tries to fill that role. Each person, from the maharajah down to the crippled beggar, is doing what is prescribed. That is what Krishna said to Arjuna on the battlefield in the Bhagavad-Gita. 'Be a warrior,' he said, 'and do not trouble yourself with the ethics of killing.' You have done over eight minutes. From now on, most patients assure me, it becomes easier. It will be downhill. Can you feel that yet?"

"At my age," Fleischer announced from the center of his burning blindness, through lips immobilized by a mask of inward-directed needles, "it's all downhill."

Each of Fleischer's three wives had borne one child—girl, boy, girl. They in turn had each produced two children, all boys, oddly. Odd, too, was the way they all, against the dispersive tendencies of American independence and enterprise, lived within an hour's drive of the Swampscott condo to which he had retired. Guilty about his inadequate grandfathering—he never, unlike grandfathers in television commercials, took his grandsons fishing or onto idyllic golf courses—he tried to visit each household once a month. In the weeks after his blue-light treatment, he would rather have hidden in his stuffy bachelor quarters, their curtains drawn to keep out any further light, while the television set in the corner muttered and shuffled its electrons like a demented person playing solitaire.

But once a parent, always a parent. Guilty habit drove him forth. His younger daughter lived in a sprawling old farmhouse that had lost most of its acres but kept its barn and long side porch. She and her husband, in what seemed to Fleischer a precarious arrangement with the real world, ran a riding stable in the barn, and an advertising firm out of their basement—rural bohemians plugged into the World Wide Web. Once his shyest, plumpest child, Gretchen had acquired in her thirties a lean, sun-hardened horsewoman's confidence, and a hearty, not always welcome frankness to go with it. "Dad," she greeted him, "what happened to your *face?* It's so *red.* Does it hurt?"

"It did. It doesn't now. You should have seen me five days ago. I looked monstrous. Not just red but all swollen, as if I'd been punched."

Gretchen blinked, but did not contradict him. How could she? She hadn't been there, in the room of merciless blue light. Nevertheless, he felt nettled, entitled to more sympathy than he was getting. He went on, "I've been trying to hide, but I remembered Tommy's birthday was yesterday, and I didn't want him to think I'd forgotten. Here. I got him that electronic King Kong game I think he said he wanted from seeing it advertised on television. The kid who waited on me in Circuit City thought this must be the one I meant, but he didn't seem to know much, and he kept staring at my poor red face."

"Poor Dad. Actually, Tommy's birthday was last week. But he'll be thrilled. I'll call him in from the barn. He was helping Greg."

"Don't bother, if he's doing useful work. I'll just leave King Kong here."

"Don't be silly, Father. Tommy's always asking, 'When is Grandpa coming to visit?' "

Grandpa—Fleischer couldn't identify with the name, but on the other hand couldn't think of a better. It was what he had called his own grandfather, with whom he had lived until the dear old man died. Tipping back his head to see through thick bifocals, his grandfather had read the newspaper and the Bible in his favorite armchair and smoked cigars on the porch and taken a nip of whiskey in his bedroom, which smelled wonderfully of bygone mores and medicines. For every day of Fritz's young life he awoke to the sounds of his grandfather coughing his tenacious tobacco cough, muttering to Grandma, walking up and down stairs in his squeaky high-top shoes, and shaking down the clinkers in the coal furnace in the basement. When the Depression had hit, his pregnant daughter and out-of-work son-in-law had taken refuge with him, and they had gratefully named their baby for him. Fritz, a solid old German name. One of the Katzenjammer Kids in the Sunday comic strip had been called Fritz.

None of Fritz's grandsons was named Fritz. Tommy, trailing his little brother, Teddy, came in from the side porch. The nine-year-old, his bare chest slick with sweat, looked disturbingly pudgy. Teddy, at six, was still wiry, but his hair, blond with bits of barn straw in it, hung uncut to his shoulders, so that only Fleischer's having seen the child being bathed at the hospital told him that this was not a girl. The boys came up to him to be hugged yet did nothing to help the embrace, standing there limply and refusing to lift their faces to give his lips access to more than their ears. "I hope this is something you don't already have," he told Tommy weakly, handing him the long flat package. It had cost him several hours in the shopping and the wrapping, plus sifting through the rack at the local drugstore for a suitably jocose but not obscene or hostile birthday card.

In a flash the boy ripped off the paper and confronted the raging gorilla on the box, its giant jaws wide open to engulf an entire lime-colored automobile. "Yippee!" he cried, in what seemed to Fleischer faked rapture. "This is just the one I asked Mom for and she didn't get me."

"It looked pretty violent," his grandfather warily observed.

"Why would even a monster chew lumps of metal?" To himself he thought that fewer computer games might take some pounds from the boy's soft, aggressively bare torso.

Gretchen, hearing the critical edge in her father's voice, maternally intervened: "Dad, the latest thinking on that seems to be that the violence, however awful, does children *good.* It gives their fantasies a form and carries them off. Isn't that Aristotle's old theory of catharsis all over again?"

"I didn't know you read Aristotle. I didn't know anybody still did." To his grandson he said, "Enjoy, Tommy. Teddy, make him give you a turn now and then."

But the boys were no longer listening. The older was whining to his mother, "I *gotta* go back to helping Dad," and the younger had given up gazing expectantly at his grandfather. "Next time, Teddy," Fleischer told him brusquely. "Today's not your birthday." Still, the boy's unspoken disappointment pained him. The girlish child reminded him not of Gretchen at that age but of the bottomless well of hopefulness he had felt within him at the age of six, against all reason, surrounded as he had been by the Depression. Optimism and a helpless dependence on being loved, he saw with the reluctant wisdom of age, are the meager survival weapons we bring with us into the world. Fleischer still wanted to be loved, however little he deserved it. He sat with Gretchen over cups of herbal tea, marvelling that his baby girl, who had hated her own thighs, should have become not only a woman but a leathery one in jodhpurs, practiced in the ways of equestrianism and advertising and motherhood and, he dismally supposed, sex.

Her good-bye kiss when his time came to leave startled him, considering their relation, by being aimed at the center of his mouth. In backing away, though, she gave him a quick sideways glance, checking on her effect, looking, for this moment, remarkably—piercingly—like her mother. Corinne had been the youngest of his wives and the least philosophical about his leaving her. She had not wanted to be left; she doubted, more than her two predecessors, her ability to enjoy freedom and create a new attachment. Her insecurity, with her watchfully qualified kisses, had been one of the initial fascinations. After his two rough-and-tumble, roughly equal matches with women his own age, Corinne brought out his protective instinct. But then her streak of panic, of fearing she could not cope, excited his capacity for impatience and, in the end, cruelty. He had grown stony under her siege, the last year, of pleas and tears.

Gretchen had been only seven, a wide-eyed innocent bystander. Corinne had, in a fashion, eventually coped, moving to the South Shore and making one of those postmodern living-together arrangements with a somewhat younger man. Fleischer was secretly offended and felt cuckolded. If only she had not shyly held back, giving kisses but then undermining them with a questioning irony—self-protective behavior touching in a daughter but hard to forgive in a wife—Corinne might still be his, a quarter of a century later. He had loved the infantile, trusting way she had slept, her bare toes sneaking out of the covers and a soft round arm wrapped around her face, its pink elbow up in the air.

Fleischer and Gretchen parted on the long side porch, tidily stacked with wood for the coming winter. His face felt hot; the oblique flash of resemblance to her mother had warmed a sore spot within him.

His second wife, Tracy, had taken a good deep tan. They had spent a lot of the days of their brief marriage at the beach together, even though Fleischer burned while she turned the color of a Polynesian. He had hoped some of her melanin would rub off on him, but she kept it all to herself. Quick to marry, once their divorces from other people came through, they had been quick to have a child—a son, Geoffrey. They took him to the beach early, in his cream-colored oilcloth bassinet, under a layer of muslin to keep off the sand flies and to soften the noontime sun. By the time he was two it became clear that his skin took after his mother's. No sun damage had been inflicted.

Or so it seemed: Fleischer observed that even in his teens, when his parents had been long divorced, the boy kept an indoor complexion, a sallow refusal of gratuitous exposure. He became as sober and cautious a man as his mother had been reckless and dazzling as a woman. At the beach, when she and Fleischer were still married to other people, Tracy's white smile in her brown face had signalled to him from far away, a beacon on the horizon. Then, when she came and stood next to him where he lay dozing, fuzzily hungover, on a blanket beside his first wife, Tracy's long naked legs had stretched, it seemed, almost to the sky. Ah, those scintillating afternoons on the sand in the sun-loving, fun-loving Sixties! People used baby oil and Bain de Soleil back then, instead of number-rated sunscreen. Tracy's long-toed bare feet beside Fleischer's groggy face had bronzed insteps and pale soles and cherry-red nails, and he wanted to lick them, every square inch, but for the scandal this would have caused, and the sand grains that would have adhered to his tongue.

Geoffrey, forty-two, and less than nine at the time of his parents' divorce, lived alone in a Boston apartment whose only disorder came when his teen-age boys visited. Their mother, Eileen, lived a few miles away, in Brighton. They had been separated for three years, with plenty of counselling but no perceptible legal action. Fleischer often wanted to ask his son why the divorce wasn't happening; but he feared the answer, which might have been that his father's impulsive behavior had set a cautionary example. In Fleischer's mind at the time, he was doing Tracy a favor, once the extent of her infidelities—ski instructors, local workmen—had become clear, freeing her to find another husband. No such considerate thoughts, apparently, urged Geoffrey forward, though Eileen was younger than he, and still beautiful. He had been, like many of his generation, slow to marry, close to thirty. The bride was twenty-two, with raven hair, edgy but demure, perfect and spectacular at the wedding, with her china-white skin. Her dark eyes and thick lashes had made smoldering spots of shadow through the veil. The father-in-law had beamed with pride, gloating, as if over an unexpected inheritance, over the genes she was bringing into the family line. The Fleischers for generations, back to Teutonic hunters and gatherers, had been a homely, knobby, unevenly ruddy race; Fritz guessed he wasn't the first psoriatic. Now Eileen's older son, Jonathan, showed her delicacy and precision of feature to rakish effect in a thirteen-year-old's lengthening frame. In his younger, blonder brother, Martin, those qualities were wed to his father's phlegmatic stolidity to achieve a gentler and more angelic handsomeness. Fritz tried to fulfill a grandfather's duty by visiting his son on the weekends when the boys were visiting.

"How's school?" he would ask them.

"O.K.," Martin would answer.

"Sucks," Jonathan would say.

Martin's silence had the innocent purity of there simply being no more he could think to say, but Jonathan's had a deliberately withheld quality. He would not even turn his head for a second to acknowledge the presence of his grandfather, concentrating instead on the television program, or book of science fiction, or piece of drawing (he was artistic) that was engaging him. Fleischer remembered very well the intensity of a child's need to concentrate down into the comic book, the model airplane, the stamp collection—deep into the miniature world that sheltered you from the larger, adult, out-of-your-control world—but his empathy was hard to express. Even Jonathan's blue-black hair, glossily brushed and eccentrically parted in the middle, emanated a desire to repulse. He and his younger brother were enduring a parental separation that must seem endless, a kind of disease eating their adolescence away, and they suspected their grandfather and his obscure sins to be behind it all. Perhaps the boy felt protective of the mother he strikingly resembled; he feared that any friendliness toward his grandfather would lead to an invasion and a betrayal of that large half of his life where she ruled. So Fleischer imagined; he imagined that his sins were as evident as the scorched, mottled look of his face.

Martin was more mechanical in his interests than artistic, and his elaborate Lego constructions and his increasingly polished ventures into carpentry gave his grandfather some slight opportunity to admire and even, through helpful practical questions, to share. But playing with blocks and tools was decades behind Fleischer, and the child's interest, kindled, flickered out as he felt his elder's momentarily roused attention wander away. Grandchildren were raised in an alien technology, an electronic one of amplified noises and simulated violence too quick and coded for an elderly eye and hand. Although he recognized his grandsons as further extensions of himself, it was Fleischer's own, enigmatically wounded son who fascinated him.

"How's it going?" he would ask Geoffrey, letting the question mean whatever his son chose it to mean.

"O.K.," he would say. "She's still fussy, but improving." The pronoun "she" inevitably referred to Eileen. "The last counsellor helped," he added.

It was apparent to anyone, even to his father and his sons, that nothing would help enough, that the marriage was over for everyone but its two principals. Perhaps it was a family failing, Fritz speculated—not knowing how to let go. In his heart he felt still married to all three of his wives: the marriages continued underground, through tunnels of fondness and mutual understanding. Sometimes it took one or another of his wives to remind him, when he overstayed or overstepped, that their connections were broken. Women, who must give more thought to their survival than men, are in the end less sentimental.

"It's hard," was all Fleischer could think to say, sitting with his only son, seeing his own features in the stubbornly sorrowing, aging face, and hearing from the next room the muffled clutter of his grandsons killing time until they were no longer children and could escape this limbo. A helpless, guilty, wordless silence between the two grown men stretched and burned. To break the silence, Fleischer asked, "Does my face look red?"

Geoffrey, after a quick glance, answered, "I guess. But it always looks sort of red."

"Really? It got blasted at the hospital two weeks ago. I felt like a sun-dried tomato."

"Nothing much shows now. You don't look that bad, Dad."

Fleischer felt exasperation. "Geoffrey, you're not looking. You're thinking of something else."

"You sound like my wife. That's what she always says."

Together, in silence, the two men contemplated the unfathomable pleasure it gave the younger to still be able to say "my wife."

"Dad, what did you do to your face? It looks *beautiful!*" So spoke his eldest child, Aurora, four weeks after his session with Sheela.

He blushed, his skin remembering the heat of the blue light. "Really? It was horrible at first—swollen, all red. I stopped looking in the mirror when it calmed down a little."

"Oh, no," his daughter said, beaming. "More than a little. Dad, I've never seen your face so smooth. You look ten years younger."

He laughed, greedily. "Ten years? That's more than I deserve."

"Why say that? Go for it, I say." Aurora was breezier than Gretchen, happier in her body. Perhaps because of her prematurely New Age name, bestowed by her young parents in the first flush of the power and joy of engendering life, Aurora took thought concerning her health and her rapport with the physical world: she jogged and did yoga, cooked along macrobiotic principles, and would have turned vegetarian but for her husband, a tradition-minded Kenyan who believed his two sons should be fed meat. She was over fifty, a fact amazing to her father, who more clearly than with his later children remembered her newborn weight in his arms, so perilously light, the tiny person so indisputably alive, that his knees had begun to tremble. For fear he would pass out and drop her, he had had to sit down on Maureen's firm, narrow bed, there in the base hospital at Fort Bliss, Texas. In those days most young males went into the Army, though there was more peace then than there is now.

Wonderingly, those first two years, as he made the passage from Fort Bliss to the Wharton School of Business in Philadelphia, he had observed the minute daily extensions of Aurora's grip, with her slowly focusing slate-colored eyes and grasping little lavender-tinged fists, on the world. She had crawled and then walked and then talked with a growing vocabulary that slowly shed her dear, irrecoverable toddler solecisms. She had been, he and Maureen had joked, an "industrial-strength" child, rarely ill and never injured, the perfect one to practice on. They had intended to have more, but the Fifties consensus was breaking up around them, as easy contraception and a new hedonism swept in. Tracy loomed on the shimmering beach, and by the time John Kennedy was shot Fleischer had attained, in private, to licking her feet, with their tan insteps and cherry-red toenails.

Aurora must have been touched by radicalism in her crib, because after her parents divorced and she entered puberty, she manifested a wide variety of erotic attachments, from other girls to college instructors twice her age to musical drug addicts and dark lovers from the Third World. Out of this shadowy mass of unsuitable mates Hector Kanogori emerged as a savior: Aurora and he met in a pottery class. He was interested in the arts only as a hobby, a holiday from his serious work as an assistant professor of economics at a state-university campus south of Boston.

Mr. and Mrs. Kanogori travel. When Fleischer, by then in the last days of his marriage to Tracy, and Maureen, herself remarried, had consulted a counselling service about their daughter's heedless, impractical involvements, the therapist, removing the pencil from her Cambridge bun, had asked them what Aurora seemed interested in, and Maureen surprised her former husband by responding without hesitation, "Travel." How do women know these things about one another? Yes, their industrial-strength baby's romances had been modes of travelling, and Hector, every other year, took Aurora to Africa and Asia on his academic investigation of developing economies. Their house in Milton brimmed with masks and beadwork and statuettes, souvenirs of their trips.

All very well, Fleischer thought, for them: one more charming black-white couple easing the West's racial conscience. But what about their two boys? Alfred and Daniel, as their grandfather called them—he had trouble pronouncing the Kikuyu names also bestowed upon them, in ceremonies both Christian and pagan—had inherited strands of their mother's blithe sturdiness and their father's prim dignity, but these qualities dangled, their grandfather felt, in air. Called black in America, they lacked, as they entered manhood, a black American's street smarts and defenses. On their trips to Africa they had been teased by other boys as *wa-zungu*—whites. In the polite society around them, once the enforced tolerance and diversity of school had been left behind, they had no tribal roots, no matter-of-fact acceptance. Bryant Gumbel had managed it, and Ralph Bunche and Tiger Woods, but how many others? Fleischer blamed himself, with his diseased white skin and reflexive liberalism, for allowing the seeds of daring in Aurora to flourish unchallenged and to bear such tender, imperilled fruit.

"The skin remembers," Fleischer's old dermatologist had said more than once, closing his eyes as he visualized the phenomenon. Sunburn your bottom once at a nudist beach, fry your nose on an all-day sail, and the insulted epidermis never forgets. Time's blue light flushes out everything immature, ill-considered, or not considered at all. The world was being populated by his mistakes. It was possible that his adventurous daughter, having seen her mother deserted for a woman who took a better tan, had presented to her father, and to the string of Fleischer ancestors bleached white in Europe's fogs, a gift of melanin fetched straight from mankind's African homeland.

Aurora's boys had been his first grandchildren. Enthusiastically he had tackled the role of grandfather. He had asked to babysit for them, insisting on it, determined "to get to know them," pushing himself in, sending Aurora and Hector out to a movie they hardly wanted to see. He would share milk and cookies with the boys, read them ethnically suitable stories from the household's large collection, and, as their parents were about to come home, demand they go to sleep. They were accustomed to sleeping in a heap, in the African manner, in their parents' bed. As an exasperated concession Fleischer would let them share the lower of their bunk beds. There they would fall asleep like bookends, their bottoms touching, bits of bare skin exposed by skimpy pajamas tugged in their final struggle against sleep—soft brown skin, a smooth latte, half and half.

Last June, having invited the Kanogoris to the Swampscott beach his condo overlooked, he watched the two boys, both taller and broader now than he, strip down to bathing suits worn beneath their jeans and, in the unison of a mutual challenge, race to the still-wintry water and dive in. He was amazed by the sight: the breadth of their backs, the flare of the shoulder blades, the oval muscles of their long legs, the erect strength of their necks' tapered columns and their tensed Achilles tendons, the flash and flicker of their naked pale soles as their feet thrashed in the icy blue water. They were grown men—magnificent, potent. If Fleischer had encountered them in a shadowy alley, he would have been frightened. Yet they were his blood. Daniel wore on his broad nose a spattering of the freckles that Fleischer had worn as a child and that Aurora had inherited.

Between his two glimpses—his mulatto grandsons in pajamas and then in bathing suits—there was almost nothing; he had not gotten to know them. Their heads were full of lore and survival strategies that had nothing to do with him. They were creatures seen at a distance, under the sea's dark horizon. When they came out of the water, shivering, towelling themselves furiously, they seemed to surround Fleischer with chilly saltwater spray and the warmth of healthy flesh.

He told them, "Boys, that was *heroic*. How could you *stand* it, for more than a second?"

"It was no big deal," Alfred reassured him. "Once you're in." He was the taller of the two, and the more quiet and solemn.

Daniel's face held a spark of mischief, to go with his freckles. "You should have tried it, Grandpa. It gets your blood moving."

"Next time," Fleischer promised.

But life runs out of next times, at least for non-Hindus. Today, as her father visited, Aurora's cheerful manner hid a sorrow: her boys were gone, Alfred a sophomore at the University of Arizona and Daniel a senior at Deerfield. "How are they doing?" Fleischer asked her.

"Well enough, but not well enough for Hector. I tell him, 'You were exceptional. Always first in your class at mission school, scholarships abroad—all that. I wasn't. Blame me,' I tell him."

"You had another agenda."

This made her laugh; she saw through this remark to the image her father retained of her, of a girl out of control. Her laugh was cut in half as she turned her head aside. Like her mother and father, she had turned gray early. *She is over fifty*, Fleischer thought. *She knows her life has been mostly lived.*

Fathering children, Fleischer had never pictured their gray hairs or their own children. He had just selfishly wanted to create little beings who would look up to him, despite his bad skin, and brighten his life with their sunny innocence. But he had abandoned them all, with their mothers, when their innocence gave out. And now each had created another generation, extending rootlets into the world's hard substance. He could not imagine what his grandchildren would do in the world, how they would earn their keep. They were immature cells, centers of potential pain.

Outage

The jolly weatherpersons on television, always eager for ratings-boosting disasters, had predicted a fierce autumn storm for New England, with driving rain and high winds. Evan Morris, who worked at home while his wife, Camilla, managed a boutique on Boston's Newbury Street, glanced out of his windows now and then at the swaying trees—oaks still tenacious of their rusty leaves, maples letting go in gusts of gold and red—but was unimpressed by the hyped news event. Rain came down heavily a half-hour at a time, then pulled back into a silvery sky of fast-moving, fuzzy-bottomed clouds. The worst seemed to be over when, in mid-afternoon, his computer died under his eyes. The financial figures he had been painstakingly assembling swooned as a group, sucked into the dead blank screen like glittering water pulled down a drain. Around him, the house seemed to sigh, as all its lights and little engines, its computerized timers and indicators, simultaneously shut down. The sound of wind and rain lashing the trees outside infiltrated the silence. A beam creaked. A loose shutter banged. The drip from a plugged gutter tapped heavily, like a bully nagging for attention, on the wooden cover of a cellar-window well.

The lines bringing the Morrises' house electricity and telephone service and cable television came up, on three poles, through two acres of woods. Evan stepped outside in the storm's lull, in the strangely luminous air, to see if he could spot any branches fallen on his lines. He saw none, and no lit windows in the nearest house, barely visible through the woods whose leaves in summer hid it entirely. The tops of the tallest trees were heaving in a wind he barely felt. A spatter of thick cold drops sent him back into the house, where drifts of shadow were sifting into the corners and the furnace ticked in the basement as its metal cooled. Without electricity, what was there to do?

He opened the refrigerator and was surprised by its failure to greet him with a welcoming inner light. The fireplace in the den emitted a sour scent of damp wood ash. Wind whistled in crevices he had not known existed, under the eaves and at the edges of the storm windows. He felt impotent, and amused by his impotence, in this emergency. He remembered some letters he had planned to mail at the post office in his suburb's little downtown, and a check he had intended to deposit at the bank. So he did have something to do: he collected these pieces of paper, and put on a tan water-resistant zippered jacket and a Red Sox cap. The burglar alarm by the front door was peeping and blinking, softly, as if to itself. Evan punched the reset button; the device fell silent, and he went out the door.

It seemed eerie that his car started as usual. Wet leaves were plastered over the driveway and the narrow macadam roads of this development; the neighborhood had been built all at once, twenty years ago, on the land of an unprofitable farm. He drove cautiously, especially around the duck pond, beside a vanished barn, where, in a snowstorm ten years ago, a teen-ager had slid through a rail fence and sunk his parents' Mercedes up to its hubcaps. The downtown—two churches, a drugstore, a Dunkin' Donuts, a pizza shop, a mostly Italian restaurant, two beauty parlors, a dress shop, a bridal shop, a few more stores that came and went in the same chronically vacated premises, an insurance agent and a lawyer on the floor above a realty office, a dentist, a bank branch, and a post office—was without electricity but busier than usual, its sidewalk full of pedestrians in this gleaming gray lull.

Evan saw two young women embracing, before they began to converse as if renewing a long-neglected acquaintance. People stood talking, discussing their fate in small groups. Shop windows usually bright were dark, and it occurred to him that, of course, people had been flushed onto the sidewalk by the outage. The health-food store, its crammed shelves of bagged nuts and bottled vitamins and refrigerated tofu sandwiches, and the fruit store, its rival in healthy nutrition across the street, were both caves of forbidding darkness behind their display windows.

But it did not occur to him that the bank, usually so receptive to his deposits, would have a taped notice on its glass doors declaring the location of the nearest other branch, and that, although he could see the tellers chatting on the padded bench where applicants for mortgages and perpetrators of overdrafts customarily languished, he could no more access his money than he could have laid hands on the fish in an aquarium. The bank manager, a bustling small woman in a severe suit, was actually patrolling the sidewalk; she told Evan breathlessly, "I'm so sorry, Mr. Morris. Our ATM, alarms, everything is down. I was just checking to see if the hardware store had any power."

"Myra, I think we're all in the same boat," Evan reassured her; yet he understood her incredulity. He himself did not expect that the little post office, though open to box users and seekers of the inside mail slots, would be also closed to transactions; everything had been computerized by a United States Postal Service zealous to modernize, and now not a single letter could be weighed or a single stamp sold, even had there been enough light to see. The afternoon was darkening. In danger of completing no errands at all, he tested the door of the health-food store. The latch released, and he heard a giggle in the shadows. "Are you open?" he called.

"To you, sure," answered the voice of the young proprietress, curly-haired, perpetually tan Olivia. Evan groped toward the back, where a single squat perfumed candle illuminated bins of little plastic bags; they shimmered with blobby reflections. He brought to the counter a bag of what he hoped were unsalted but roasted cashews. "The register's out. All contributions accepted," Olivia joked, and made change out of her own purse for what he, holding it close to his eyes, verified was a five-dollar bill.

The transaction had felt flirtatious to him, and the atmosphere of the downtown, beneath its drooping festoon of useless cables, seemed festive. Automobiles paraded past with their burning headlights. The ominous thickening in the air stirred the pedestrians to take shelter again. There was a brimming, an overflow of good nature, and a transparency: something occluding had been removed, baring neglected possibilities. Hurrying back into the shelter of his car, Evan laughed with an irrational pleasure.

. . .

Fresh drops speckled his windshield as he turned into his neighborhood, through a break in the stone wall that had once marked the bounds of the farm. PRIVATE WAY, a painted sign said. A woman in white—a shiny vinyl raincoat and swollen-looking white running shoes—was walking in the middle of the narrow road. With fluttering gestures she motioned him to stop. He recognized a newish neighbor, a wispy blonde who had moved a few years ago, with her husband and two growing boys, into a house invisible from the Morrises'. They only met a few times a year, at cocktail parties or zoning-appeals-board hearings. She looked like a ghost, beckoning him. He braked, and lowered the car window. "Oh, *Evan*," she said with breathy relief. "It's you. What's *hap*pening?" she asked. "All my electricity went out, even the telephones."

"Mine, too," he said, to reassure her. "Everybody's. A tree must have fallen on a power line somewhere, in this wind. It happens, Lynne." He was pleased to have fished her name up from his memory: Lynne Willard.

She came close enough to his open window for him to see that she was actually trembling, her lips groping like those of a child near tears. Her eyes stared above his car roof as if scanning the treetops for rescue. She brought her eyes down to his face and shakily explained, "Willy's away. In Chi*ca*go, all week. I'm up there all alone, now the boys are both off to boarding school. I didn't know what I should do, so I put on my sneakers and set off walking."

Evan remembered those boys as noisy and sly, waiting in their little blazers for the day-school bus at the end of the road, just outside the tumbled-down fieldstone wall. If they were now old enough for boarding school, then this woman was not as young as she seemed. Her face, narrowed by a knotted head scarf, was pale, except for the tip of her nose, which was pink like a rabbit's. Her eyelids also were pink; they looked rubbed, and her eyes watered. He wondered if she was a daytime tippler. "I like your hat," she said, to fill the lengthening silence. "Are you a fan?"

"No more than normal."

"They won the World Series."

"That is true. Get in the car, Lynne," he said, his powers of reassurance deepening. "I'll drive you home. There's nothing downtown. Nobody knows how long the outage will be. Even the bank and post office didn't know. The only thing open was the health-food store."

"I was taking a walk," she said, as if this hadn't been quite established. "I can keep going."

"Don't you notice? The rain is starting up again. The skies are about to let loose."

Blinking, pressing her lips together to suppress their tremor—the lower had a trick of twitching sideways—she walked around in front of his headlights. He leaned across the car seats to tug at the door handle and push open the passenger door for her, as if she couldn't do it for herself. Sliding in, with a slither of white vinyl, she confessed, "There was a beeping in the house I had to get away from. Willy's not even in Boston, where I could call him."

"I think that's your burglar alarm," Evan told her. "Or some other alarm that doesn't like losing current. I'll come inside, if I may, and look at the problem."

She had brought a pleasant smell with her into the car, a smell from his childhood—cough drops or licorice. "You may," she said, settling back on his leather car seat. "I got so afraid," she went on, with a wry twist to her mouth, as if to laugh at herself, or at the memory of a long-ago self.

He had never been to the Willards' place. Their driveway was fringed with more elaborate plantings than the Morrises'—gnarly little azaleas, already bare of leaf, and euonymus still blaring forth that surreal autumnal magenta. Their parking area was covered in larger, whiter stones than the brown half-inch pebbles that Camilla had insisted on despite their tendency (which Evan had pointed out) to scatter into the lawn during winter snowplowing. But the basic house, a good-sized clapboarded neo-colonial twenty years old, with a gratuitous swath of first-floor brick façade, looked much like his. Lynne hadn't locked the front door, just walked out in her panic. Trailing behind her, Evan was surprised by the lithe swiftness with which she climbed the steps of the flagstone porch and let herself back in, holding the storm door for him as she opened the other.

Inside, the beeping was distinct and insistent, but not the urgent, ever-louder bleating of alarm mode. He turned the wrong way at first; the floor plan of this house was different from his, with the family room on the left instead of the right, and the kitchen beyond it, not beside it. The furnishings, though, looked much the same—the modern taste of twenty years ago, boxy and stuffed, bare wood and monochrome wool, coffee tables of thick glass on cruciform legs of stainless steel, promiscuously mixed with Orientals and family antiques. These possessions looked slightly smarter and less tired than those in his home; but Evan tended to glamorize what other people had.

"Over here," Lynne said, "next to the closet"—the very front-hall closet in which she was hanging up her raincoat of white vinyl. The snug knit gray dress she wore beneath it looked to him as if she had come from a ladies' luncheon that noon. Using her toes, she pried off her bulky sneakers without bothering to unlace them—perhaps to avoid bending over, ass up, beneath his eyes—and kicked them onto the closet floor.

"Yes," he said, moving to the panel in stocking feet. "It's just like mine." He lifted his hand to touch it, then took thought to ask, "May I?"

"Help yourself," she said. Her voice, in her own house, had become almost slangy, shedding its quaver. "Be my guest."

He pushed the little rectangular button labelled Reset. The beeping stopped, sharply. Coming close up behind him, she marvelled. "That's all it takes?"

"Apparently," he said. "That tells it the current shut-off wasn't a home invasion. Not that I'm much of a hand with technology."

She giggled in obscure delight. What he had smelled in the car, he realized, had had alcohol in it, mixed with a licorice scent from long ago. "Willy's such a prick," she told Evan. "He knows all this stuff but never shares it. Tell me," Lynne said, "as a man. Do you think he *really* has to spend all this time in Chicago?"

Cautiously, he offered, "Business can be very demanding. At a certain level men—and women in business, too, of course—have to look each other in the eye. I used to be on planes all the time and have meetings and all that myself, but I found working at home was more efficient. With all this electronic communication everywhere there's really no need to get out that much. But, then, I don't know Will—Mr. Willard's business." His words, nervously excessive, seemed to have an echo in the unfamiliar house—or, rather, felt absorbed by its partial strangeness, the sounds falling into the many little differences between this house and his own.

The rain, as he had foretold, had returned, whispering and drumming outside, and bringing inside a deeper shade of afternoon. The wind whipped bursts of wet pellets across the windows.

"Me, neither. Could I offer you a drink?" this woman asked, nervous herself. She added with another giggle, "Since you've *got*ten out." She gestured toward her becalmed kitchen. "I can't offer you coffee."

"What have *you* been drinking?" Evan asked her.

Her eyes widened, as if to compensate for the lack of light. "How did you know it was anything? Some girlfriends and I had wine and finished off lunch with anisette."

"In the car," he answered her, "you smelled sweet," and moved closer, as if to verify.

Her kisses did not taste of licorice. There in the family room, where the great plasma-TV screen stared blankly and the morning *Globe* lay, still in its plastic wrapper, where it had been tossed onto the sofa unread, Lynne kissed dryly, tentatively, as if testing her lipstick. Then her lips warmed to the fit; her face pushed up at his and her fidgety hands went around his back, to its small and the nape of his neck, and Evan dizzily wondered if he wasn't too far, too suddenly, out on a limb. But no, he reassured himself, this was human and harmless, this sheltered contact while the rain thrashed outside and the light inside the rooms dimmed by imperceptible notches. His impulse was to keep smoothing her hair, where it had been tangled and pressed flat beneath her head scarf. His hands trembled, as her lips had. Their faces grew hot; their caresses through their clothes began to feel clumsy. "We should go upstairs," she said huskily. "Anybody going by could look inside."

"Who would go by in this weather?" he asked.

"He gets a lot of FedExes," she said. Climbing the stairs ahead of him—carpeted in pale green, where his and Camilla's were maroon—Lynne continued the unidentified pronoun. "He calls me every day, often around now. I guess it leaves his nights free."

Evan, slightly winded at the head of the stairs, from having held his breath while admiring this woman's surprisingly muscular haunches as they moved in the snug knit dress, asked, "Did you mean it, that your phone doesn't work, either?"

"Yeah, some penny-pinching system he got installed, so it's all the same wires. I don't understand it exactly. In our new car, I can't do the radio stations. They give you too many options now."

"Exactly," he agreed.

The rooms upstairs had a different layout from those in his house, and the one she led him into was barer and smaller than the master bedroom would have been. Photographs on the bureau showed her boys, at various stages, and older people, though still young, in Fifties clothes, perhaps her parents, or Willy's. The color in various framed vacation snapshots had bleached out, shifting register. On the wall a paper poster showed a woman, draped only in a python, stretched out on a Lamborghini. Lynne stood a moment by the window. "Look," she said. "You can see your house, now that the leaves are down." It took Evan some seconds to make it out—a pale shadow, the tint of smoke, through the intervening trees.

"You have good eyes," he told her. He did not want to feel that this neighbor was much younger than he, but an age difference was declared in how calmly and quickly she shed her clothes, as if it were no big deal. Oh, but it *was* a big deal, she was so lovely, all bony and downy and fat in the right places, drifting back and forth in the shadowy room to put her folded clothes on chairs, simple straight-backed boys' chairs. When he had seen her in the center of the road he had thought for an instant she was a ghost, and there was a ghostly betranced quality in the way she moved, her lips crimped in that twist of self-criticism he had noticed in the car, when she had slid in beside him.

She came to him to help him undress, something Camilla never did. This servile act, her small face frowning as she worked at his shirt buttons, excited him so that he ceased to feel nervous, out on a limb—ceased to listen to the rain and wind. The storm of blood inside him drowned them out. The tip of her tongue crept between her lips in her concentration. The front fringe of her hair, which the scarf had left uncovered, showed a few gleaming droplets and smelled of rain, another scent from boyhood. "God," he said. "I love this." He had kept himself, with an effort, from saying "you."

"It's not over," she promised, in the light voice of a woman talking to a girlfriend. "There's more, Evan."

The electricity came on. All over the upstairs, wallpaper patterns and wood moldings popped into clarity. Downstairs, in the kitchen, the dishwasher surged into its next phase. By the front door, the burglar alarm resumed its beeping, at a shriller pitch. The furnace in the basement, at a pitch below that of the wind, ignited and began, with a roar steadier than the wind, to reintroduce warmth into the cooling house. Amplified, eager voices downstairs proclaimed that Lynne had been watching television an hour ago, before she panicked. Her face, so close to his that their breaths mingled, jumped back, like a cut to the commercial. "Oh dear," she said, her rubbed-looking eyes coming back into focus.

"To the rescue," he said. He began to redo his buttons.

"You don't have to go." But she, too, in her nakedness, was embarrassed; her cheeks blazed as if with a rash.

"I think I do. *He*," he said, "might call. Even *she* might, if the outage has made the news in Boston. You'll be fine now. Listen, Lynne. The alarm has stopped beeping. It's saying, 'All is well. All is normal.' It's saying, 'Get that man out of my house.' "

"No," she weakly protested.

"It's saying, 'I'm in charge now.' " Evan turned his eyes from her nakedness, his wispy blonde's. "It's saying," he told her, " 'This is how it is. This is the real world.' "

The Full Glass

Approaching eighty, I sometimes see myself from a little distance, as a man I know but not intimately. Normally I have no use for introspection. My employment for thirty years, refinishing wood floors—carried on single-handedly out of a small white truck, a Chevrolet Spartan, with the several sizes of electric sanders and the belts and discs of sandpaper in all their graded degrees of coarseness and five-gallon containers of polyurethane and thinner and brushes ranging from a stout six-inch width to a diagonally cut two-inch sash brush for tight corners and jigsaw-fitted thresholds—has conditioned me against digging too deep. Balancing in a crouch on the last dry boards like a Mohican steelwalker has taught me the value of the superficial, of that wet second coat glistening from baseboard to baseboard. All it needs and asks is twenty-four undisturbed hours to dry in. Some of these fine old New England floors, especially the hard yellow pine from the Carolinas that was common in the better homes a hundred years ago, but also the newer floors of short, tongued pieces of oak or maple, shock you with their carefree gouges and cigarette burns and the black scuff marks synthetic soles leave. Do people still give that kind of party? I entered this trade, after fifteen years in a white-collar, smooth-talking line of work, as a refugee from romantic disgrace, and abstain from passing judgment, even on clients arrogant enough to schedule a dinner party six hours after I give their hall parquet the finish coat.

But now that I'm retired—the sawdust gets to your lungs and the fumes eat away your sinuses, even through a paper mask—I watch myself with a keener attention, as you would keep an eye on a stranger who might start to go to pieces any minute. Some of my recently acquired habits strike me as curious. At night, having brushed my teeth and flossed and done the eye drops and about to take my pills, *I like to have the water glass already full.* The rational explanation might be that, with a left hand clutching my pills, I don't want to fumble at the faucet and simultaneously try to hold the glass with the right. Still, it's more than a matter of convenience. There is a small but distinct pleasure, in a life with the gaudier pleasures levelled out of it, in having the full glass there on the white marble sink-top waiting for me, before I sluice down the anti-cholesterol pill, the anti-inflammatory, the sleeping, the calcium supplement (my wife's idea, now that I get foot cramps in bed, somehow from the pressure of the top sheet), along with the Xalatan drops to stave off glaucoma and the Systane drops to ease dry eye. In the middle of the night, on the way to the bathroom, my eye feels like it has a beam in it, not a mote but literally a *beam*—I never took that image from the King James Version seriously before.

The wife keeps nagging me to drink more water. Eight glasses a day is what her doctor recommended to her as one of those feminine beauty tricks. It makes me gag just to think about it—eight glasses comes to half a gallon, it would bubble right out my ears—but that healthy sweet swig near the end of the day has gotten to be something important, *a tiny piece that fits in:* the pills popped into my mouth, the full glass raised to my lips, the swallow that takes the pills down with it, all in less time than it takes to tell it, but bliss.

The bliss goes back, I suppose, to moments of thirst satisfied in my childhood, some states to the south of this one, where there were public drinking fountains in all the municipal buildings and department stores, and luncheonettes would put glasses of ice water on the table without your having to ask, and drugstores served Alka-Seltzer up at the soda fountain to cure whatever ailed you, from hangover to hives. I lived with my grandparents, a child lodged with old people thanks to the disruptions of the Depression, and their house had a linoleum floor and deep slate sinks in the kitchen, and above the sinks long-nosed copper faucets tinged by the green of oxidation. A child back then had usually been running from somewhere or other and had a great innocent thirst—running, or else pumping a fat-tired bicycle, imagining it was a dive-bomber about to obliterate a Jap battleship. Filling a tumbler with water at the old faucet connected you with the wider world. Think of it: pipes running through the earth below the frost line and up unseen from the basement right through the walls to bring you this transparent flow, which you swallowed down in rhythmic gulps—down what my grandfather called, with that twinkle he had, behind his bifocals, "the little red lane." The copper would bead with condensation while you waited for the water to run cold enough.

The automobile garage a block away from my grandparents' backyard had the coldest water in town, at a bubbler just inside the overhead sliding doors. It made your front teeth ache, it was so cold. Our dentist, a tall lean tennis player already going bald in his thirties, once told me, after extracting an abscessed back molar of mine when I was fifteen, that no matter what else happened to me dentally I would have my front teeth till the day I died. Now, how could he know that just by looking every six months into a mouth where a Pennsylvania diet of sugar doughnuts and licorice sticks had already wreaked havoc? *But he was right.* Slightly crooked though they are, I still have my front teeth, all the others having long since gone under to New England root canals and Swedish implantology. I think of him, my primal dentist, twice a day, when I do my brushing. He was the beloved town doctor's son, and had stopped short at dentistry as a kind of rebellion. Tennis was really his game. He made it to the county semi-finals at least twice, before dropping over with a heart attack in his mere forties. In those days there was no such thing as a heart bypass, and we didn't know much about flossing, either.

The town tennis courts were handy to his office, right across the street—a main avenue, with trolley tracks in the middle that would take you in twenty minutes the three miles into the local metropolis of eighty thousand working men and women, five first-run movie theatres, and a surplus of obsolescing factories. The tennis courts, four of them, were on the high-school grounds, at the stop where my grandmother and I, back from my piano lesson or buying my good coat for the year, would get off the trolley car, to walk the rest of the way home because I had told her I was about to throw up. She blamed the ozone for my queasiness: according to her, the trolley ran on ozone, or generated it as a by-product. She was an old-fashioned country woman who used to cut dandelions out of the school grounds and cook the greens into a disgusting stew. There was a little trickling creek on the edge of town where she would gather watercress. Farther still into the countryside, she had a cousin, a man even older than she, who had a spring on his property he was very proud of, and would always insist that I visit. It was his idea of a good time for a citified boy.

I disliked these country visits, so full, I thought, of unnecessary ceremony. My great-cousin was a dapper chicken-farmer who by the time of our last visits had become noticeably shorter than I. He had a clean smell to him, starchy with a touch of liniment, and a closeted mustiness I notice now on my own clothes. With a sort of birdy, cooing animation he would faithfully lead me to the spring, down a path of boards slippery with moss from being in the perpetual shade of the droopy limbs of a great hemlock. In my memory, beyond the shadows of the hemlock the spring was always in a ray of sunlight. Spidery water striders walked on its surface, and the dimples around their feet threw interlocking golden-brown rings onto the sandy bottom. A tin dipper rested on one of the large sandstones encircling the spring, and my elderly host would hand it to me, full, with a grin that was all pink gums. He hadn't kept his front teeth.

I was afraid of bringing a water strider up to my lips. What I did bring up held my nostrils in the dipper's wobbly circle of reflection. The water was cold, tasting brightly of tin, but not as cold as that which bubbled up in a corner of that small-town garage, the cement floor black with grease and the ceiling obscured by the sliding-door tracks and suspended wood frames holding rubber tires fresh from Akron. The rubber overhead had a smell that cleared your head the way a bite of licorice did, and the virgin treads had the sharp cut of metal type or newly ironed clothes. That icy water held an ingredient that made me, a boy of nine or ten, eager for the next moment of life, one brimming moment after another.

Thinking back, trying to locate in my life other moments of that full-glass feeling, I recall one in Passaic, New Jersey, when I still wore a suit for work, which was selling life insurance to reluctant prospects. Passaic was out of my territory, and I was there on a stolen day off, with a woman who was not my wife. She was somebody else's wife, and I had a wife of my own, and that particular fullness of our situation was in danger of breaking over the rim. But I was young enough to live in the present, thinking the world owed me happiness. I rejoiced, to the extent of being downright dazed, in this female presence beside me in the rented automobile, a red Dodge coupe. The car had just a few miles on it and, as unfamiliar automobiles do, seemed to glide effortlessly at the merest touch of my hand or foot. I felt like that, too. Being with this woman made my blood feel carbonated. She wore a broad-shouldered tweedy fall outfit I had never seen on her before; its warm brown color, flecked with pimento red, set off her thick auburn hair, done up loosely in a twist behind—in my memory, when she turned her head to look through the windshield with me, whole loops of it had escaped the tortoiseshell hair clip. We must have gone to bed together at some point in that day, but what I remember is being with her in the interior of the car, proudly conscious of the wealth of her hair and the width of her smile and the breadth of her hips, and then in my happiness jauntily swerving across an uncrowded, sunny street in Passaic to seize a metered parking space along the left-hand curb.

A policeman saw the maneuver and before I could open

the driver's door was standing there. "Driver's license," he said. "And car registration."

My heart was thumping and my hands were jumping as I rummaged in the glove compartment for the registration, yet I couldn't wipe the smile off my face. The cop saw it there and it must have further annoyed him, but he studied the documents I handed him as if patiently mastering a difficult lesson. "You crossed over onto the left side of the street," he explained at last. "You could have caused a head-on collision."

"I'm sorry," I said. "I spotted the parking space and saw no traffic was coming. I wasn't thinking." I had forgotten one of the prime axioms of driving: a red car attracts the police. You can get away with almost nothing in a red car.

"Now you're parked illegally, headed the wrong way."

"Is that illegal? We're not from Passaic," my passenger intervened, bending down low, across my lap, so he could see her face. She looked so terrific, in her thick shoulder pads and pimento-flecked wool, that I thought another man must understand and forgive my intoxication. Her long oval hands, darting up out of her lap; her painted lips, avidly tensed in the excitement of argument; her voice, which slid past me almost palpably, like a very fine grade of finish sand-paper, caressing away my smallest imperfection—the police-man must share my own amazed gratitude at what she did for me with this array of erotic instruments. And she was gen-teel, too. Her husband had money.

The cop handed the documents back to me without a word, and bent down to say past my body, "Lady, you don't cut across traffic lanes in Passaic or anywhere else in the United States to grab a parking space heading the wrong way."

"I'll move the car," I told him, and unnecessarily repeated, "I'm sorry." I wanted to get going; my sense of fullness was leaking away.

My companion took a breath to tell the cop something, perhaps of some idyllic town back in Connecticut, where we came from, where cutting across traffic lanes was perfectly legal. But my body language may have communicated to her a fervent wish that she say nothing more, for she stopped herself, her lips parted as if holding a bubble between them.

The policeman, having sensed her intention and braced to make a rejoinder, silently straightened up into his full frowning dignity. He was young, but it wasn't his youth that impressed me; it was his uniform, his badge, his authority. We were all young, relatively, as I look back at us. It has taken old age to make me realize that the world exists for young people. Their tastes in food and music and clothing are what the world is catering to, even while they are imagining themselves victims of the old, the enforcers of the laws.

The officer dismissed me with "O.K., buddy." Perhaps in deference to my giddy condition, he added, "Take it easy."

The lady and I were not young enough to let our love go, the way teen-agers do, knowing another season is around the corner. We returned to our Connecticut households unarrested, and persisted in what my grandfather would have called evildoing until we were caught, with the usual results: the wounded wife, the seething husband, the puzzled and frightened children. She got a divorce, I didn't. We both stayed in town, after her husband went to the city to survey his new prospects. She and I entered upon an awkward afterlife of some ten years, meeting at parties, in the supermarket, at the playground. She kept looking gorgeous; woe had thinned her down a little. It was a decade of national carnival. At one Christmas party I remember, she wore red hotpants and green net stockings, with furry antlers on a headband and a red ball, alluding to Rudolph the Reindeer's nose, stuck in the middle of her heart-shaped face.

Parties are theatre in Connecticut bedroom towns, and the wife and I did nothing to make her performances easier, the wife giving her the cold shoulder and I sitting in a corner staring steelily, still on fire. She had taken on a new persona, a kind of fallen-woman persona, laughing, brazen, flirting with every man the way she had with that cop in Passaic. I took a spiteful pleasure in watching her, from my distance, bump like a pinball from one unsuccessful romance to another. It enraged me when one would appear to be successful. I couldn't bear imagining it—the nakedness I had known, the little whimpers of renewed surprise that I had heard. She brought these men to parties, and I had to shake their hands, which seemed damp and bloated to me, like raw squid touched in the fish market.

Our affair had hurt me professionally. An insurance salesman is like a preacher—he reminds us of death, and should be extra earnest and virtuous, as payback for the investment he asks. As an insurance agent I had been proficient and tidy in filling out the forms but less good at tipping the customers into the plunge that would bring a commission. The wife and I moved to a state, Massachusetts, where nobody knew us and I could work with my hands. We had been living there some fifteen years when word came from Connecticut that my former friend—her long looping hair, her broad bright smile, her elegant oval hands—was dying, of ovarian cancer. When she was dead, I rejoiced, to a degree. Her death removed a confusing presence from the world, an index to its unfulfilled potential. There. You see why I am not given to introspection, to digging deep. Scratch the surface, and ugliness pops up.

Before we were spoiled for each other, she saw me as an innocent, and sweetly tried to educate me. With her husband's example in mind, she told me I must learn to drink more, as if liquor were medicine for grown-ups. She told me the way to cure a cold was to drink it under. Rather shyly, early in our love life, she informed me my orgasms told her that this—sex—was important for me. "But isn't it for everybody?" I asked.

She made a wry mouth, shrugged her naked shoulders slightly, and said, "No. You'd be surprised." There was a purity, a puritan clarity, to her teaching, as she sought to make me a better person. At some point in the ungainly aftermath of our brief intimacy, she let me know—for I used to seek her out at parties, to take her temperature, as it were, and to receive a begrudged bit of the infinite wisdom a love-object appears to possess—how I should have behaved to her if I "had been a gentleman." *If I had been a gentleman:* it was a revelatory slur. I was not a gentleman, and had no business putting on a suit each morning and setting off to persuade people wealthier than I to invest in the possibility of their own deaths. I had begun to stammer on the mollifying jargon: "in the extremely unlikely event" and "when you're no longer in the picture" and "giving your loved ones financial continuity" and "let's say you live forever, this is still a quality investment."

My clients could sense that to me death was basically unthinkable, and they shied away from this hole in my sales pitch. Not being a gentleman, I could move to a new state and acquire a truck and heavy sanders and master the modest science of penetrating slow-drying sealers, steel-wool buffer pads, and alkyd varnishes. Keep a wet edge to avoid lap marks, and don't paint yourself into a corner. Brush with the grain, apply your mind to the surface, and leave some ventilation if you want to breathe. Young men now don't want to go into it, though the market for such services keeps expanding with gentrification. Everybody wants to be gentry. Toward the end, I had so many clamoring clients that retiring was the only way I could escape them, whereas selling insurance had always been, for me at least, an uphill push. People are more concerned about the floors they walk on than the loved ones they leave behind.

Another curious habit of mine can be observed only in December, when, in the mid-sized sea-view Cape Ann colonial the wife and I moved to thirty years ago, I run up on the flagpole five strands of Christmas lights, forming a tent-shape that at night strongly suggests the festoons on an invisible tree. I have rigged two extension cords to connect with an outside spotlight so the illusion can be controlled from an inside switch. Before heading up to the bedroom—"climbing the wooden hill," my grandfather used to say—I switch it off. I could do it without a glance outdoors but in fact I move to the nearby window with my arm extended, my fingers on the switch, *so that I can see the lights go out.*

In one nanosecond, the drooping strands are burning bright, casting their image of a Christmas tree out into the world, and in the next, so quick that there seems no time at all while the signal travels along the wires from the switch, the colored, candle-flame-shaped bulbs—red, orange, green, blue, white—are doused. I keep imagining, since a pair of one-hundred-foot extension cords carry the electrons across the yard, through the bushes and frozen flower beds, that I will perceive a time lag, as with a lightning flash and subsequent thunder. But no; the connection between the lights and my hand on the switch appears instantaneous. The lights are there, imprinting the dark with holiday cheer, and then are not. *I need to see this instant transformation occur.* I recognize something unhealthy in my need, and often vow beforehand just to touch the switch and forgo peeking. But always I break my vow. It's like trying to catch by its tail the elusive moment in which you fall asleep. I think that, subconsciously, I fear that if I don't look the current will jam and reverse and it is I who will die, and not the lights.

The wife and I are proud of our homemade Christmas tree. We see it loom vividly from the beach below and, stupid as children, imagined we could even see it from Marblehead, eight miles away. But, though we took along our younger son's telescope—abandoned now in his room, with all his toys and posters and science fiction and old *Playboy*s—we couldn't make out our festooned flagpole at all, amid so many other shore lights. Our faces hurt in the December wind; our eyes watered. What we, after much searching, thought might be our illusion of a tree was a blurred speck in which the five colors and the five strands had merged to a trembling gray as slippery in the telescope as a droplet of mercury.

My hoping to see the current snake through the extension cords possibly harks back to my fascination, as a boy, with pathways. I loved the idea of something *irresistibly travelling along a set path*—marbles rolling down wooden or plastic troughs, subway trains hurtling beneath city streets, water propelled by gravity through underground pipes, rivers implacably tumbling and oozing their way to the sea. Such phenomena gave me considerable joy to contemplate, and, with the lessening intensity that applies in my old age to all sensations, they still do. They appeal, perhaps, to a bone-deep laziness of mine, a death-wish. My favorite moment in the floor-finishing business used to be getting out the door and closing it, knowing that all that remained was for the polyurethane to dry, which would happen without me, *in my absence*.

Another full moment: Beginning in kindergarten, all through grade school and high school, I was in love with a classmate I almost never spoke to. Like marbles in parallel troughs we rolled down the years toward graduation. She was popular—a cheerleader, a star hockey player, a singer of solos in school assemblies—with many boyfriends. She had big breasts on a lean body. My small-town grandparents had kept many country connections, and through them I was invited to an October barn dance five miles out of town. Somehow I got up my nerve and invited this local beauty to go with me, and she absorbed her surprise and surprisingly accepted. Perhaps, reigning so securely in the tightly built-up streets of our small town, she was amused by the idea of a barn dance. The barn was bigger than a church, and the fall's fresh hay bales were stacked to the roof in the side mows. I had been to barn dances before, with my country cousins, and knew the calls. Bow to your partner. Bow to your corner. All hands left. Women like all that, it occurs to me this late in life—connections and combinations, *contact*. As my partner got the hang of it, her trim waist swung into my hand with the smart impact of a drum beat, a football catch, a lay-up off the reverberating backboard. I felt her moist sides and the soft insides beneath her rib cage, all taut in the spirit of the dance. Sexual intercourse for a female has always been hard for me to picture, but it must feel to be all about *you*. You, at the center of everything. She might have gone on a date with me before, if I had asked. But that would have spilled her, for me, into too much reality.

From a geographical standpoint, my life has been a slow crawl up the Eastern seaboard. The wife and I joke that our next move is to Canada, where we'll get the benefits of universal health care. A third curious habit I've fallen into is, when I get into bed at night, having been fending off sleep with a magazine and waiting in vain for the wife to join me (she is deep into e-mail with our grandchildren and English costume dramas on public television), I bury my face in the side of the pillow, stretch out down to my toes in the hope of forestalling the foot cramps, and *groan loudly three times*—*"Ooh! Ooh! Ooh-uh!"*—as if the bliss of letting go at the end of the day were agony. At first it may have been an audible signal to the wife to switch off whatever electronic device was keeping her up (I'm deaf enough to be totally flummoxed by the British accents in those costume dramas) and to come join me in bed, but now it has become a ritual that I perform for an immaterial, invisible audience—my Maker, my grandfather would have said, with that little thin-lipped smile of his, peeping out from under his gray mustache.

As a child I would look at him and wonder how he could stay sane, being so close to his death. But actually, it turns out, Nature drips a little anesthetic into your veins each day that makes you think another day is as good as a year, and another year as long as a lifetime. The routines of living—the tooth-brushing and pill-taking, the flossing and the water glass, the matching of socks and the sorting of the laundry into the proper bureau drawers—wear you down. And the *shaving*.

I shave every morning. Athletes and movie actors leave a little bristle now, to intimidate rivals or attract cavewomen, but a man of my generation would sooner go onto the street in his underpants than unshaven. The very hot washcloth, held against the lids for dry eye. The lather, the brush, the razor. The right cheek, then the left, feeling for missed spots along the jaw line, and next the upper lip, with that middle dent called the (did you know this?) philtrum, and finally the fussy section, where most cuts occur, between the lower lip and the knob of the chin. My hand is still steady, and the triple blades they make these days last forever.

The first time I slept with the woman who got me nearly arrested in Passaic, I purred. That detail had fled my memory for years, but the other day, as I held somebody else's cat on my lap, it came back to me. The lady and I were on a scratchy sofa, covered in that off-white Haitian cotton that was once fashionable in suburban décor, and when I had pumped her full of myself—my genetic surrogate, wrapped in protein—I lay on top of her, cooling off. "Listen to this," I said, and laid my cheek against hers, which was still hot with the love-flush, and let her listen to the lightly rattling sound of animal contentment that my throat was producing. I hadn't known I could do it, but I had felt the sound inside me, waiting for my happiness to overflow enough to produce it. She heard it. Her eyes, a few inches from mine, flared in astonishment, and she laughed. I had been a dutiful, religious child, but there and then I realized that the haven where life was rounded beyond the need for any further explanation had been opened up, and I experienced a peace that has never quite left me, clinging to me even now, in shreds.

Years before, before our affair, a group of us young marrieds had been sitting and smoking on a summer porch, and when she, wearing a tennis dress, crossed her legs, the flash of the underside of her thigh made my mouth parch—go as sharply dry as if a desert wind had howled in my skull. She was to me a marked woman from that moment on. And I to her, it may be, a marked man.

Until the wife leaves off her electronic entertainments and comes to bed, I have trouble going to sleep. Then, at three o'clock, when there's not a car stirring in town, not even a drunken kid or a sated philanderer hurrying home on rubber tires, I wake and marvel at how motionlessly she sleeps. She has taken to wearing a knotted bandana to keep her hair from going wild, and the two ends of the knot stick up against the faint window light like little ears on top of her head. Her stillness is touching, as is the girlishly tidy order in which she keeps her dressing room and kitchen and would keep the entire house if I would let her. I can't fall back into unconsciousness, like a water strider held aloft on the surface tension of her beautiful stillness.

I listen for the first car downtown to make a move toward dawn; I wait for the wife to wake and get out of bed and set the world in motion again. The hours flow forward in sluggish jerks. She says I sleep more than I am aware. But I am certainly aware of when, at last, she stirs: she irritably moves her arms, fighting her way out of some dream, and then in the strengthening window light pushes back the covers and exposes for a moment her rucked-up nightie. I see in silhouette her torso lift through a diagonal to a sitting position. Her bare feet pad around the bed, and, many mornings, now that I'm retired and nearly eighty, I fall back asleep for another hour. The world is being tended to, I can let go of it, it doesn't need me.

The shaving mirror hangs in front of a window overlooking the sea. The sea is always full, flat as a floor. Or almost: there is a delicate planetary bulge in it, supporting a few shadowy freighters and cruise ships making their motionless way out of Boston Harbor. At night, the horizon springs a rim of lights—more, it seems, every year. Winking airplanes from the corners of the earth descend on a slant, a curved groove in the air, toward the unseen airport in East Boston. My life-prolonging pills cupped in my left hand, I lift the glass, its water sweetened by its brief wait on the marble sink-top. If I can read this strange old guy's mind aright, he's drinking a toast to the visible world, his impending disappearance from it be damned.

read more

JOHN UPDIKE

If you enjoyed this book, there are several ways you can read more by the same author and make sure you get the inside track on all Penguin books.

Order any of the following titles direct:

9780141027845 TERRORIST £7.99
'Updike displays his mastery of the psychic topography of his homeland... Flashes with intelligence' *The Times*

9780241140918 MORE MATTERS: ESSAYS AND CRITICISM £25.00
'Attests to Updike's remarkable versatility, and to his ardent drive to turn all his observations into glittering, gossamer prose' *The New York Times*

9780141011165 SEEK MY FACE £8.99
'A wonderful tour de force and a meditation on the dying of the light,' *Independent*

9780241143353 STILL LOOKING: ESSAYS ON AMERICAN ART' £25.00
'Glorious, a true pleasure. Updike's prose is incandescent' *Herald*

9780141016085 THE EARLY STORIES £18.99
'No one can make magic out of the mundane with the ease of Updike' *Observer*

9780141188973 THE WITCHES OF EASTWICK £9.99
'A strange and marvellous organism' *The New York Times Book Review*

9780141038032 THE WIDOWS OF EASTWICK £7.99
'Funny, yet also terrifying' *Irish Times*

Simply call Penguin c/o Bookpost on **01624 677237** and have your credit/debit card ready. Alternatively e-mail your order to **bookshop@enterprise.net**. Postage and package is free in mainland UK. Overseas customers must add £2 per book. Prices and availability subject to change without notice.

Visit www.penguin.com and find out first about forthcoming titles, read exclusive material and author interviews, and enter exciting competitions. You can also browse through thousands of Penguin books and buy online.

IT'S NEVER BEEN EASIER TO READ MORE WITH PENGUIN

Frustrated by the quality of books available at Exeter station for his journey back to London one day in 1935, Allen Lane decided to do something about it. The Penguin paperback was born that day, and with it first-class writing became available to a mass audience for the very first time. This book is a direct descendant of those original Penguins and Lane's momentous vision. What will you read next?

read more

JOHN UPDIKE

ENDPOINT AND OTHER POEMS

John Updike was always as much a poet as a storyteller and the poems in this, his final collection, celebrate the everyday, even as they address his own imminent mortality. It is in this connected series of poems, written on his last few birthdays and culminating with the illness that killed him, that Updike's work is at its most touching and poignant.

'Deeply affecting, elegant and eloquent' *Sunday Times*

'Superbly skilful, effortlessly able to delineate the sweep of a lifetime in a few pages' *Evening Standard*

'Urbane, worldy and robustly sane, the late Updike's poetry bears comparison with writers such as Auden, James Merrill and Seamus Heaney' *Daily Mail*